Alan walked to t⟨...⟩
water. It could ha⟨...⟩
His reflection mi⟨...⟩
etal. His skin was white as stone, his eyes huge and dark and
seemingly recessed into deep pockets. He could easily make
out the apostrophe-shaped cut above his right eyebrow and the
bruise on his cheek.

He dropped to one knee and reached out, sticking two
fingers into the water—

*(ice-cold!)*

—only to pull them quickly out, hissing between clenched
teeth. A bundle of muscles at the small of his back tightened
from the cold. He flexed his fingers, working the feeling back
into them, amazed at how numb they'd become from no longer than a split second beneath the water. It was July and the
water was ice-cold . . .

His reflection stared up at him.

Rippling.

Things moved in the trees. *Large* things.

Alan stood and stared at them: black silhouettes framed
against the night sky. Only the ones on the branches that
passed in front of the moon were clearly outlined.

*Birds*, he thought, though the realization afforded him
little relief and did not do the birds justice. *Buzzards.*

There were scores of them, whole families, multitudes.
Carrion birds, stooped over like hunchbacks in bell towers.
And although he knew it was crazy, he had the disquieting
feeling that they were all watching him.

*Carnivorous birds.*

It was insane, sure . . . but if they all decided to simultaneously
swoop down off their perches and attack . . .

# CRADLE LAKE

# CRADLE LAKE

## RONALD MALFI

**MEDALLION**
P R E S S

Medallion Press, Inc.
Printed in USA

For the Mermaid and the Sailor

Swim, kids.

Published 2013 by Medallion Press, Inc.

The MEDALLION PRESS LOGO
is a registered trademark of Medallion Press, Inc.

Typeset in Adobe Garamond Pro
Printed in the United States of America
Title font by James Tampa

ISBN# 978-160542510-8

10 9 8 7 6 5 4 3 2 1
First Edition

## ACKNOWLEDGMENTS

Special thanks to Charles J. Sailey, MD, MS, for his assistance in answering this author's questions regarding all things medical; if there are any inaccuracies concerning these issues throughout this book, those mistakes are mine alone. Thank you, Chuck.

Further thanks to my wonderful editor, Lorie Jones, whose expertise continues to be my fail-safe; this is the third novel we have worked on together, yet she still manages to open my eyes. Thanks, Lorie.

Lastly, thanks to my wife, Deb, and my daughter, Madison—two gals who have taught me that being an author is the second-best thing a man can be. I love you guys.

—RM
11/29/2012
Annapolis, MD

# BOOK ONE
# THE PATH

# CHAPTER ONE

He had been to the house once before, in his youth, for some ancient relative's wake or maybe an Easter dinner. Who could remember? Those memories were mostly lost on him now, faded like the faces of those long forgotten relatives he had seen so infrequently throughout his childhood.

At that time, the house itself was unimportant to him; he recalled the vastness of the property and the surrounding woods with more relish than the run-down, butter-colored ranch with the wraparound porch and the roof that sloughed shingles like reptilian scales. It had been his uncle's place. Like all his other relatives who never saw fit to leave the security of their birthplaces—in this instance, the embrace of the Great Smoky Mountains in rural North Carolina—he had met his father's brother on very few occasions. Uncle Phillip. He could not even summon a face.

Nearly two decades since that first visit, Alan Hammerstun returned. He crept down from New York City where he'd spent his entire life, the rattling Toyota Celica packed to the gills, his wife, Heather, in the passenger seat and Jerry Lee in the back, perpetrating the occasional dog fart. For much of the ride there had been no talking. The times when he stopped for gas gave him some relief, and he found himself gibbering at the cashier like a fool, hungry for human interaction. He watched through one of the gas station windows as Heather took Jerry Lee to the edge of the parking lot where the old dog urinated in the sunburned weeds. Heather wavered beside the dog like a ghost, and when the sun hit her a certain way, for a moment Alan thought he could see right through her.

*If I stare at her long enough, she'll blink out of existence. I know it. I can feel it.*

As they drew closer to his uncle's house, he told Heather about the place and the immense forest that climbed from the rear of the property out to the early ridges of the great mountain chain. He surprised himself with the clarity of some of these memories that had been lost to him just moments ago, as well as with the emotional impact they had on him. Alan's father, Bill Hammerstun, had been the family pariah. He'd skipped out of North Carolina when he was young and against all odds carved a niche for himself in Manhattan as the owner of a small but popular nightclub in the Financial District that catered to Wall Street cokeheads and organized crime. It had been the latter who had eventually punched Bill Hammerstun's card with a gunshot to the temple. Alan had been just a teenager.

"I don't remember much about the house," Alan said, "but I remember being impressed with the property. I'm sure it isn't as big as it is in my head, but I was a kid from the city, and I couldn't comprehend how someone could actually *own* acres of grass."

"What killed him?" Heather said. She did not look at him; she hadn't turned away from the passenger window for about an hour.

*The first thing she's said all afternoon and it has to do with death,* he thought, feeling a cold sickness climbing around in his stomach.

"Time, I suppose," he said eventually. "Age. More specifically, a stroke, I think. That's what the lawyer said, anyway. I never saw any cause of death paperwork or anything like that. Phillip's kids must know all the details."

He waited for his wife to pick up the reins and add something to the conversation, to perhaps ask why Phillip had left the house to Alan instead of his two grown children. When she didn't speak, he said, "I only met Uncle Phillip a couple of times when I was a kid. He and my dad weren't very close, not that my dad was close with anyone. There was almost a twenty-year difference in their ages. To be honest, I'm surprised old Uncle Phillip even remembered me after all these years."

Again, he waited for a response. But Heather was done talking. *Ghost*, he thought. Alan stole a glance at her profile, the contours of her delicate face. She looked startlingly young sitting there, even though she was three years older than him at thirty-five. His gaze slipped down to her hands, which she had buried in her lap. Silver rings with colored stones on her fingers. She wore a long-sleeved cardigan, but he could still see the bandages on her wrist . . .

"Alan!" she shrieked.

Alan jerked his head forward. Something darted out in front of the car. He slammed on the brake. The car shuddered to a stop, the mounds of boxes crashing into one another in the backseat. Jerry Lee howled in anguish.

A young boy in a red baseball cap and striped polo shirt stood directly in front of the car. Large brown eyes, tawny hair in need of trimming, deer-in-the-headlights look on his face . . . the kid had come out of nowhere. Only the mere whim of fate—and Heather's shout—had saved him from sudden death. The boy's eyes, more surprised than frightened, locked onto Alan's through the windshield. Alan could taste his heart in his throat. Clenching the steering wheel in a death grip, the palms of his hands were suddenly bleeding sweat.

A second later, something flew out of the sky. Its arrival practically underscored by a comic whistling sound, the object struck the hood of the Toyota with a hollow *gong* before leaping back up into the air and completing its arc to the pavement. It was a baseball.

"Oh, Jesus," Alan uttered, his heart hammering away like some piece of industrial machinery. He glanced at Heather. Her eyes were wide and trained on the little boy, who couldn't have been more than ten years old. There was a slight quiver to her lower lip. "You okay?" he asked her.

"That boy." Her voice came out in a strangled gasp. "You almost hit that boy."

As if cued by this statement, the boy scooped up the baseball off the ground and darted across the street. He rejoined a group of kids playing baseball on a nearby lawn. Not once did he look over his shoulder to acknowledge how close to death he'd come.

"Stupid kid," Alan said. "He came out of nowhere."

"Oh, my God," Heather sighed.

"Are you all right?" he asked again. He reached out for one of her hands but accidentally ran his fingers along the gauze bandage on her left wrist. As if zapped by a current of electricity, he jerked his hand away.

"I'm fine," she said after a moment. Catching her breath, she looped a loose strand of black hair behind one ear.

Alan turned and faced the backseat. He scratched the golden retriever under his grayish-white muzzle. "You okay, boy?"

The dog whined.

When Alan turned back around, he realized he was looking at his uncle's house just ahead of them and off to the left. At first he hadn't realized it was the same place because it had gone to pot. In fact, the whole structure looked like a giant frown sinking into the ground. Perhaps in his old age, his uncle had given up trying to maintain it.

"That's it," he said, easing the car down the road. Out of the periphery of one eye he watched with caution the kids playing baseball on the other side of the street. "My uncle's place."

"It's ours now." Heather said this with such eerie prophetic detachment that it caused a shiver to race down Alan's spine.

He pulled into the driveway and shut the car down. Jerry Lee perked up, panting heavily. Alan knew the poor beast was probably busting a kidney, ready to water some lawn. Alan climbed out of the car and let the dog out of the backseat. Sure enough, Jerry Lee trotted to the nearest bush and relieved himself. There was almost a comical and somewhat human look of satisfaction on the dog's face.

Heather still sat in the car. Alan poked his head in. "You gonna get out, or should I just drive us into the living room?"

His attempt at levity went right through her. Emotionlessly, she opened the passenger door and stepped out onto the driveway.

Gone was the butter-colored gingerbread ranch from Alan's memory. It was now a dirt-colored shoe box with a sagging roof and a frowning wraparound porch. The front windows looked blind with cataracts, and the yard was horribly overgrown. Most disturbing was the network of sturdy vines that climbed all over the exterior of the house, as if in an embrace. Alan went to one of the stalks of vines, this one as thick as two fingers, and tugged on it. It held securely to the side of the house by small thorns. Alan followed the vine down with his eyes where he could see it sprouting from a bundle of wormlike roots in the ground. He thought of corpses reaching up out of the earth from their graves.

Jerry Lee padded over to Heather and sat down at her feet. She stared at the house with a look of utter detachment.

*She's lost more weight, too*, Alan thought. *I have to make sure she's eating.*

"So?" he said. He was wearing one hell of a mask now, trying desperately to pretend all was fine between them. *Dance, boy, dance!* "What do you think?"

Without emotion, Heather rolled her shoulders and said, "It's a house."

Alan dug around in his pocket for the key. When he mounted the front porch, he thought the floorboards would play the traitor, opening up and swallowing him whole. But they held.

He unlocked the door and pushed it open on squealing hinges. Glancing over his shoulder, he tried to force a smile for Heather's benefit but found his reserve temporarily empty. In that moment, he couldn't even look at her. Instead, he said, "Come on, boy," and patted his thigh.

Faithful Jerry Lee arthritically climbed the porch steps and wove around Alan to gain access to their new home.

Alan's eyes finally locked with Heather's. There was a nonspecific deadness in them, a deadness he had become all too familiar with. His mind slipped back to that night in the apartment when he'd awoken in a cold sweat to find Heather's side of the bed empty. The strip of light at the other end of the hallway issuing through the bottom of the closed bathroom door . . .

*No*, he warned himself. *Not here, not now. We left all that in the city. This is a time for new beginnings, goddamn it. I won't bring those nightmare memories here.*

"Heather," he managed, her name nearly sticking to the roof of his mouth.

After a moment, she crossed the lawn and mounted the porch steps. She paused beside him, so close he could count the creases at the corners of her dead eyes, the conch shell contours of her ear. Then she entered their new home.

*New beginnings*, he thought again and wondered, with a deepening sense of dread, if he was only fooling himself.

Twenty minutes later, after the movers arrived and began lugging Alan's and Heather's personal effects into the house, Alan took time to survey the place. His memory of what it had been like based off one childhood visit was not to be trusted. It was much smaller than he remembered (which

9

was understandable since he was, after all, much taller now). The walls sloughed paint chips, the tiles were cracked and broken in the bathroom, and the kitchen's linoleum floor was carpeted in dust.

The estate sale had cleared out most of his uncle's belongings, although random photos still decorated some walls and the odd coffee mug or lamp could still be found. In the master bedroom, Alan opened the closet and was momentarily dumbstruck at a parade of bedroom slippers on the floor. The entire house smelled *old*, and he was overcome by the peculiar notion that the house had been sitting here since his uncle's death, holding its breath while awaiting new occupants.

The thought made him uncomfortable.

Heather hadn't left the living room since she entered the house. She stood now, hugging herself as she looked out the sliding glass doors that faced the backyard. Thick vines segmented the glass. The doors led onto a small concrete slab that served as a patio. Beyond the slab, the vast backyard climbed toward a heavy forest. In the distance, like dinosaurs coming awake from their ancient slumber, the jagged peaks of the Great Smoky Mountains were visible.

Alan came up behind Heather, touched one shoulder. He felt her recoil inwardly. Her skin was cold. "That's some backyard, huh?" He was whispering.

No answer.

"This will be good for us, honey. We can make this work. New beginnings."

He kissed the side of her face, and it was like kissing a wax dummy.

# CHAPTER TWO

Two hours later, when the movers had finally finished, Alan watched the big moving van shudder down the road and vanish in the cool mist of an early evening. Producing a pack of menthol cigarettes from the rear pocket of his pants, Alan shook one of the smokes out of the cellophane. He lit it and inhaled deeply, casting his head far back on his neck, nearly in ecstasy. He had quit five times in the past year. But, of course, the past year had been a nightmare. *Fuck it.*

At his feet, Jerry Lee whimpered and sat on his haunches.

"Let me have my habits, you judgmental bastard," Alan said to the dog.

Jerry Lee looked up at him, as if considering a rebuke.

He was about to turn around and head back inside the house when a police car, its lights off, slid by and came to an eventual stop across the street. Its engine idled, and its tailpipe sputtered out great belches of black exhaust.

Alan waited for the officer to climb out of the cruiser, but there was no movement inside. He crossed the yard to the edge of the street and raised a hand in his most neighborly gesture, anticipating a reaction from the driver.

But the driver did not respond except for switching the cruiser into gear and slowly rolling away from the curb. As the vehicle completed a U-turn, Alan could see the emblem on the door—a gold shield decaled with the words *Groom County Sheriff's Department*. Alan stepped into the street and watched the car coast back up the way it had come. Its taillights flared when it approached the nearest intersection. Then the cruiser turned right and disappeared.

*Strange. I wonder what that was all about.*

Across the street the kids were still playing baseball. There resounded another *tink* as one of the boys struck the baseball squarely with the bat, launching the fist-sized white sphere a good distance into the air. Alan glanced up at it, the overcast sky heavy enough with clouds to shield any glare from the sun. The kids were shouting, and the runner was already bounding down an invisible baseline.

Alan got under the ball and, pushing his hand up through his T-shirt to soften the impact, caught it.

The shouts of the children died in midair. Even the runner slowed to a jog before coming to a full stop between second and third base.

Alan suddenly felt like a comedian who had just bombed onstage, hearing nothing from the audience but the chirping of crickets. No doubt these kids were wondering who the hell this strange guy was—a guy wearing a Megadeth T-shirt and camouflage BDUs, smoking a cigarette, and boasting a smattering of tattoos and an unshaven face. What had he gotten himself into?

"Hey!" one of the kids shouted. "Nice catch, mister!"

"Thanks!" Alan lobbed the ball across the street.

The kid hunkered down on his knees and snatched it up in his glove.

"Does that mean he's out?" one of the other kids wanted to know.

"I'd say it's more like a home run," Alan suggested.

The runner—a chubby kid in a gray sweatshirt and baggy jeans—pumped a fist in the air and continued loping toward an oversized wicker purse that obviously served as third base.

But the outfield wasn't having any of it. "Interference!" the center fielder yelled. "Doesn't count! Interference!"

"No way!" one of the runner's teammates shouted. "You wouldn't have caught that in a million years. Automatic home run."

"Yeah," said the runner. "You heard the old guy."

*Old guy*, Alan thought with some humility. *Christ. When did that happen?*

"Do-over!" the pitcher demanded. "Do-over!"

The runner groaned in protest. Slouching, dejected, he turned around and dragged his feet back to home plate. Casting a glance over his shoulder, the kid eyeballed Alan from across the street. He'd been the kid's savior just a moment ago, but now the kid looked at him as if he'd just ran over his dog. "Shouldn't smoke, mister," he said. "Bad for your health."

Alan nodded, somewhat surprised by the kid's effrontery. He even considered tossing the cigarette to the ground and crushing it beneath his sneaker, setting a good example and all, but then decided to hell with it and finished it off as he walked around to the backyard. "Come on, Jerry Lee."

The retriever padded after him, tongue lolling out like a circus pennant.

The grass was thick and green, patches of it almost as high as his hips. Colorful swells of wildflowers blossomed up from the ground. Jerry Lee's upraised tail cleaved through the grass like the dorsal fin of a shark. Alan walked several yards into the field until his left foot snagged on a tangle of thick grass low to the ground. He tugged it free with a popping sound. With a little loving care, it promised to be a wonderful yard. He would need a lawn mower, of course—he'd never owned one in his life and, in fact, had never *operated* one—and maybe Heather would plant a vegetable garden close to the house in the spring. Fresh tomatoes, asparagus, parsley . . . whatever. It was amazing just how different their lives would be now that they'd left the city behind.

*You can escape the city, but you can't escape what happened there*, said a voice in his head. It sounded frighteningly like his dead father. *You can run away, but darkness has quick feet and large wings, and it will follow you.*

There was a rustling off to his left. He looked up and was shocked to see a deer staring at him from the edge of the pine forest. Its moist dark eyes were like pools of India ink, its hide a sleek sorrel hue. It was a doe, its head absent of antlers, and it looked much bigger than Alan would have suspected a female deer to be. (Until now, the only deer he had ever seen had been on television or in magazines.) A world of difference from the diseased squirrels that scavenged from trash cans and shat black marbles in the alleyways back in Manhattan . . .

"Hey," he cooed. Made kissing noises. "Hey, there . . ."

At his heels, Jerry Lee whimpered and lowered his head on his front paws.

"Coward," he said to the dog.

He took a tentative step in the doe's direction. Except for the rotating, bovine-like motion of its jaw as it chewed grass, the animal did not move. He hazarded another step, but this time his sneaker caught under another tangle of weeds; the ripping sound it made as he liberated his foot from the tangle was enough to send the doe bounding off into the forest. The last thing he saw was its white tail flitting good-bye.

In the deer's wake, Alan noticed a dark impression in the wall of trees. He trumped through the tall grass and realized he was looking at a parting in the trees, like the opening in a curtain. A rutted dirt path cut through the opening and, from what he could estimate, wound deep into the woods. Had the day been sunnier he might have been able to see farther into the woods, but as it was the woods were dense with shadows. He thought he could make out the shape of the deer arcing through the underbrush, obscured by shadows and the green-blue arms of evergreens.

It was a man-made path; he realized this the moment he stepped onto it and through the opening in the trees. The ground had been worn down to dirt from the traction of human feet. Around him, the world grew unusually quiet, the thickness of the inner firs providing natural insulation against outside noises. Even the quality of the air seemed different: constricted somehow. Motionless.

*Like being in a sealed tomb*, he thought. Then reconsidered: *Like being in outer space.*

There was *one* sound, he noticed. But it took him several seconds to learn it was the sound of his own respiration. Then, a moment after that, the forest seemed to instantly come alive with an arrangement of bird caws, buzzing insects, the crunch of dead leaves underfoot—or, more accurately, under *paw* or *hoof.* Up ahead, the dirt path twisted through the trees, vanishing behind a thick stand of bluish firs so dense they practically formed a wall. The silvery sky was crisscrossed by a canopy of interlocking tree limbs.

He turned and beckoned to Jerry Lee to follow him, but the dog only whined and did not move from where he had hunkered down in the grass. Alan felt a pang of compassion for the old beast; a city dog all his life, Jerry Lee probably had no clue what to make of their new surroundings.

Alan turned around and moved farther down the path, having to bow his head several times to clear the overhanging limbs. *Good way to lose an eye*, he thought. When he came to the place where the path cut through the firs, he noticed a smooth white stone sitting at the apex of the path's bend. It was roughly the size of a football, and there was something carved into it: an upside-down triangle. Was it supposed to be an arrow instructing which way to go? Because the path led in only one direction—

A giant bird burst into flight no more than two feet in front of him, forcing a startled cry from his throat and causing him to stagger backward. He fell down hard on his ass, the right side of his face skimming the bark of the nearest tree. Fireworks exploded before his eyes, and his cheekbone felt as though someone had addressed it with a swatch of sandpaper.

The bird cut easily through the tangled canopy of tree limbs overhead. Alan heard it squawking as it vanished into the air, its visage a blurred hieroglyphic approximation.

"Son of a bitch." He brought one hand up to the side of his face. His right cheek burned and felt twice its normal size. When he fingered the tender spot just above his right eyebrow he winced. His fingers came away slick with blood. Nonetheless, he couldn't help but shake his head and grin like an asshole. He was such a goddamn city boy. What the hell was he doing out here in Bumfuck, North Carolina, anyway?

He returned to the house, Jerry Lee trailing behind him in a cloud of his own cowardice, hoping to locate the first-aid kit in one of the bathroom boxes without much difficulty. But when he opened the front door, he was surprised to find they had guests.

Heather stood in the middle of the living room holding a ceramic dish tented with tinfoil and a bottle of wine. Beside her stood a handsome couple and a girl about ten years old.

"Well, hey, here he is now," said the man, a wide smile nearly cracking his face. He extended a hand to Alan. Alan shook it. "I'm Hank Gerski. This is my wife, Lydia, and my daughter, Catherine."

"Alan Hammerstun. Hello."

"Lord," said Lydia Gerski. "What happened to your face?"

Alan pawed at the fresh wound as if he'd forgotten about it. "It's nothing. I was a little careless out in the yard."

"Looks like someone sucker punched you good, partner," Hank Gerski said.

"Violent trees around here."

Hank laughed. Lydia cocked her head and smiled like someone out of an Ira Levin novel about creepily perfect housewives. Catherine twisted her hands together in front of her, looking just as out of touch and aloof as Heather.

"We saw the moving truck earlier and just wanted to welcome you both to the neighborhood," Lydia said. She had a squeaky, birdlike voice.

"It's good to have new neighbors," Hank added, giving Alan a toothy smile. Hank was tall, his skin nicely tanned, his black hair cropped short and turning gray at the temples. He wore an IZOD polo tucked into his overly tight jeans, and reflective sunglasses hung around his neck by a nylon cord. "Old guy who used to live here was a real curmudgeon."

Alan, who had never heard any adult male use the word *curmudgeon* in his life, forced a smile and said, "He was my uncle."

Hank's face seemed to drop like an elevator crashing through floors. "Oh, hey . . . jeez . . ."

Lydia slapped her husband on the arm. "See that? Always opening your mouth."

"Didn't mean anything by it . . ."

Alan shrugged. "It's no big deal. I hardly knew him. In fact, I'm surprised he left us this place in his will."

"They brought us food and wine," Heather said.

The detour in conversation was as loud as an explosion. Everyone turned and looked at her.

"Ah yes," Lydia said, still maintaining her perfect smile. "Some tuna casserole and a bottle of Pinot."

"Well, thanks," Alan said. "That was very nice."

"We were going to invite you over for supper," Hank

said, "but we didn't want to impose on your first night in your new home—"

"We really went around and around about it," Lydia interrupted. "Should we invite them or shouldn't we."

"Should we or shouldn't we," Hank parroted. It was like watching a tennis match. "Moving is a hectic thing. We didn't want to add any confusion. And it looks like you've got a lot of boxes to go through, too."

"Yeah," Alan said.

Lydia touched Heather's arm. "Maybe later in the week we can have you both over. We're just across the street."

*Wonderful*, Alan thought.

Heather smiled wearily, her eyes unfocused. It looked like one of her hands was beginning to tremble slightly. He would have to give her more Ativan.

"So what do you do?" Hank asked, perhaps discomforted by Heather's obvious detachment.

"I'm an English professor," Alan said. "I took a job at the community college. I'll be starting in the fall."

"Wow," Hank said. "A professor, huh? Way cool."

Alan just nodded and thought, *Way cool? What the fuck?*

"Oh, hey, great tats," Hank said, suddenly noticing the tattoos on Alan's arms.

Lydia tugged on her husband's elbow. "Come on. Let's get out of their hair."

Hank Gerski clapped Alan on the shoulder as his wife pulled him toward the front door. "I'll give you a shout later, Alan," Hank said, his smile like the chrome grille of an eighteen-wheeler. "Fill you in on the neighborhood's tawdry secrets."

"Sounds inviting," Alan said, feigning a smile of his own.

As they filed through the door, Catherine went to pet Jerry Lee on the top of his head. The dog took a step backward and growled deep in his throat. The girl's hand froze in midair, her eyes wide.

Alan got down on his knees and raked his fingers along the dog's head. "Cut that out." To Catherine, he said, "He's a friendly guy, really. He's probably just a little scared, being in a new house in a new town."

"What's his name?" Catherine asked.

"Jerry Lee. Like the piano player."

"Oh," said Catherine. As if she had any clue about piano players.

"Come on," Hank called to her. He and Lydia stood in the doorway, a mutual look of distaste on their faces as they stared at Jerry Lee.

"Really," Alan promised, "he's a big old dummy. Perfectly harmless."

"I'm sure." Hank cleared his throat and put one hand on the back of his daughter's neck. "Well, anyway, you folks have a good night."

They left.

"Hey," Alan said, looking into the dog's sloppy eyes. Jerry Lee seemed perfectly fine now. "What's gotten into you, huh, bud?"

"He's probably cranky from the car ride." It was the first thing Heather had said to him without being prompted in what seemed like forever.

"Probably." Alan went to the front windows and peeked

out past the latticework of vines that veined the windowpane. "I don't think I've ever heard a grown man use the word *tawdry* before." He watched the Gerski family cross the street toward their house. They looked like the perfect middle-class *Leave It to Beaver* family. Well, *almost* perfect: he noticed Hank walked with a slight limp.

When he turned away from the window, Heather was gone. *Blink—right out of existence.* Yet he could hear her in the kitchen, setting the food down on the stove. Alan went to the bathroom and peered at his reflection. Even without the peppery sprinkle of a bruise on his right cheek, which indeed had swollen to nearly twice its normal size, and the bleeding laceration above his eyebrow, he was surprised to find his reflection looking haggard and run-down.

*I'm thinking too much about it,* he told himself. It was the truth. *I'm thinking too much, and I'm going to cause the goddamn ulcer to act up again. Stop it already.*

The ulcer had developed last year after the second miscarriage. At the time he had thought it fitting that he should suffer with stomach pains after Heather's womb had equally suffered. But what was so easily rectified in him with antacid tablets and misoprostol could not take away the memory of the miscarriages nor fix whatever was inside Heather that had caused them.

After scrounging around in a number of cardboard moving boxes, Alan finally located the little white first-aid kit with the red cross on the lid. He applied peroxide to the gash above his eyebrow, gritting his teeth at the sting.

Five minutes later, when he felt somewhat better and

his face was cleaned up, he went into the living room and found Heather sitting on the sofa, right in the middle of the room where the movers had left it, staring blankly at one wall.

"Hon," he said, "you hungry?"

He waited several moments until the silence grew intolerable.

Then he went into the kitchen and uncorked the bottle of wine.

# CHAPTER THREE

Long before Alan Hammerstun had ever dreamt he and his wife would be living in his uncle's house in North Carolina, they had spent five months trying to get pregnant. They had talked long and hard about children, though they both agreed early on that they wanted a big family.

One question, among myriad others, was that of location. Heather had grown up in the Midwest, with sprawling acres on which to run and play, lots of animals and friends and well-meaning neighbors at every turn. Alan, on the other hand, had been a child of Manhattan and knew of no other life. There was some brief talk, initiated by Heather, about relocating outside the city for the benefit of their future children. Alan had insisted city life would be good for their unborn progeny, citing the importance of learning how to deal with different types of people while attaining certain street smarts that he didn't believe were easily come by outside a major metropolitan area.

Those conversations died down, however, after months and months of trying to conceive without result. Each time Heather had her period there was a definite gloom that overtook them but nothing serious. Not in the beginning, anyway. They didn't truly start to worry until, ironically, they went to the doctor to see if there was a problem and found out Heather *was* pregnant—that her missed period did indeed signal the arrival of new life. They scheduled an appointment with an obstetrician who inserted a gelled rod into Heather's body. Squiggly, ill-defined shapes, like the suggestive presence of ghosts, appeared on the ultrasound monitor.

Mommy books came quickly. Hasty phone calls were made to close family and friends. Alan bought a stack of classical music CDs, which they played on rotation on the portable CD player by their bed at night, because they had heard playing classical music made your fetus smart.

Then, two months into the pregnancy, Heather sat up in bed—

"Alan?"

"Yeah?"

"Alan . . . Al—Alan—"

"Babe—"

"I think—"

"Heather—"

"I *think*—"

Under the blankets, his right foot slid in something wet.

Heather screamed, jumped out of bed, and raced to the bathroom down the hallway of their tiny Manhattan apartment.

Alan hopped out of bed as well, the sheets tangling around his ankles, and flipped on the light switch. As he listened to Heather's moaning from the bathroom, he stared in horror at the mattress. A dark crimson smear of blood stood out obscenely on the white sheet. At its center was what looked like a small twist of black fibrous tissue. Alan thought of bloody noses blown into Kleenex.

In the bathroom, Heather was curled in a fetal position on the floor. Her inner thighs were wet with blood, and there were dark red asterisks on the yellow linoleum tile.

It had been a horrible evening that segued into a horrible two weeks. Neither of them wanted to talk about what had happened. And neither of them did. Heather put in extra hours at the art gallery, and Alan buried himself in his work at the university.

Time continued to move on. Clocks ticked.

(There was no explanation and these things sometimes happened. It was nature's way, Mother Nature up to her old tricks, and anyway, it was just one of those things and they would get past it and move on from there, everyone said so.)

They did not make the effort to try as hard this time. They let things happen naturally. Perhaps, Alan thought on occasion, it was the stress of trying to get pregnant that had caused the pregnancy to end prematurely. Even the obstetrician agreed that it was certainly a possibility.

So there was no stress, no effort to make things happen. *(these things happen)*

Several months later, Heather discovered she was pregnant again. She told Alan one night over dinner, after having already gone to see the doctor for confirmation on her own. Everything looked fine. They were happy again. More phone calls were made.

As time progressed, Alan moved his computer and desk out of the spare bedroom and painted the walls a neutral yellow because it was too early to determine the sex of the baby. Heather watched what she ate—no deli meats, no sushi or undercooked food, no more coffee—and, because that was sometimes hard to do, Alan watched what *he* ate in an effort to support her and put up a unified front. So they suffered caffeine withdrawal together. In bed at night, they thought of names. Heather suggested William if it was a boy, but Alan didn't want to name his child after his father.

"The first one was a mermaid," she told him one night as he was about to fall asleep. He was half-dreaming of pastel paintings and great seagoing vessels. Lighthouses and cresting waves.

"How do you know?" he mumbled.

"I just know." She pressed her face against him, warm in the cool night. "This one will be a sailor."

Heather carried the baby midway through the second trimester before she collapsed one afternoon at the art gallery and was rushed to the hospital. Alan arrived to find her gray and withdrawn in the hospital bed, nearly catatonic. He talked to her and tried to get her to respond, but it was futile. She could do nothing, it seemed, except stare at the blank wall across the room. Touching her hand was like touching a mannequin's. A nurse had disposed of Heather's slacks, which were apparently soaked in blood. None of the doctors could give him a suitable reason for why any of it had happened.

Out in the hospital corridor, Alan stopped one of the nurses whom he'd recognized going in and out of Heather's room. She was a heavyset black woman with a lacquered coiffure and neon orange talons for fingernails.

"I want to see it," he said.

The nurse said she didn't understand.

Calmly, Alan said, "Then I will explain it to you." And he did—that he wanted to see it, needed to see it. Where was it?

"We don't do that." She seemed disgusted by the idea.

"Then get me someone who will," he said and waited.

Other nurses filtered by, and some of them tried to give Alan coffee or take him down to the cafeteria for something to eat. Tried to distract him, change his mind. But he wouldn't be distracted, wouldn't change his mind. He wanted to *see* it.

Eventually, a grizzled old doctor with rimless glasses and hair like a nest of copper wires approached. He spoke in a low voice. His breath reeked of onions. He used phrases like *highly unorthodox* and *would not change what happened*.

"I know that. I'm not a fool," Alan said. "I want to see it."

The doctor nodded. "Then follow me."

He would suffer nightmares from what he saw that afternoon in a small room at the end of the long corridor. A very clean, antiseptic room. The thing itself was in a clear plastic bag, vacuum-sealed and with a biohazard sticker on it. He could *see* it . . . the suggestion of delicate limbs, the misshapen cranium, the vagaries of all the things that make humans human. A single foot, tiny toes splayed, five of them, all five . . .

Back at the apartment, Heather refused to leave the bedroom. She quit her job and spent her days in bed, reading

27

trashy romance novels and watching daytime television with the volume turned all the way down. She refused to come out for dinner; like a prison guard, Alan simply left food on the nightstand.

For two weeks he slept on the pull-out sofa in the living room. A needling white-hot pain began to spread in his guts. He thought of nonspecific cancers and ravenous tapeworms; of African orphans with bloated bellies whose faces served as banquets for giant, flesh-hungry flies. He thought, too, of exploding fireworks and bloody stool. Half-dreaming, half not.

Then one night he was jarred awake on the pull-out sofa by something that may or may not have been a dream. He crept down the hall to the bathroom. A sliver of tallow light radiated from beneath the closed door. Gently, he knocked. "Heather?"

No answer. It sounded like someone shaking a single maraca on the other side of the door.

"Heather? Honey?"

The maraca stopped.

Alan tried the knob and found the door unlocked. Pushed it open . . .

She sat naked on the edge of the tub, her hands between her knees clutching a bottle of pills. The pills shook as her hands shook: the maraca sound. She looked up at him, her face blotchy and indistinct, her eyes messy in their sockets. There was a slight tremble to her lower lip.

He rushed to her, dropping to his knees while simultaneously grabbing her head in both hands. The plastic bottle of pills fell to the floor and rolled against the toilet. He sobbed into her hair. "Christ, hon . . ."

"I didn't take any," Heather said, and it was the voice of the recently deceased. Her hands continued to shake. Her eyes could not focus on him—could not focus on anything. "I thought about it but I didn't take any."

"Shhhh," Alan said into her hair, gently rocking her. "Shhhh, babe. Shhhh."

And the next morning she was fine. She even got her old job back at the art gallery. Just like that. As if it had all been a dream.

The stabbing, burning pain worsening in his gut, Alan went to his own doctor who diagnosed him with an ulcer. The doctor prescribed misoprostol and antacid tablets and told Alan to cut back on the drinking and smoking and try not to be so stressed out, maybe take a vacation.

Alan could only smirk and assure the doctor that he would try to relax.

When Alan picked up the misoprostol from the pharmacy, the plastic bottle had one phrase mockingly printed across the label in all capital letters—PREGNANT WOMEN SHOULD NOT INGEST. The pharmacist looked at him as if he were crazy when he started laughing like a loon at the counter.

With the medication lulling his ulcer into semidormancy and Heather seemingly back on track, the nightmare appeared to be behind them. (Just to be on the safe side, Alan collected all the pills from the bathroom medicine cabinet, including Heather's antidepressants and an ancient tub of Tylenol, and hid them in the hallway closet behind a bundle of towels.)

The doctors found nothing physically wrong with either of them, so there was really no reason they couldn't try again, couldn't eventually have children. There were all sorts of reasons why the body aborts a fetus—they were told this dozens of times—and, in the long run, it was usually for the best. Mother Nature's way of righting herself, one doctor had said. Alan and Heather had mumbled to each other, "Mother Nature's a whore. Mother Nature never did nothin' for nobody" until their laughter filled the apartment.

They went out to dinner and to the movies, read books in Central Park, visited their favorite café for Sunday brunch. When Alan got word that his uncle Phillip had died and he had inherited the old man's house, he and Heather never even considered the possibility of leaving the city and moving to rural North Carolina. In truth, he was not only surprised that his uncle had remembered him from the few times they had seen each other when Alan was just a boy, but Uncle Phillip had two grown children, Maryanne and Keith, who would have been more appropriate recipients of the property.

In an effort to do the right thing, Alan attempted to track down both cousins, a task that was difficult to say the least, and finally managed to locate Keith in Rhode Island. He offered Keith his condolences to which his cousin made a snuffling, snorting sound on the other end of the line that reminded Alan of hogs nosing through slop. There was a cold, distant air about his cousin. The distance only increased when Alan brought up the house. Of course, Keith had already known the house had been left to Alan.

"I'm not quite sure why he left it to me," Alan

confessed. "I didn't think he remembered me."

"I'm not sure why, either." Keith sounded like he wanted to get off the phone quickly. "Doesn't matter. That dump is your problem now."

"I was going to see if you wanted it. I've got no use for a house in North Carolina."

"So sell it."

"What about Maryanne? Do you think she'd have any interest in—?"

"She moved to London ten years ago. I've heard from her maybe a dozen times since then. She's got no interest in that old place, either. Believe me."

When Alan got off the phone, he felt like he needed to take a shower. Something about talking to his cousin had left him feeling dirty. "I guess I'll eventually have to take a trip down there and check the place out," he said to Heather one morning over breakfast. "You know, before we can sell it."

Then one random night, Alan was jarred awake by a horrible nightmare, the details of which he could not remember the instant he sat up in bed.

Heather's side of the bed was empty.

Through the darkness, he peered down the hall. The bathroom door was closed, the sliver of buttery light visible beneath the door.

His heart began to race. He tried to calm himself. Thought, *She's taking a leak. Chill out.* He waited. Waited.

"Babe?" he called.

No answer.

He flipped the bedsheets off and hurried down the hall, twisted the bathroom doorknob.

Locked.

"Heather!"

He slammed one shoulder against the door. The frame splintered on impact. He stumbled into the cramped bathroom and froze as he saw her in the tub, the water around her stained pink, a razor in the soap dish. Her gaze shifted in his direction. He could see the life draining from her eyes even as he stood there.

He rushed to her, gathered her up out of the tub. Examining her wrists was like facing his worst nightmare. He wrapped her arms in towels and called 911. Twice she started to pass out, but he slapped her face and talked to her and made her eyes stay open.

*You tricked me*, he thought. *You had me believing everything was all right so I'd drop my guard. And then you tried to leave me again.*

He was sobbing like a baby into her hair by the time the paramedics came in through the front door.

# CHAPTER FOUR

Alan awoke covered in sweat, the memory of the past year clinging to him like a web. It took him a few moments to recall his surroundings: the new house, the new master bedroom. Their bed shoved against one wall, boxes still strewn about the bedroom half unpacked. Beside him, Heather slept soundly. The house was silent, not even the ticking of a clock to disturb the void. Alan stared at the rectangular panel of bluish moonlight along the ceiling while he listened to his own heartbeat.

*(I didn't take any. I thought about it but I didn't take any.)*

He pawed sweat from his eyes. He had been dreaming of the babies, the dead babies, and how the one had looked in the vacuum-sealed biohazard bag. The splayed foot, each toe perfectly and undeniably identifiable . . .

The memory of those events caused his ulcer to claw at the walls of his intestines. He groaned and rose creakily from the bed. His jeans were draped over a nearby chair. He climbed into them as Jerry Lee, who'd been asleep on the floor at the foot of their bed, lifted his head and watched him with lazy detachment. Too tired to follow his master, the dog dropped his head back down on his paws while Alan made his way out of the room to the hall.

Stumbling in the unfamiliar darkness and fumbling for light switches he couldn't readily locate, he arrived in the bathroom just as the pain in his stomach tightened into a tiny burning fist. He found his antacid tablets and downed two of them. His reflection stared wearily back at him.

*Being eaten from the inside out*, he thought. Grimaced. And on the heels of that, he couldn't help but think of wombs, broken and infertile . . .

As quietly as a cat, he slipped on his Nikes in the foyer and eased open the front door, stepping onto the porch and already poking a cigarette into his mouth. The porch floor-boards groaned beneath his feet. Lighting one of the cigarettes, he looked out across the front yard. It was late. All the houses on the other side of the street were asleep. He listened, wondering what was wrong, what was missing . . . then realized with half a smirk that it was the commotion of the city. He had grown so accustomed to city sounds that the rural silence was nearly deafening. Manhattan was alive in that electrical-current-through-wires way. Out here, it was as quiet and desolate as an ancient tomb.

From out of nowhere, he caught a strange yet oddly familiar scent on the air. Oddly *nostalgic*. It took him only two seconds to place the smell: his father's cologne. That cheap, medicinal Aqua Velva smell. It had come down on the wind and infiltrated his nose as sharp as a slap across the face.

Bill Hammerstun, who had been a miserable human being up until the day he died from a bullet in the brain, had tried to warn Alan against marriage. Women ran around on you. They were selfish and they cheated. And if they weren't running around on you, they stuck by your side just to make your life unbearable. (Alan had often wondered how his old man had come upon this second bit of wisdom as no woman, as far as Alan could tell, had ever stuck by his side—including Alan's mother.) Bill Hammerstun had been positively brimming with words of wisdom.

Alan remembered coming home from high school one day in late May, just a few weeks before graduation, to a squad car parked outside the Upper West Side tenement where he lived with his old man. Two cops were standing on the stoop with Jimmy Carmichael, one of his father's drinking buddies. The sight of the police car and the cops didn't alarm Alan; he had come home to such things before. It was Jimmy's presence that struck him as unusual. Jimmy did not associate with cops.

As Alan mounted the steps of the tenement, Jimmy had eased off the porch railing with a grunt. The man's considerable bulk shifted beneath his too-tight, sleeveless undershirt. Grinning sourly around a short black cigar, trying desperately to appear approachable, Jimmy had placed a heavy hand on Alan's shoulder and exhaled fetid breath into his face. *Hey there, sport,* he'd said. *Hey there, kiddo.*

Both cops had taken a simultaneous step forward, their arms folded. For one fleeting second, Alan thought they were there to arrest him. He thought of shoplifting from the 7-Eleven and stealing money from the tip jar at the Afghan

Kebab. Also, there had been the silver BMW with the cryptic vanity plates—MRBBALL. Alan and his friend Ritchie Ulrich had smashed the passenger window and pried the stereo out of the dashboard with a screwdriver. Before running away, they had even glommed the loose change from the cup holders between the front seats.

*Hey there, sport. Hey there, kiddo.*

The cops had shuttled him off, along with Jimmy, to the city morgue where his father had already been pronounced dead. Jimmy stood behind him with one fat hand on his shoulder as Alan looked at his old man dead on the stainless steel table in the basement. Bill Hammerstun's skin had already gone a fishy, sallow color. His face looked like a mold of himself made out of vulcanized rubber. There was something that resembled blue pool chalk on his cheek. And, of course, the dime-sized bullet wound in his right temple. Blessedly, the blood had been cleaned away.

Alan had looked to Jimmy and, with little emotion, asked him what the hell he was supposed to do now.

Jimmy rolled his big, meaty shoulders and said he didn't know. *You're eighteen now, ain't you, sport? Guess you can do whatever you want. Happy trails.*

He had contacted his mother, who had been estranged from him since his early childhood. He had never fully understood what had gone wrong in his parents' relationship, though he often wondered how any woman could have put up with Bill Hammerstun for the entirety of a marriage, so he didn't necessarily blame her for leaving. He had located her somewhere in Michigan, and she passed along unemotional condolences over the telephone—a bad connection, the line popped and hissed with static for the duration of the phone call—but she did not invite him to live with her. The call lasted no longer than five minutes, and toward the end of it, Alan paid more attention to what sounded like a crying baby in the background than to the actual words coming out of his mother's mouth.

He received money from the sale of his father's nightclub, which paid for the funeral costs and even set him up in an apartment in Manhattan. He took on two roommates—punk rockers with dyed hair and an affinity for clove cigarettes and fuzzy music with garbled lyrics—and Jimmy Carmichael gave him a job as a bicycle courier in Midtown while he put himself through college with the remainder of the nightclub money.

Only once did Alan think he saw his dead father, and it was a cold, rainy late afternoon. He'd tethered his bike to a No Parking sign and rushed into an office building to deliver a package. On his way out, an eerie calm seemed to overtake him. Strangely, there wasn't any traffic along the street, though he could see the flaring of taillights at the nearest intersection through the drizzle. Tugging the hood of his nylon jacket over his head, he began running the combination to his bike lock, anxious to get home and out of the rain.

But then something had caused him to look up. Across the street and hidden within the shadows of a narrow alley that cut between two buildings, a pale visage emerged from the gloom. At first, Alan thought it was a homeless man, but then he recognized the face, floating there in the darkness of the alley like a moon hanging in space, and a cold dread coursed through his veins. He hurriedly undid the bike lock and jumped onto the seat, his legs already pedaling in the air before they had a chance to settle onto the pedals themselves. Once he hopped down the curb and gained speed, he risked a glance over his shoulder. The pale face was gone, having retreated into the shadows. Or perhaps, he would think later that night, it had never existed in the first place.

*Happy trails*, he thought now, smoking the cigarette down to the filter. Contrary to what his doctor had told him, smoking actually made his ulcer feel better. Fuck doctors. Happy trails, indeed.

He stepped off the porch and cut through the yard on his way around to the back of the house. Momentarily, the scent of his father's cologne grew stronger. The sky was a country sky, afire with an abundance of stars. The moon was fat and full, the color of bone. Lighting a second cigarette, Alan crossed the yard while trailing the palms of his hands over the high grass. It was warm enough for fireflies, and this night they were out in multitude, filling the sky with their peculiar brand of visual Morse code.

Alan's gaze fell upon the dark hollow in the curtain of trees. It looked like the mouth of a cave in the side of a mountain. He exhaled a cloud of smoke out of the corner of his mouth and tromped down the tall grass on his way over to the stand of trees. Stupidly, it caused him to think of the alley between the two buildings and the pale moon face that had floated there, watching him from across a Manhattan street.

*Quit it.*

A cool, summery breeze cascaded down into the yard, rustling his hair and causing gooseflesh to spring up on his bare chest. The breeze passed through the branches of the pines, too, making them undulate. As if waving him closer, beckoning him. A ghostly moan rose out of the woods: the wind funneling through hollow trees.

He passed through the opening between the trees and stepped onto the path.

Darkness rushed in to greet him. Just a few paces down the path, he paused and glanced up. Despite the brilliance of the moon and the clear sky, the overlapping branches above his head were plentiful enough to keep much of the moonlight off the path and out of the woods. Yet as his eyes grew accustomed to the dark, he made out something glowing dimly in the shadows of the woods just a few yards ahead of him on the path. He walked toward it, keeping his knees bent and one hand in front of his eyes to swipe away errant tree branches. As he drew closer he realized it was the smooth white stone he had seen earlier that day, the one with the strange upside-down triangle carved into it. And even though the moonlight was limited here in the woods, the stone glowed faintly, as if radioactive.

Alan crouched before the stone and waved one hand in front of it. His fingers left psychedelic trails in their wake. Looking up, he saw more white stones staggered at intervals along the path, which appeared to wind deeper and deeper into the woods.

*Happy trails*, he thought again and continued down the path.

Even with the stones guiding his way, he nearly got lost. If the stones were supposed to serve as directional markers, they could have been arranged in a better fashion. Some of the stones sat on the edge of the path while others veered off into the underbrush, causing him to step clumsily and blindly into a bush or to bark his shins on moss-covered deadfalls. All the stones had a symbol, each one different, carved into them, and they seemed to radiate with that same phosphorescent light. *It's reflecting the moonlight; that's got to be it.* When he touched one, it was as cold as ice. He pulled his hand away and felt a timorous laugh quake through his body.

He stood there for a moment, the reality of the situation settling upon him. Wandering around out here in the dark was foolish. He could trip over something, break an ankle. Or fall down a blind ravine and break his neck. If he was so curious about where this path led, he could follow it tomorrow in the daylight.

Yet something refused to let him turn around and return to the house. He could convince himself that he swore he smelled his father's cologne again, stronger here in the woods, but he didn't necessarily think that was true. Whatever was urging him to keep going was inexplicable.

Alan continued down the path. The antacid began working on his ulcer, dulling it into stupid submission. By the time he reached the end of the path, all the glowing white stones behind him now in the darkness, he'd forgotten about the pain.

The trees opened up on an immense moonlit clearing of low grass, billowy ground fog, and pockets of tiny white flowers. He stepped into the clearing and looked around in awe.

The trees seemed much older than the ones in the woods, their trunks an impressive circumference, like the trees in the redwood forest off the Pacific Coast, and they were as white as polished bone in the moonlight. They were staggered in a rough circle around the perimeter of the clearing, glossy and seeming to drip wetly with moon glow. Their bare branches reached high into the night sky and passed like a network of veins across the colorless face of the moon. They were towering, tremendous, mind-boggling things.

In the center of the trees was a small lake.

Its surface covered by a blanket of roiling mist, the lake didn't appear to him all at once. The mist slid slowly off the surface of the water in a rolling, smoky fashion, dense as wool. As it reached the edge of the lake, the mist thinned out until it clung low to the ground where it continued to undulate as if alive. Motionless, Alan stood and watched as the mist dissipated throughout the clearing, slowly spreading out to the surrounding corral of trees. It took several seconds before he realized he was holding his breath.

*It's beautiful . . .*

Alan walked to the edge of the lake and peered down at the water. It could have been tar or smoked glass it was so black. His reflection mirrored up at him, looking ghastly and skeletal. His skin was white as stone, his eyes huge and dark and seemingly recessed into deep pockets. He could easily make out the apostrophe-shaped cut above his right eyebrow and the bruise on his cheek.

He dropped to one knee and reached out, sticking two fingers into the water—

*(ice-cold!)*

—only to pull them quickly out, hissing between

clenched teeth. A bundle of muscles at the small of his back tightened from the cold. He flexed his fingers, working the feeling back into them, amazed at how numb they'd become from no longer than a split second beneath the water. It was July and the water was ice-cold . . .

His reflection stared up at him.

Rippling.

Things moved in the trees. *Large* things.

Alan stood and stared at them: black silhouettes framed against the night sky. Only the ones on the branches that passed in front of the moon were clearly outlined.

*Birds*, he thought, though the realization afforded him little relief and did not do the birds justice. *Buzzards*.

There were scores of them, whole families, multitudes. Carrion birds, stooped over like hunchbacks in bell towers. And although he knew it was crazy, he had the disquieting feeling that they were all watching him.

*Carnivorous birds.*

It was insane, sure . . . but if they all decided to simultaneously swoop down off their perches and attack . . .

A noise somewhere off to his left collected his attention. Alan turned and squinted. For a second he thought he could see the pale shape of a man wending through the trees. But the harder he looked for the figure, the more he became convinced it was just his imagination.

When he looked up again he noticed some of the buzzards had moved closer together on a number of the lower branches of the giant, skeletal trees. That many birds and the night should have been a cacophony of shrill, earsplitting shrieks. But these birds were silent. They'd gathered on the lower branches of the trees while he wasn't looking, as if creeping up on him for an ambush . . .

Out of nowhere the absurdity of the situation struck him. Nervous, he laughed maybe a bit too loud, his eyes still on the collection of large birds—they didn't seem disturbed by the sound—before retreating across the clearing toward the wooded path.

But Alan could not find the path. The opening in the trees was now obscured by a dull mist. In fact, it appeared as if the mist itself had gotten caught in the boughs of the trees and tangled around their trunks like smoky strands of gossamer. A disturbing thought suddenly struck him: *The mist doesn't want me to leave.* Trapped, captive, imprisoned forever. It was ridiculous, of course, but it still caused a cold butterfly to flutter to life in his stomach. He wanted to laugh again, if for no other reason than to fool his addled brain into clearheadedness, but decided against it. He had been lucky with the birds thus far. He didn't want to press his luck further by startling them with mad laughter.

For several minutes he wandered around the perimeter of the clearing, peering through the soupy mist in hopes of locating the path. He couldn't retrace his footsteps because he'd left none behind. None that he could see, anyway. He knew *approximately* where the opening should be, as he had pretty much walked in a straight line from the end of the path to the clearing. But as he swam through the fog toward the place he assessed the path should have been, parting the cloudy air with his hands, he stumbled over and over again into a profusion of pine needles.

Finally, when it seemed he would never find the path

RONALD MALFI

again and he started deliberating whether or not he should push his way through the goddamn trees and keep walking until he eventually staggered into his own backyard, he spied the dark hollow through the wall of fog. He went to it and crossed between the trees, stepping onto the dirt path. He spotted one of the luminous white stones up ahead in the woods.

*I checked here already*, he thought. *I know I did.*

Disquieted, he pushed on through the woods, refusing to look back over his shoulder the entire way.


Alan wasn't sure how long he'd actually been outside, stumbling through the clearing to find the path, but by the time he stepped into his backyard, the moon had repositioned itself in the sky. The night had cooled considerably, causing a chill to ripple through his body and his bare chest to prickle. For some reason, he felt fatigued, as if he had just returned from a long, arduous journey.

He lit one final cigarette, taking his time walking around the side of the house toward the front porch. A strong breeze rustled the remaining leaves high in the trees. Finishing the cigarette, he looked across the street. All remained still and quiet. *Ghost town*, he thought. Which made him think of Heather.

There was a police car parked farther down the street, a couple of houses away from Alan's. He just happened to glance up and see it. Its lights and engine off, it looked abandoned. From this distance, he couldn't tell if there was anyone sitting inside it or not. Was it the same car from earlier that day? He tried to make out the sheriff's department emblem on the door, but it was too dark.

Alan tossed the cigarette butt and walked to the edge of the property. One of the neighbors was probably a police officer and parked his car in the street at night to deter burglars. No big deal. Yet on the other hand, if there was something going on in the neighborhood—something that required around-the-clock police surveillance, in other words—he wanted to know about it.

There was movement from inside the police car. He was positive he saw something. The shape of someone sitting up behind the wheel . . .

Alan stepped into the street and walked toward the police car. The cruiser's headlamps flared on, startling him. He froze, spotlighted in the glow of the headlights. His shadow became an elongated scarecrow on the pavement behind him.

The cruiser's engine coughed to life. The car pulled away from the curb and nearly hopped the opposite one as it spun around and took off down the street toward the nearest intersection.

Alan watched the cruiser's taillights disappear in the darkness.

# CHAPTER FIVE

Hank Gerski's basement was a shrine to the Baltimore Orioles. Theatrical-sized posters of Cal Ripken Jr. hung from the paneling; a conga line of autographed baseballs sat on the mantelpiece, hermetically sealed in clear plastic globes; a scuffed pair of cleats hung from a bronze peg above a coffee table, the tabletop itself a patchwork of baseball cards housed in Lucite. Hank had played a single season with the O's in the early nineties before an auto accident ruined his left knee. He worked now as a bookkeeper for a law firm and didn't seem bitter about settling for a life of mediocrity.

Alan surveyed the paraphernalia. "Do you miss playing?"

"I did early on. Thought my life had ended. Not so much anymore, though."

"I'd be devastated."

Hank shrugged. "Family keeps me busy enough, I guess."

"Yeah, but still . . . I mean, that had to have been one

hell of a ride, playing professional ball."

"It's only a game," he said, grinning goofily. He was dressed in a ridiculous Hawaiian shirt and overly starched chinos and sipped noisily from a can of beer. "You guys planning to have kids?"

Outside, laughter from the backyard could be heard as Lydia entertained the rest of their guests. Alan hadn't wanted to attend the barbecue, but he thought it might be good for Heather to get out of the house and meet some of the neighbors, so he had accepted Hank's invitation.

"I don't know," Alan said dryly.

"It's a great neighborhood, a great place to raise kids," Hank went on. "Everyone's real friendly. Fourth of July we have a parade down Market Street, and at Christmas all the shops in town are decorated real nice. Santa comes through on a fire engine and everything, throwing candy canes to the kids. You'll see how crazy it gets at Halloween soon enough, too, so make sure you guys get plenty of candy. Your doorbell will be ringing all night. And trust me, man, you don't want to clean up toilet paper from the trees the next morning."

"Anything bad every happen in this great neighborhood?" Alan said. He hadn't meant to sound sarcastic, but Hank didn't seem to notice.

"What do you mean?"

"Well, I've noticed a cop car sitting across the street on two different occasions. Once in the middle of the night. I was wondering if there'd been some burglaries or vandalism in the neighborhood. Anything like that."

"Oh," said Hank, "you're talking about Sheriff Landry. It's

nothing to worry about. Just the standard neighborhood patrol."

"The sheriff does his own patrolling?"

Hank shrugged. "We're a small town. There's only him and two deputies."

"They don't recruit you all for that sort of thing? Citizens on patrol and neighborhood watch and whatever else?"

Hank raised his eyebrows and examined his beer can. His expression relayed that he had never given it much consideration before. "Landry likes to keep pretty hands-on. One of those perfectionist types."

"I hate those," Alan commented, only half-joking.

"Guess you can't shake your own upbringing," Hank said. "Can't take the boy out of the city, that kind of thing."

Now it was Alan's turn to shrug and look overly casual. "Where I come from, a cop car slides past your house, you close your windows and hope the stray bullets don't come through the drywall."

"Was it really that bad?" There was genuine fascination on Hank's boyish face. "Like, shoot-outs in the streets and things like that? The stuff they show on those *CSI* programs?"

It hadn't really been that bad growing up in the city, but Alan deliberately hesitated before he answered, hoping the moment of empty silence would fill Hank's head with all sorts of images of urban violence and moral decay.

"I guess it's just gonna take me a while to get used to things around here," he confessed. "Even the air smells funny."

"Funny?"

"Clean. Like, I've never smelled fresh air before."

Hank didn't so much laugh as make a nasally *gah* sound way back in his throat.

"The trees, the fields, the mountains," Alan went on. "It's like a Bob Ross painting set to a Louis Armstrong soundtrack."

Hank leaned forward and, with one bronzed thumb, wiped a smear off one of the plastic baseball globes. "It's the untouched land. The fresh air coming down off the mountains."

"Yeah." Alan let this sink in. "Speaking of the land, there's a path cutting through the trees at the back of my yard." Since he'd followed the path to the clearing on that first night, he found himself waking up in bed at random hours every night for the past week, just thinking about it. As if he'd been dreaming about it—dreaming of *something*—but was powerless to remember anything about it as he came awake. "You know the one I'm talking about?"

"Yeah," Hank said. "I think so."

"There are these white stones along the path. A dozen or so, maybe more. They each have different symbols carved into them."

Hank turned away from the mantelpiece and leaned back against a bookcase, folding and unfolding his arms. His thumb made irritating popping sounds on the beer can.

"I guess I was just curious what they were."

"The stones?"

"The stones and the symbols, too. You've seen them, right?"

"I don't know," Hank said. "I'm not sure."

"You don't know if you've seen them?" He hadn't meant for his words to come out so combative, but once again Hank didn't seem to notice.

"No," Hank said. "I mean, I don't know who put them there. Probably kids. Anyway, what's the big deal?"

"They seemed so precise, so deliberate. I didn't get the impression that kids carved those symbols," Alan said. One was a triangle, one was two circles attached by a horizontal line, and another resembled the crenellated tower of a medieval castle. For a moment he thought about mentioning the strange birds, too, but realized there was no way to bring them up without sounding paranoid.

"Did you follow the path?"

"I did, yeah. It led to a small lake in a clearing. No bigger than a large pond, really."

"It's probably best to keep out of those woods," Hank said. His tone was matter-of-fact but almost forcibly so. He continued to fold and unfold his arms as he spoke. "We get bears coming down from the mountains in the summer and fall. They've been known to go through people's trash, and one even killed someone's dog on Broad Street last year."

"No kidding? Bears?"

"Anyway, you don't want to accidentally run into one of those suckers going through the woods."

"Have you ever seen one?"

"No. But I've seen the messes they leave behind. Garbage strewn all over the streets."

"But you know nothing about those stones, huh? The ones with the symbols on them?"

Hank once again flashed his toothy grin. "That's the college professor in you, isn't it?" His big head looked like a pumpkin with sideburns. "Always trying to find answers to the unexplained? I mean, I totally envy you academic types. I wish I had it in me to be so smart."

Footsteps sounded on the basement stairs. Don Probst,

who lived with his wife, Jane, two houses up from the Ger-ski house, appeared at the foot of the stairs. Alan had been introduced to him earlier that afternoon as the neighbors slowly gathered in Hank's backyard. Don was stocky, well-muscled, tan. A beer bottle sweated in one meaty paw.

"This some meeting of the special boys' club?" Don asked.

"Don the bomb," said Hank.

"Seriously, am I interrupting?"

Hank waved a hand at him. "Heck, no. I was just show-ing Alan my baseball junk. And telling him how envious I am that he gets to sit around the house all summer until school starts."

"Oh yeah," Don said, crossing over to them. "At the community college, right?"

Alan nodded.

"Hope you don't get my kid," Don said, rolling his eyes dramatically. "For the sake of your own sanity."

"I get my students to listen pretty well," he countered. "I take a gun to class."

Don's sense of humor was about as sharp as a balloon. But after a few beats his face creased in some suggestion of a smile. He laughed, which sounded like the backfire of an old pickup, and jabbed a stubby finger in Alan's direc-tion. "This guy," he said, turning to Hank. "This guy, he shouldn't be a professor; he should be a comedian."

When the three of them returned to Hank's backyard, the other neighbors were drinking around a large picnic table while Hank's barbecue sizzled in the background. The world smelled of hamburgers, onions, potato salad, char-coal. Young Catherine was making the rounds performing card tricks for anyone who'd grant her ten seconds of attention.

The men passed around cigars and swilled beer. Most of the women had gathered around one young woman whose swollen abdomen became the center of attention. Jane Probst had her hand on the woman's pregnant belly, and she was grinning like an idiot. Never quite able to understand how one person could just walk up and touch another person's stomach, Alan watched the women with a combination of distaste and sheer puzzlement.

*Belly touchers*, he thought. *The whole lot of you.*

His eyes connected with Heather's. She sat alone in a lawn chair, an unopened can of beer in her lap. Her stare caused his testicles to retreat into his abdomen. At that moment he was all too clearly aware of his ulcer.

Thankfully, Lydia broke the tension when she clapped and told them all that it was time to eat.

That night, at some ungodly hour, Alan awoke to find Heather's side of the bed empty. Fear shook him. He thought he could hear the shudder of pipes and the sounds of running water. Terrified, he thought of locked bathroom doors and tubs half-filled with pinkish water.

Blood pumping, he sprung from bed and called Heather's name. It was like shouting into an empty steel chamber. He raced out into the hall and found the bathroom door standing ajar, the light from the bathroom spilling onto the floor and the opposite wall in a crooked rectangle. A curl of steam roiled into the hallway from the bathroom, like fog rolling across a graveyard.

But the bathroom was empty. Water emptied into the tub, which was half full. The water was crystal clear.

Yet this didn't set his mind at ease. He staggered into the hallway, wondering if he was actually still dreaming . . .

"Heather? Baby?"

Still no answer.

Down the hall, the kitchen lights were off. So were the living room lights. He clicked on the lamp beside the couch, hoping to find his wife curled up there, but the couch was empty.

Jerry Lee whined from across the room, startling him. The dog stood by the sliding glass doors that led to the backyard, though the creature—seemingly equally as frightened as Alan—was looking at his master with moist, dark eyes that struck Alan as oddly human. Jerry Lee typically slept on the floor at the foot of the bed, as he had done in the apartment for many years, and Alan was surprised to find the dog standing here now, tail wagging.

Alan went quickly to the doors. Jerry Lee whined again but moved out of the way. Beyond the glass was nothing but pitch-black space. Alan ran his hand along the light switch that controlled the patio lights; they came on, casting white light onto the cement patio and the surrounding grass.

At first he didn't see anything. But then he noticed Heather standing in the tall grass, her back toward him and wraithlike in a sheer white nightgown, a vampire from an old Hammer film. She faced the line of trees at the edge of the yard, seemingly staring at the opening in the trees that marked the entrance to the dirt path.

Beside him, Jerry Lee barked. It was like a gunshot going off in an airplane hangar.

Alan unlocked the door and slid it open. He was wearing

nothing but a pair of pajama bottoms, and the cool summery wind suddenly chilled his bones and caused his chest
to break out in gooseflesh. "Heather!"

She didn't acknowledge him.

He stepped onto the patio, the concrete rough and cold
beneath his bare feet.

Behind him, Jerry Lee whimpered but did not follow
him outside.

"Honey?"

Still no acknowledgment. In fact, as if in direct disobe-
dience, Heather began walking toward the opening in the
trees, toward the dirt path.

For whatever reason, this caused a hard lump to rise in
Alan's throat. He broke into a sprint and closed the distance
between them before she could disappear within the trees.
He dropped a hand on her shoulder and spun her around.

Her face was frightening—a blank canvas. "Oh," she
uttered in a small voice. It was like waking a somnambulist.

"What are you doing out here?"

The question seemed to confuse her. She looked disoriented. He stared hard at her until recollection filtered into
her eyes.

"Oh," she said, though more clearly now. "I was looking for you."

"Me?"

"Yes."

"Out here?"

"I didn't know."

"Didn't know what?"

Heather looked confused. "I just . . . I didn't know . . ."

"Why would you think I'd be out here in the middle of the night?"

"Because you whispered something to me. I was half-asleep. You whispered something in my ear about going down to the lake." A small fissure formed in the center of her forehead as she frowned. "Didn't you?"

"No," he said.

"*Someone* did."

"It wasn't me."

"But *someone* . . ."

"No one did. Maybe you dreamt it."

"No," she said simply. "I heard it."

"Of course you dreamt it." His heart was bursting.

"No." She was calm but adamant. "I didn't dream it. I heard it. It was you."

"Come on." He slipped an arm around her waist and led her across the yard toward the house.

# CHAPTER SIX

Sunday afternoon, a full week after they'd moved into the house, Alan found himself alone for the first time since arriving in town. Lydia had come by earlier and, after much prodding, convinced Heather to go shopping with her. Heather had pulled on a pair of wrinkled slacks and a blouse and, after searching around the house for her purse for nearly fifteen minutes, left with Lydia without saying good-bye to Alan. He was certain Lydia noticed the awkwardness between them—she wasn't blind—but she didn't say anything. Heather's bandages were gone now, and she took to wearing heavy silver bracelets to cover the scars, but Alan wondered if Lydia had noticed the bandages that first day when she brought over the casserole and the bottle of wine.

Nonetheless, he savored the solitude. He hadn't realized how much he had begun to feel like Heather's babysitter—no, Heather's goddamn *keeper*—since her suicide attempt. It hadn't even been a conscious thing; he just knew that he never felt right leaving her alone. And the night he'd found her standing in the yard, staring at the trees? Even now in the relative safety of daylight, it chilled him to recall that event. What the hell had she been doing? When he questioned her about it the following morning, she couldn't even remember doing it let alone provide a reasonable explanation. With much unease, he wondered what he was going to do when school started in the fall.

*Maybe that night in the yard was just a fluke and things will be different here*, he thought. *Maybe things will get better. This is a nice town and the people, however tedious, are nice, too. Heather might even find a friend in Lydia or one of the other neighbors and start living her life again. We can beat this; we can get past all the badness.*

He hoped.

In the kitchen, he heated up some of the coffee from that morning in the microwave and listened to the silence of the otherwise empty house.

Jerry Lee poked his head into the kitchen, sniffed around, then admonished Alan with solemn eyes. Then the dog licked his chops and retreated down the hall, yawning.

"Lazy bastard," Alan called after him.

He was contemplating cutting away some of the vines that crept along the house when he happened to notice one of those very vines crawling up the wall from behind the refrigerator. It startled him at first, as it looked nearly snake-like in its appearance. Only a few inches were visible, thin and curling at the tip, but he imagined it must have come up from the floor behind the refrigerator and was probably several feet long and thick as an electrical cord at its base.

"Son of a bitch, you buggers are stubborn."

He leaned against the wall and peered behind the refrigerator. Sure enough, the vine ran down the wall and vanished into a crack in the molding at the bottom. A second vine, much thinner, had branched off the first and had wrapped itself around the grate at the back of the refrigerator. The vines reminded Alan of a video he'd seen about Humboldt squid in the Sea of Cortez and how their tentacles would splay out and make grabs at the cameramen.

The microwave beeped, making him flinch. He laughed nervously and retrieved the steaming mug, smelling the rich aroma. The doctor had cautioned him about drinking too much coffee, as it promised to aggravate the ulcer, but for Christ's sake, he couldn't give up all his worldly pleasures, could he?

Through one of the kitchen windows, Alan caught sight of something dark moving in the forked trunk of a tree in the side yard. He approached the window for a better look and felt his bowels clench. His blood suddenly turned to ice.

It was enormous—perhaps the size of a car's spare tire—and the enormity of it made the thing look almost ridiculous hunkered down in the crook of the spindly little tree. Since that night in the clearing off the path, Alan had managed to convince himself that in his sleep-deprived state he had either exaggerated the size of the birds or possibly even imagined them altogether; but here in the daylight, staring straight at one of the beasts, the truth of it all came crashing back down on him. The thing was *huge*.

Alan drummed his fingers on the windowpane.

The giant bird cocked its fleshy head but did not take

its eyes from him. Alan tapped the glass harder. The damn thing refused to fly away.

In the foyer, he strapped on his sneakers, then went into the front yard just as thunder rumbled overhead. Across the street, a number of neighborhood kids were getting in their baseball game before the storm hit.

Mr. Pasternak from farther up the block jogged by on what Alan had come to learn was his usual midafternoon run. Mr. Pasternak raised a hand, his sweat-soaked tank top and nylon running shorts hanging from his narrow skin-and-bones frame. Mr. Pasternak was eighty-seven though he looked twenty years younger. Alan had met him earlier in the week while the old man jogged by, and they'd shared a short but pleasant conversation by the mailbox.

"My young friend," Mr. Pasternak cawed as he strode by.

"Hey," Alan returned, not pausing to talk this time. He crossed to the side of the house only to find the little dogwood tree empty. The big, ugly bird had disappeared. Fishing his cigarettes from his jeans and lighting one, he approached the tree with an overly sensitized sense of apprehension, as if the bird was going to spring out at him at any moment. Peck his eyeballs out or some such nonsense. God-damn thing was large enough to swoop down and snatch up a small child . . .

He leaned closer to examine the trunk of the tree. It had left behind claw marks in the shape of lightning bolts in the bark.

"Hey," Hank said from behind him, causing Alan to jump and turn around. Hank was leaning against a tree, two cans of Coors in his hands. He offered Alan his trademark grin, then handed him one of the beers. "Doing some yard work?"

"Something like that."

"You look like you're looking for somebody."

"Big fucking bird," he said, popping the top on the Coors.

"Oh yeah. You'll get those, sure. There's like fifteen hundred acres of forest behind your house in case you hadn't noticed. Remember what I said about the bears, too?" He winked. "Wild animals, dude."

For the first time, Alan thought he might actually come to like Hank. There was a goofy, brotherly quality about him that was warm and inviting.

"By the way," Alan said, knocking his beer can against Hank's, "thanks for the barbecue. We enjoyed meeting the rest of the neighborhood."

"No sweat. Glad to do it. Seems like Lydia and Heather have hit it off, too, huh?"

He couldn't tell if Hank was feeling him out, curious about Heather's rather obvious state of detachment, and Alan wondered if he should try to mitigate Hank's curiosity right off the bat. Not that he had any intention of filling him in on what he and Heather had been through and what she had done to herself . . .

There came the sound of screeching car tires followed by a vague *whump* from across the street. The shouts of the children playing baseball, which had been a constant cacophony since Alan had stepped from the house, now rose to a frenzied urgency that caused his stomach to clench like a fist. Both he and Hank dropped their beers and raced across the yard.

"Oh, Christ," Alan uttered, skidding to a stop.

There was a child on the ground, unmoving. A few yards away, a red Audi with a dented front fender had come to rest crookedly in the center of the street. The driver's door opened but no one came out. Through the glare across the Audi's windshield, Alan could make out only subtle, indistinct movements behind the steering wheel.

Hank rushed past him and over to the fallen child.

It took a few heartbeats for Alan to snap back to reality. He forced his legs to move toward the injured child. With each stride bringing him closer and closer, the horror of the scene grew more pronounced. Finally, when he reached the child, he had to quickly avert his eyes. The boy's legs were at funny angles, and there was a trickle of blood along one pant leg. Worse still was the way the boy's head was turned on his neck . . .

Hank crouched down and pressed his ear to the boy's face. "Jesus, Hank. Is he . . . ?"

"He's alive," Hank said. Then he shouted it, as if to attract the attention of anyone holding a phone. "He's alive!"

The crowd of neighborhood kids closed in, their faces slack, their eyes wide in a combination of fear and disbelief. Among them Alan recognized the boy *he'd* nearly hit with his car on that first day in town. For an instant, the boy's big, dark eyes met his. The boy's stare was accusatory, as if this had all somehow been Alan's fault.

"Get back, guys," he told the kids. His voice shook. "Give them room."

While Hank touched the side of the boy's throat, perhaps checking for the strength of his pulse, Alan took a step back. His foot came down on something. He looked down and found himself standing on a baseball glove. He suddenly thought he was going to be sick.

Neighbors stood on their porches. Some of the men gathered around the fallen boy. The boy wasn't moving. Aside from the splash of blood on his pants, there was some blood on his T-shirt as well, but Alan held out hope that the minimal amount of it was a good sign. One of the kid's sneakers was missing, leaving behind a foot within a floppy white sock pointing at the sky. Absently, Alan wondered where the sneaker had gone.

*And his neck, oh God, the poor kid's neck . . .*

He hurried around the emergent crowd of men and peered into the Audi's open door. A woman, no more than thirty years of age, sat behind the wheel. She would have been attractive had her face retained any color, had it not been stricken by the sudden horror of what she had done. White-knuckled, she squeezed the steering wheel in both hands. She was mumbling something under her breath as he approached.

He bent down and said "Ma'am" a number of times through the open door, but she didn't respond.

"Move!" one of the men shouted from the huddle.

Alan looked up and watched the huddle begin to separate, amazed at just how *far* the boy had been thrown.

"He's breathing! The kid's breathing!"

". . . nowhere," said the woman.

Alan looked at her. "What?"

"Came out of nowhere." Her voice was barely audible.

"It'll be okay." It was a stupid thing to say—the sort of

stupid thing people say in movies that cause the audience to groan—but it was the only thing that came to his mind. So he repeated the stupid thing: "It'll be okay."

"Ask the woman her name." It was Don Probst, coming up behind him. Don looked about as gray as the sky. "We should get her name."

Alan reached into the car and turned off the engine, sliding the gear to Park. The last thing he wanted was for the woman to freak out and accidentally gun the accelerator, plowing through the crowd of men trying to help the injured boy. He withdrew the keys from the ignition. The woman didn't even look at him.

"Someone should call an ambulance," he said, backing away from the Audi. He slammed into Don, who hardly uttered a sound. Turning to face the neighbors who were still standing on their porches, Alan shouted, "Someone call an ambulance!"

He turned and, to his horror, saw Hank and two other men *lifting* the injured boy off the ground. The boy's head pivoted awkwardly. His limbs hung limply, and that white sneakerless sock was like a finger pointing straight at the heavens. A large smear of blood was soaking into the concrete.

"Don't *lift* him!" Alan shouted, already backing away in the direction of his house. "Are you crazy? Wait for a fucking ambulance!"

Of all the absurd things and despite the gruesomeness of the scene, the group of kids recoiled at his language. One of them even pointed at him in astonishment, then covered his ears. It would have been comical under different circumstances.

Alan rushed across his lawn and into the house, wondering where the hell he'd put his goddamn cell phone when, blowing past the kitchen, he realized there was a phone on the wall.

Ramming one shoulder against the side of the refrigerator, he yanked the receiver off the cradle and punched 911. The operator came on and he stammered, "Ambulance! Ambulance!" Once he was connected, he prattled off what had happened, answering the questions he could while stumbling over the ones he didn't know, such as the name of the boy who'd been hit and the woman's name—

*(ask the woman her name we should get her name)*

—who'd hit him.

Like earlier, something out the window caught his attention. He slammed the phone down on the handset and practically pressed himself up against the kitchen window.

Two boys from the baseball game stood in his yard, their hands weighted down with oversized gloves, their baseball hats too big for their heads. They were staring in the direction of the backyard. Don appeared from around the rear of the house and bent to speak to one of the children. He held the boy's shoulder and talked very close to his face, the brim of the boy's baseball cap nearly touching Don's forehead. The boy nodded and took off toward the street, leaving his friend behind. Don ran his hands through his thick black hair, then dipped back behind the house.

Alan bounded down the hallway and cut through the living room, heading for the sliding patio doors at the rear of the house. The commotion roused Jerry Lee from semi-consciousness; the dog began barking as if at an intruder.

Alan ignored him. Pulling the blinds back from the doors revealed a file of neighborhood men disappearing into the trees at the edge of the backyard. Don brought up the rear, hurrying now in a panicked jog.

Alan yanked on the door handle but it wouldn't budge. Futilely, he repeated this action two more times before he realized that the goddamn door was *locked*. He flipped the lock and the door whooshed open. Apparently, he'd been sweating for the past couple of minutes because the stormy breeze descending from the mountains froze the perspiration to his skin, causing a series of shivers to race down to the small of his back. He shouted Don's name, but the man had already disappeared through the trees and down the rutted dirt path.

Rushing outside, he nearly slammed into the boy who'd remained standing, wide-eyed and motionless, in the yard. The boy looked about eight years old. He stared up at him, disbelief still tattooed on his face. His ears bent under the weight of his oversized baseball hat.

"What's going on?" Alan shouted, his voice loud enough to cause the boy to flinch. It was a ridiculous question to shout at an eight-year-old, anyway.

The boy pointed at the dark gap between the trees where Don and the rest of the men had vanished just moments ago. A strong wind shook the trees, swinging the branches in front of the hollow. As if trying to close it up, hide it from sight.

"They took Cory," said the boy.

Without another word, Alan took off toward the opening in the trees. Shoving branches out of his way, he stepped onto the path and passed into the depths of the woods.

Hardly any sunlight permeated the trees. Ahead, he could see Don bringing up the rear as the line of men hurried along the wooded path. Alan thought he spotted Hank among them, but it was too hard to tell because the man he believed to be Hank was surrounded by two other men— the two men who'd helped him lift the boy off the pavement—and all three were moving in synchronized strides.

"Don!"

Don froze and whirled around, his eyes nearly bugging out of his head. "Jesus, Alan . . ."

"What the fuck's going on?"

"Look," he said, placing a hand on Alan's chest, "go back to the house, round up a bunch of towels. I'll come back and get you when—"

"What are you talking about? Where are they taking him?"

"We're not—"

"What the hell do you guys think you're *doing*?" Alan's voice shook the trees. He brushed past Don and tore off down the path in pursuit of the congregation. For a moment, he thought he could see that floppy white sock protruding out from the procession like a banner in a parade.

He broke into a full-fledged run, but the men were still a good distance ahead of him. And whereas they seemed to be continuing down the path in an unencumbered straight line, it appeared that he was left to contend with sharp turns and switchbacks, fallen limbs obstructing his passage, and low-hanging, clawlike branches reaching down to snag his clothes or draw blood from his skin. At one point, a formidably contentious tree limb snatched hold of his T-shirt and yanked him off his feet. He crashed to the ground in conjunction with an unsettling ripping sound. He hoped it was only his T-shirt and not a ligament tearing in his ankle, which he twisted in the fall. Glancing up, he spotted a strip of black T-shirt fabric flapping from the angry branch, and he felt his breath shudder from his abraded throat.

By the time Alan reached the end of the path, Hank and the rest of the men were already crossing the clearing toward the lake. The men carried the injured boy—Cory?—like island natives carrying a virgin sacrifice up the side of a volcano.

*What the hell do they think they're doing?*

He opened his mouth to shout Hank's name, but the wind was knocked out of him as Don rushed by.

Don offered a somewhat conciliatory glance from over one shoulder as he ran to catch up with the others, but something told Alan the bump wasn't completely accidental.

Righting himself against the nearest tree, Alan shook his head and paused while his vision cleared. His throat was on fire and his hands wouldn't stop shaking.

Hank—he was sure it was Hank now—splashed into the lake. Icy steam rose off his body, his muscles seeming to convulse at the touch of the water. He waded backward until he sank down to his chest, his empty arms outstretched toward the other men. Another one of the neighbors— Gary Jones, a car dealer Alan had met at Hank's barbecue—clutched one of Hank's wrists. Crazily, Alan thought they might begin chanting while forming a human circle until he realized Gary was just trying to steady Hank and help keep his balance.

The injured boy appeared like a casket carried by pallbearers. The men fed him through the crowd, his small, frail body quite visibly unconscious, until Hank was able to grab the boy's narrow, rounded shoulders. The poor kid's head hung too far back on his neck. Hank gripped the kid under both arms and dragged him backward into the lake. Gary followed, plodding down into the water.

For one insane moment, Alan thought they were going to drown the boy, hide him beneath the black waters of the lake. Bury him in the silt like a town secret. Perhaps they were covering up for the careless driver—*What happened to her, anyway?*—and were disposing of the body, getting rid of the evidence . . .

*What the hell . . . ?*

The boy's body floated briefly on the surface of the water. A third man climbed into the lake. Hank smoothed the boy's hair back on his forehead. The boy's skin looked sickly white and bloodless, the underbelly of a boa constrictor. When a fourth man tried to get into the water, Hank and Gary held up their hands and shook their heads. Don took the man by the elbow, as if to make sure he abided by the command to stop. The man looked around, wide-eyed and confused. Again, Don firmly yanked the man's elbow. Then Hank and Gary pressed down on the boy's chest, submerging him.

Alan uttered a strangled moan, which succeeded only in causing Don to turn and shoot a cold glance in his direction. Alan hurried over to the edge of the lake, finally managing an articulate "Hey!"

Don was quick for a man of his girth, whirling around to catch Alan by both shoulders just as he reached the huddle of men.

"Get the fuck *off* me," he groaned, knocking Don's hands free.

"Calm down." Don's voice sounded impeccably calm. "Just take a few deep breaths and relax."

"The *fuck* do you—?"

The boy's face broke the surface of the water. A gout of water burst from his lips as he coughed.

Alan stared in disbelief at the boy, who was now rapidly blinking, his mouth working soundlessly as he floated on his back in the water.

There was a collective sigh from the populace.

Hank gathered the boy against his chest, still smoothing back the child's wet hair. He hugged the boy to his chest, and Alan could see that both he and the child were shivering, their teeth rattling like—

*(maracas)*

—slot machines despite the summery temperature. Fleetingly, Alan recalled how cold the water had been when he'd touched its surface that night.

"Here, here, here," beckoned one of the men as he leaned over the edge of the lake. He took hold of one of the boy's hands, pulling him from Hank's grasp. Hank placed his hands on the boy's buttocks and hoisted him out of the water. The boy went limply but he was very much conscious.

Off to the side, both Gary and the third fellow climbed out of the lake. Their skin looked an ungodly grayish blue, and they were hugging themselves. Gary peeled off his shirt as one of the other men handed him his.

The boy's eyes were wide, roving around the circle of men. Disoriented, he groped blindly at Hank's sopping pant leg as Hank pulled himself from the lake. In a sour and gravelly voice, the boy muttered, "Lost my . . . glove . . ."

Hank laughed nervously and embraced the kid's head in a one-armed hug.

It was then that Alan noticed all the men staring at him. Their glares seemed to linger for an eternity, almost accusatory in their gravitas, as if he'd been the one behind the wheel of the red Audi. Even Hank glanced in his direction with a look of disapproval.

"Towels!" someone yelled, breaking the spell. "Anyone bring any towels? These guys are freezing their asses off!"

Don shot Alan an angry look. Don had told him to get the towels, of course. However, this hardly registered with him. He was rendered too dense and stupid to think or speak. Because of what he'd just seen . . . what he'd just *seen* . . .

# CHAPTER SEVEN

They wrapped Cory up in extra shirts, and someone draped a Windbreaker over his shaking shoulders. The boy followed them back through the woods along the path, his hands clenched together and pressed to his breastbone as if in prayer. His lips were colorless and they shivered feverishly, even in the heat of midday. The blood on his clothes had faded to a pinkish smear from the water, and his skin, to which the color was quickly returning, glistened with water diamonds. Despite his disorientation, the boy seemed to be wholly unfazed.

Alan followed them. Hank came up beside him and lightly squeezed his elbow.

"You okay?" Hank's voice was solemn. Hank's gait was tedious and slow, his limp more pronounced than before, and the rest of the men were far ahead of them on the dirt path. With some detachment, Alan recalled how Hank had run to the injured boy's side without much difficulty, despite his limp. As if his own pain and the injury suddenly didn't matter.

"You're asking *me*?" Alan surrendered a humorless chuckle. "That kid . . ."

"Is fine," Hank finished. He wore someone else's polo shirt, which was too small for his elongated, sinewy frame, and carried his own sopping wet shirt balled up in one fist. Like the boy, Hank was shivering. "There's an explanation for what happened here."

"But that *kid* . . ." He couldn't shake the image of the boy from his mind: sprawled out on the pavement, legs at crooked angles, blood soaking through his shirt and down his pants, the one blaringly white sock sticking straight up. When they lifted him, there'd been the smear of blood, dark as motor oil, on the pavement, and the back of the kid's shirt had been wet with it.

The way his head had turned funny when they lifted him . . .

"What the hell just happened?" he managed.

"He was stunned, that's all," Hank said.

"Stunned? But what about the blood?" He couldn't stop seeing the limp way they'd lifted him off the pavement, the way the kid's shirt *peeled* off the pavement, sticky with blood. "I think *I'm* the one who's stunned."

Hank looped an arm around Alan's neck. It was an oddly fatherly gesture. Alan thought of his dead father and how he could probably count the number of times the man had hugged him on one hand.

"You've got some imagination," Hank marveled, grinning from ear to ear.

*What the hell is that supposed to mean?* Alan wanted to say. *Are you trying to convince me that I didn't see what I just saw? That what happened didn't actually happen? That it's all in my head?* He wanted to say all of that, but his mind was still reeling.

Back in the street, the driver of the red Audi was crying and hugging herself while surrounded by a group of women from the neighborhood. The door was still ajar, its front grille still grinning at the arch of black blood on the pavement several yards in front of it. As Alan approached the vehicle, he glared at the sizeable dent in the fender. Absently, he wondered if it had been there before the accident.

The group of men disbanded, each of them milling slowly away in the directions of their respective homes.

The injured boy, his fists still clenched to his chest, shuffled into the arms of a sobbing, red-faced woman who must have been his mother. She squeezed him within her embrace, which did not seem to hurt the boy, then held him at arm's length to scrutinize every inch of his soaking wet body. She mumbled something as she touched one of the noticeable pink spots on the boy's shirt. Then she broke out into fresh tears. Pulling the boy against her chest, she proceeded to squeeze him all over again.

One of the men from the lake walked up to her and, putting his hand on her shoulder, bent and said something into her ear. Still sobbing, she didn't look as if she was listening to him.

Two women—one of them Jane Probst, Don's wife—hurried down a sloping brown lawn. Jane had a stack of dark-colored towels beneath one arm. The other woman carried two industrial scrub brushes. As Alan watched, they dropped to their knees on either side of the bloodstain in the street and, to his utter astonishment, began to scrub away the blood.

*Is this for real? Am I dreaming? Wake the fuck up!*

Hank squeezed Alan's forearm, creeping up behind him like a shadow. Another woman—one of the belly touchers from the barbecue—now stood a few paces behind Hank, watching them both with the terrified eyes of a defenseless animal. When Alan's gaze met hers, she quickly looked away.

"What?" Alan pulled his arm free of Hank's grasp.

"The keys."

"What fucking keys?"

Again: that goofy, brotherly grin. "The keys in your hand," he said.

Alan looked down and realized he was still holding the woman's car keys. In fact, he'd squeezed them so hard they left key-shaped impressions in the pink flesh of his palm. He handed them to Hank who carried them over to the women standing in a semicircle around the hysterical driver.

Hank leaned in close to the driver, turning her around so Alan could no longer see her face (and whether this was deliberate or not, he couldn't tell). He heard Hank's voice coming out in smooth, soothing murmurs, though he could not make out what he was saying. Yet Hank seemed to calm the woman, whose hysterics subsided to a series of hitching breaths and shuddering exhalations.

Eventually, he returned her keys and even walked her to her car. But before she got in she said something to him, the look on her face almost pleading. In return, Hank nodded and pointed to the boy she'd struck with her car. The boy's mother was leading him by the hand up the street. A few of the other kids trailed closely behind, shuffling their feet and kicking at stones. Now that the best of the action had subsided, they looked terminally bored.

"See?" Hank said, the timbre of his voice astonishingly cheerful. "He's fine."

The woman watched the boy retreat with his mother for several seconds more. Finally, she nodded and swiped at her eyes with the heels of her hands. Hank rubbed one of her shoulders as she crawled back into the Audi. The engine started up with no trouble. There was a slight rattling sound beneath the hood as the woman turned the wheel and rolled in an excessively slow half circle. She executed a tedious three-point turn, even though she had ample room to drive forward without hopping a curb, then seemed to idle in the middle of the street, no doubt catching her bearings, for an uncounted period of time. Then the Audi eased up the street toward the intersection. She sat at the stop sign with her blinker on for what seemed like an hour before turning right and vanishing.

On the ground, Jane and the other woman had done their best with the bloodstain and were now covering it up with the towels. A man in khaki shorts and a striped golf shirt was dragging a garden hose from the back of his house to the street.

"This is unbelievable." Alan's voice was no louder than a hoarse whisper.

"This must look like a circus to you," Hank said, running his fingers through his wet hair. He could tell Hank was trying his best to sound affable. "You must think we're all a bunch of nutcases."

"You're certainly getting closer to the bull's-eye," he deadpanned. "Who was the woman? The driver?"

"Motorist from out of town. She got lost on one of the back roads."

"What was her name?"

"Doesn't matter."

"Shouldn't she stick around and wait for the cops?"

Looking bored, Hank rolled his shoulders. "What cops?"

"I mean, won't someone have to file a police report or something?"

"Who would file it?"

"That kid's mother, for one."

Hank chuckled. "Look, you need to relax. You're all shaken up, man."

"No shit."

"Listen, some of us are gonna head into town and have a few beers, try to cool down a bit. Why don't you come along? I'll do my best to fill you in on what just happened. Looks like you could use a beer, too, to say the least."

*Fill me in? What the hell does that mean?*

Despite a strong desire to have this whole situation explained away, Alan felt instantly uncomfortable at the thought of going anywhere with Hank and the rest of the neighborhood men. For whatever reason, they'd just covered up a crime, and he still couldn't wrap his mind around what he'd witnessed at the lake. He was trying to think of a way to back out of the invitation when Lydia's station wagon pulled into the driveway and Heather climbed out of the passenger seat.

"Gals are home," said Hank.

"I think maybe I'll take a rain check," Alan said, his words ironically underscored by a grumble of thunder. "I told Heather I'd help her with dinner tonight."

"Oh. Okay, sure." Hank didn't seem bothered or surprised by the declination.

Heather walked soundlessly up the drive and did not look at Alan. He watched her the whole way, feeling the weight of her depression on him, suffocating him, like a physical presence.

"You don't have to tell her what happened," Hank said. It came out like an afterthought. "No sense hanging a dark cloud over the neighborhood."

Alan calmed a bit over dinner, though a needling disquiet at the base of his animal brain persisted. He had decided not to say anything to Heather about the incident after all. They plodded through dinner mostly in silence. Heather seemed content to stare at her plate. Alan could see the scars on her wrists and wondered if Lydia had questioned her about them. He considered asking her but bit his tongue at the last minute. He didn't want to talk about scars, didn't want to think about dead babies.

*Maybe Hank was right. Ridiculous as it seems, maybe the kid was just stunned and knocked unconscious. Dragging him into the lake had been the equivalent of splashing cold water on someone's face after they'd passed out.*

He wasn't so sure he could completely convince himself . . .

"I saw a hunter yesterday morning," Heather said. She was still staring down at her plate. "Did I tell you?"

"No. Where?"

"In the backyard. It was early. You were still asleep."

"I didn't realize you could hunt back there."

"He just stood there. He had a gun over his shoulder. He watched the house for a long time. Then he turned and went into the trees."

"What do you mean, he watched the house?"

"Staring," Heather said. "Out in the yard. I thought maybe he could see me from the window, but I'm sure he was too far away."

"For how long?"

"How long what?"

"How long was he standing there?"

"I don't know. A little while."

"That's strange." He frowned, turning back to his plate. "I don't like the idea of guys toting guns through our yard."

"He was barefoot."

"What?" He looked up at her.

"No shoes, no socks. Barefoot. And his pants were rolled up."

*No*, Alan thought, *that can't be right.* And on the heels of that: *Please, God, don't let her be cracking up again. Not here, not now. Please fix whatever is broken inside her. I don't think I can stand it if she's hallucinating.*

Before dinner had ended, someone knocked on the front door. The sound startled him, and he nearly knocked over his glass of iced tea.

Heather peered out the nearest window. "It's a police car."

A hot ember sparked to life in the pit of his stomach. He thought of the police car he'd seen on two occasions across the street. He stood, the chair scraping the floor. "I'll get it."

A formidable man in his early fifties, dressed in a khaki sheriff's uniform and a wide-brimmed hat, stood on the other side of the door. His upper lip was covered in a bristling, gingery mustache, and his eyes were small, lucid, and bright blue. Dark crescents of sweat bled from his armpits and soaked his uniform. "Good evening," he said, nodding. "I'm looking for Alan Hammerstun."

"That's me."

"You make an emergency phone call earlier this afternoon? A boy getting struck down by a vehicle?"

In all the excitement he'd completely forgotten about dialing 911. "Shoot, yeah, I did."

The guy looked like he wanted to come inside, but Alan didn't want Heather to overhear their conversation, so he stepped onto the front porch and closed the door behind him. "I'm sorry. I'd forgotten."

"I'm Hearn Landry, county sheriff," he said, leaning back on the porch railing. His knuckles looked like the forked hooves of a hog, all pink and fatty. "You folks are new in town, ain't that right?"

"Moved in a week ago. We're from Manhattan."

Alan half-expected the sheriff to say something about how he didn't cotton much to city folk in these here parts, but, to his surprise, he said, "No kidding? I got a brother works as a bouncer at one of them strip clubs up there." He laughed deep in his throat—a sound akin to someone crushing gravel beneath a heavy boot. "Real nasty place, too."

"About the boy," Alan began.

"Right," said Landry. "What was his name?"

"Cory, I think."

"First or last name?"

"Uh, I guess first. Not sure."

"Little squirt, about to here?" Landry said, holding his hand perhaps four feet off the ground. "Could be the Morris kid." Tipping his hat back on his square head, he said, "So what happened?"

In truth, he didn't know exactly what to say. Obviously, the kid had been struck by a car . . . but he had also walked home as if nothing had happened, clutching his mother's hand, and that had been the end of it.

He took a deep breath. Said, "I think maybe I overreacted."

Landry knitted his eyebrows together. "Overreacted?"

"Well, I mean, the kid *was* hit by a car. I saw it happen. But then—"

"Do you have a description of the vehicle?"

"It was a red Audi."

"And the driver's name?"

"Well, no, I didn't get a name. She was from out of town."

"Driver was a woman."

"Yes."

"License plate, perhaps?" The tone of his voice said he didn't hold out much hope.

Alan shook his head, feeling like a fool. "Sorry."

"And the boy?"

"I guess, uh," he stammered, searching frantically for the words, "I guess he was just stunned."

"Stunned?"

"You know, like—"

"Like hitting a deer with your car. Sometimes you just shake 'em up a bit. Scramble the marbles. That it?"

"Yeah." The word eked out of him like squealing hinges on an old door.

"In other words," Landry said, "the kid's okay?"

"Yes."

"You sure?"

"He got up and went home."

"Just . . . got up?"

"Yes."

"Just like that?"

"Yes."

The sheriff rubbed his mustache. "Cory, you said his name was?"

"I think so."

He jerked a thumb toward the street. "Happened right out there, yeah?"

"Yes."

"You grow up in Manhattan, Mr. Hammerstun?"

"I did."

"Bet you've seen a few people get hit by cars in the city, huh? Crossing the street, not paying attention, jaywalkin' and whatnot?"

"I've seen a few."

"Still," Landry said, tugging down the brim of his hat, "guess you got a little riled up for nothing this afternoon. See some kid get whacked by someone maybe going a bit too fast, figure you'd call the fuzz." He winked. "Just, you know, in case. Ain't that right?"

He couldn't think of anything to say other than, "Sure."

"Well," Landry huffed, turning toward the porch steps, "guess I'll go pay the Morris house a visit, see how little Cory's doing. Maybe he got the license plate number stamped onto his forehead. How about that?" Again: that rumbling, gravel-crunching chortle.

*Jesus*, Alan thought, and actually winced.

"All right, then," Landry said, moseying down the steps.

"Sheriff?"

Landry paused at the bottom of the steps and, tipping his hat back again, turned around. "Yeah?"

"How come it took you so long to come out here?"

"What do you mean?"

"I called 911 over two hours ago."

If Sheriff Landry was contemplating the magnitude of the question, his face did not show it. He remained stoic and unapologetic, like the wooden masthead of a great ship. After a few seconds he set his jaw and said, "One of my deputies came on the scene after your call. Checked around the neighborhood, took a couple statements. Folks said they'd witnessed the accident but the kid was okay. Said it was no big deal. Said they were surprised to hear someone'd called the cops over it, really, seein' it was such a small, inconsequential thing."

"Inconsequential?"

"My deputy didn't think anyone had moved into your house yet, so he didn't bother knocking on your door for a statement. Figured I'd come by this evening and extend the courtesy myself."

"Oh." His voice was suddenly small, nonexistent.

"So don't worry about the boy. He's fine. And, of course, we appreciate your concern in the first place." Landry nodded, his expression unchanged. "Welcome to the pumpkin patch."

# CHAPTER EIGHT

Around nine o'clock that evening, Heather went in for a bath. Alan grabbed a pack of cigarettes and snuck out to the back patio. Jerry Lee tagged along. Outside, the sky was an electric parade of stars. Alan smoked while Jerry Lee found a cool spot to snooze in the grass.

It wasn't long before Alan's gaze drifted across the yard to the opening in the trees. Heavy boughs swayed before the mouth of the opening.

A noise off to the side of the house caught his attention. Jerry Lee raised his head and emitted a deep, resonant growl. Alan froze, the cigarette jutting from his lips, and watched as the ill-defined shape of a man materialized from out of the darkness.

It was Hank. He carried a six-pack of Miller Lite bottles. "You feel like some company?" There was tremulous uncertainty in his voice. "I just wanted to apologize."

"For what? Scaring the shit out of me just now?"

Hank crossed the yard and set the six-pack down on the picnic table Alan had been meaning to scrub clean for the past several days. Hank pulled out one of the plastic lawn chairs but cast a speculative look at Alan and did not move.

"Have at it."

"Thanks," Hank said, dropping into the chair. "Mind if I bum one, too?"

"You smoke?"

"Sometimes. Don't tell Lyds."

In a gesture of amnesty, he handed Hank a fresh cigarette, then nodded toward the beer. "How about a trade?"

Hank smiled. His oversized teeth looked like tombstones in the moonlight. "Heck, I insist on it."

Alan dragged another chair around to the other side of the picnic table and sat in it. He hadn't realized how exhausted he was until that very moment; his entire body seemed to sigh as he came off his feet. "So what was it you wanted to apologize about?"

Hank popped the cap off a bottle of Miller Lite and handed it to him. "About earlier. About insulting your sensibilities by lying to you."

Alan took a swig of the beer. It was cold and tasted fantastic. "Lying to me," he said. It came out more as a statement than a question. "You mean about what exactly happened to the kid?"

"That," Hank said, "and some other stuff."

"What other stuff?"

Hank sighed. All of a sudden he looked miserable. "Today after everything happened, I went into town with a few of the guys for some beers. We wanted to discuss what to tell you. We knew you'd have questions, and we wanted to give you a suitable explanation without having you think we were all . . . I don't know . . ." A playful smile creased his face. "Bat shit crazy?"

"Fair enough."

"It's always been here," Hank went on after a moment of silence. "Old-timers called it Cradle Lake, because it's embraced and protected by the forest. There were other names for it, too. Ancient names. You find an old Cherokee sitting on a barstool in some cruddy watering hole, buy him a beer, and he'll tell you about the magical healing lake his ancestors talked about before the days of the white man."

Hank turned away from him and stared at the darkened opening in the wall of heavy trees. "Woods surrounding the lake are said to be haunted, too, but that's just superstition. Maybe the Indians used to believe that—and maybe those woods *were* special back when they used them—but I've never seen anything out of the ordinary in there."

"What are you saying?"

Hank was working a thumbnail under the label on his beer bottle. "The boy's neck was broken. His pulse was weak, and I knew he didn't have much time. It was a risk lifting him, moving him like that, and I wasn't sure his neck was broken until I saw the way his . . . well, the way his head turned—"

"Stop it." He didn't need Hank's recount of the horrible story; the image was already in front of his eyes.

"He would have died waiting for an ambulance. Either that or spend the rest of his life in a wheelchair."

"I don't understand."

Hank set his bottle down on the picnic table. In the

darkness and beneath the moon, his face was a luminous white orb, his eyes as black as bottomless pits. "Maybe the Cherokee knew what they were talking about, or maybe it's all just a coincidence. Maybe there's no good explanation for it. All *you* need to know is that the lake is *special*. It's a gift. Today you've witnessed what it's capable of."

Alan uttered a nervous laugh; it came out as a squeak. "Jesus Christ, I'm not sure *what* the hell I witnessed today."

"Just what you saw," Hank said calmly. "Exactly what you saw."

Alan stared at him. "So you're saying the lake saved that kid's life today. It's got the power to . . . what? Heal people, fix them, make them better?"

"Not everyone." Hank tapped his bum knee with two fingers. "I've been in that lake exactly seven times since I've moved to town, including today, and this damn leg of mine has never healed." He shrugged. "Had I known of the lake when I was younger and the injury was still fresh, things might have been different. What I'm saying is maybe there was a time when it *could* have fixed me. But probably not. I don't think age has anything to do with it. Nor do I think it's dependent on the type of injury. To be honest, I can't say why it hasn't fixed my leg. I *will* say I haven't used reading glasses in three years, and the little bald spot I'd had for nearly a decade no longer exists. My cholesterol's as perfect as you could hope for, and overall I've never felt better. But this leg?" Again, he shrugged. They could have been talking about baseball scores or the weather. "Hell if I know why some things are fixed and others aren't."

"So how did you know the lake would fix the Morris boy?"

"I didn't. It was a gamble. But I knew the kid wasn't gonna make it if we didn't try." Hank leaned across the table. "Once you're dead there's no fixing it. The lake can't help you anymore." He selected another beer from the six-pack.

In the grass, Jerry Lee made a slight whimpering sound but didn't move.

Alan's sharp laugh was like a whip crack in the silence. "You're fucking with me, right? That's what this is? Hazing the new kid on the playground?"

Hank's eyes remained sober. His expression did not change. He popped the cap off his fresh beer and took a long pull.

"Come on," Alan said. "A lake in the woods with magic healing powers? That's what you want me to believe, isn't it?"

Hank didn't answer. He looked away. In the distance, the mountains were enormous black crenellations speckled with moonlight against the night sky.

"Yeah, okay, I saw the car hit that kid." Alan couldn't deny that. "But seriously, man." Yet he recognized the slow surrender in his voice and knew he was having a hard time convincing himself that it was some sort of joke. Eventually, he held up one hand in a show of surrender. "Okay, fine. If that's the case—if what you're telling me is true—then how come we don't bottle up that water and cure fucking AIDS across the globe? No more cancer, no more heart attacks, no more pain and suffering."

"We can't do that," Hank said flatly. "The lake is a gift. It's also our secret. It's our responsibility to keep it that way. And now you're part of that secret, too."

"Why?"

"You saw what it can do."

"But why does it need to be a secret?"

"Because there's no such thing as utopia. Bad things happen in life which allows us to appreciate the good things. We get sick and it makes us appreciate being healthy. We work a nine-to-five all week and enjoy the weekends more than the guy who sits home on unemployment." Hank took another swig of his beer. His eyes had grown distant, as if he were in the midst of recollecting a childhood memory. "But there's a more practical reason, too."

"Yeah? What's that?" Far off, a whip-poor-will cried out. Alan had read somewhere that whip-poor-wills were the harbingers of death.

"Georgie O'Rourke goes to the lake to mend a broken bone. The bone heals but he begins having seizures. Less than a year later he's dead. Massive brain hemorrhage. Or one of the Finto kids—who found the lake one afternoon and thought it would be a great place to swim—goes mad for no apparent reason and tries to stab his old man with a fork while the family's sitting down for supper." Hank shrugged, suggesting perhaps the lake had everything or nothing to do with these bizarre incidents. "Or last summer, Lily Breckenridge backed over her Doberman with her car, broke the poor dog's hip. She carried it to the lake and the hip was healed. But later that winter, the dog gave birth to a litter of puppies that all came out . . . well, they came out wrong."

"What does that mean?"

"It means there is a *give* and there is a *take*."

"Those stories are just coincidences. They don't mean anything."

"Sure enough," Hank said. Then, after a pause, he said, "I want to tell you about Owen Moreland."

"Owen and Sophie Moreland were your average middle-class couple in their late forties, and they lived on Cedar Avenue in one of those little A-frame houses. Owen was a pharmacist who opened up shop on Market Street. He was a quiet, kinda nerdy guy but nice enough that he'd say hello whenever he passed you on the street. Sophie worked as a claims adjuster for a big insurance firm in the next town, but she did most of her work out of the house." Hank took a breath and asked for another cigarette.

Wordlessly, Alan shook one from the pack and extended it to him along with a book of matches.

Hank lit it and looked at the glowing red eye of the ember for what seemed like an eternity before he spoke again. "It became obvious that Sophie found the lake a few months after moving to town. To the best of my knowledge, no one had ever told her about it, so I assumed she had been out hiking and happened to find the path that leads to it. She lost ten or twenty pounds seemingly overnight, and even her skin looked healthier, her eyes more alert. Younger. She began running these charity races, and she even got first place in one of them. Was in the newspaper and everything. One of the judges, a guy named Botts who lives on Tulane, clocked her at a steady six-minute mile for the entirety of the race. He said she wasn't even out of breath when she crossed the finish line."

"Isn't it possible she was exercising, and that's why she lost the weight and became a good runner?"

"Sure. Anything's possible. Personally, I was hoping that was the case when people first started talking about her. But then Sheriff Landry began keeping an eye on their house at night. Sure enough, he caught Sophie leaving her house in the middle of the night, all decked out in her running gear. At first Landry assumed she was going for a night run, but he followed her anyway. Followed her right here, in fact."

*Landry,* Alan thought. *That's why I've been seeing the goddamn police car outside the house. The son of a bitch has been spying on me.*

"He watched her go through the trees and onto the path until she disappeared," Hank continued. "When she reappeared about an hour later, it was obvious she'd been out having a midnight swim."

"What'd Landry do?"

"He stopped her and told her to stay away from the lake. He didn't need to explain its power to her as she'd already figured it out. He said she was abusing its power, using it frivolously, and it had to stop."

"Did she stop?"

"Sort of but not because of Landry's warning." Hank crushed out the cigarette on the sole of his sneaker and said, "Her husband killed her."

Alan's beer froze halfway to his mouth. He stared at Hank.

"Turns out they'd both been going to the lake together," Hank said. "Thing is, for all the good those little midnight swims did for Sophie, they didn't have the slightest effect on Owen. Or, more accurately, poor Owen seemed to get *worse.* He couldn't give up smoking, and by the time his wife won that race, old Owen had actually strapped on another ten to twelve pounds. And whether it was from the long hours he'd been putting in at work or from his frustration at watching his wife grow younger and healthier while he got older and heavier, he seemed to be plagued by unshakable fatigue."

"How come it didn't work for him?"

"I couldn't say. Sometimes it rejects someone for no good reason. Like my bum leg. Or old man Pasternak's wife who couldn't beat the goddamn cancer no matter how many midnight treks to the lake she took."

For whatever reason, Alan pictured his father—blue skinned and massive looking on the stainless steel table in the basement of the morgue, that hideous yet subtle dime-sized bullet hole at his temple. From the top of his chest down he'd been covered in a flimsy white sheet, the twin tombstones of his feet pointing straight up at the acoustical tiles in the ceiling. And remembering this made him think of Cory Morris's single shoeless foot, the tip of his white sock curled over like a deflated balloon, flapping as Hank and the other men hurried him through the woods to the lake.

Hank repositioned himself in the lawn chair. "As one might expect, their marriage had already deteriorated. It was like Owen woke up one morning married to a much younger woman—a woman he was unable to keep up with. It wore on him, ate him up from the inside. Made him feel inferior. Even his work suffered and he stayed home sick more and more. Soon he shut down his shop and wouldn't come out of the house. Not that his wife noticed. While it wasn't exactly, you know, common knowledge, Sophie had taken up with a young fellow from the firehouse, a kid in his late twenties. I don't suppose there's any need to go into much detail on *that*," he added, a sly glint to his eye.

A chilly summer breeze stirred the trees. In the grass, Jerry Lee whimpered but did not move.

"Mr. Pasternak went over to the Moreland house one afternoon and knocked on the door. It wasn't anything any of us had conspired to do, and we didn't even know Pasternak was doing it until he told us later that evening at The Moxie. He said Owen answered the door wearing a pair of filthy boxer shorts and an armpit-stained T-shirt, his hair all screwed up into tight mattress curls and the stirrings of a lumberjack beard creeping up his jawbone. Pasternak asked him to come to The Moxie with him because he wanted to talk, but Owen shook his shaggy head and, without opening his mouth, shut the door in Mr. Pasternak's face.

"About a week after that, toward the middle of August, I was carrying some firewood down Market Street in Jonathan Nasbee's pickup—Jonathan's a good guy, works at the quarry—when I happened to catch sight of the Morelands' old blue Duster parked slantways outside the Laundromat. It was Owen's car, really—Sophie always said she wouldn't be caught dead in it—so I knew he was out and about. I pulled the pickup into the next available space outside the Laundromat and hopped out.

"As you've seen, that whole downtown section of Market Street is nothing but storefronts, each one family owned and passed down through the generations. Everybody knows everybody else's business in other words. I'd imagine it's quite a bit different than what you're used to, coming from New York and all, but we like it that way."

Alan thought of the little no-name place in the East Village where he used to buy cigarettes and newspapers and of the proprietor, a grizzled old black man with salt-and-pepper muttonchops, who called himself Felix Gumdrop. Though he didn't interrupt Hank's story, it occurred to him that there were more similarities than differences between big cities and out here in rural nowhere. What was that story about the city mouse and the country mouse? He couldn't remember . . .

"Anyway," Hank said, "before I could even get my fingers around the door handle at the Laundromat, I see him standing at the end of the narrow brick alley. I called out to him but he didn't answer. He was standing toward the end of the alley, which is just a little brick walkway that runs between the Laundromat and the hardware store, the back of which is lined with Dumpsters and employee parking. Owen stared at something on the roof of the Laundromat. His gaze was so intense it was no surprise he didn't hear me call his name, so I did it again, taking a step or two toward him.

"This time he turned around. With Christ as my witness, there was such a look of empty depravity in his face I could feel my stomach muscles clench and my blood turn to ice. And then he *smiled* at me." Hank laughed nervously and swiped at the side of his face with one big hand. "There was a children's program on when I was a kid, narrated by Shelley Duvall, about nursery rhymes and fables and—"

"*Faerie Tale Theatre*," Alan said, with more excitement than he would have thought. "I watched it, too."

Hank grinned, still rubbing the side of his face, and

said, "Yeah, that's it. Anyway, there was this one episode about Aladdin and his magic lamp. James Earl Jones plays the genie. Do you remember it?"

"Afraid not."

"Well, there's a part in the show where the genie, who's really fucking bent out of shape, just turns to the camera and gives this fucking *smile*. Scared the shit out of me. Even today, I cringe whenever a phone book commercial comes on TV." Another nervous laugh. This time, Alan couldn't help but smile at him. "When Owen turned and smiled at me in that alley, that was what he looked like—fucking James Earl Jones done up as Aladdin's genie. Had I been in worse shape, I could have had a heart attack right then and there.

"'How you been?' I asked him. 'Haven't seen you in a while.'

"'Been around,' he says, his voice gravelly. Thankfully, he turns away from me, and I don't have to look at that hideous smile anymore.

"'Folks been worried about you,' I tell him. 'You been going down to the lake?' Because, see, this was well before Landry followed Sophie to the lake that night. Jury was still out.

"'Do you see it?' he says, ignoring my question. He's staring at the roof of the Laundromat again with that same intense expression. In fact, he's squinting while practically standing on his tiptoes.

"'See what?' I say.

"'It's gone.' And there's some resignation in his voice. 'You must have scared it off.'

"'Must have scared what off?'

"'They're all over the place now. Been following me. You just missed one up there.' Owen points to the roof.

'Must have heard you call my name. They're temperamental like that.'

"'I don't know what you're talking about,' I say. And suddenly I didn't care, either, because I knew he was about to face me— and offer that hideous genie's smile. Which he did. And my blood ran cold all over again.

"'It don't matter,' he says calmly enough.

"'You and Sophie been going down to the lake, haven't you?' I say again—only this time I made the mistake of mentioning his wife. I knew it was a mistake the second the words came tumbling out of my mouth, but there was nothing I could do about it.

"'Don't talk about her,' he practically growls at me.

"I could see the discolored patches under his eyes and his sallow complexion, and for one split second, he seemed to *age* right there in front of me. Like those time-lapse films that show the entire life of a flower in a matter of seconds? He just seemed to grow old.

"And later that night, lying in bed and unable to sleep, I would think about how he looked so old and wonder if the lake did that to him—that it wasn't only his worsening depression about his wife's affair, which half the town already knew about, but the lake itself. As if the lake was physically draining him. For the first time I wondered if in order to heal some people the lake had to drain that energy from others." Hank paused, almost as if he wanted those words to sink in.

"Either way," Hank said after a moment, "I don't say another word to Owen. He shuffles by me, one shoulder dragging along the brick alley wall, until he reaches the mouth of the alley where it spills onto Market Street. He pauses there and cranes his neck. *Please don't smile. Please don't smile*, I'm thinking, mentally crossing my fingers. Thankfully, he doesn't. He just peers at the roof of the building and screws his face all up, as if lost in contemplation.

"'You didn't see it?' he asks me. I shake my head and this seems to suffice, because he rolls his shoulders in return—oddly casual, I remember thinking—and hobbles back to his old Duster and drives home. That was three days before Landry followed Sophie out of the house and about a week before Owen killed her."

"How'd he do it?" Alan said, the words nearly sticking to his throat.

"Put the barrel of a pump-action Winchester to the center of Sophie's forehead and spread her brains along the front hallway of their home. She'd come from visiting her sister in West Virginia and had just walked through the door to find him standing there with his scattergun. One single trigger pull and Owen was a widower. Then he dragged her body down the hall and up the stairs into the bedroom. A few nights later, over some beers at The Moxie, Sheriff Landry said there was a glistening path of blood trailing through the house and up the stairs that reminded him of those red carpets they roll out for movie stars on their way to the big premiere."

"Jesus."

"Owen hoists her onto their bed and crawls in next to her. Then he pumps another shell into the chamber and sticks the barrel of the shotgun under his own chin. Sheriff Landry said Owen had taken off his shoes and socks and had his big toe stuck in the trigger guard when they found him, so that's probably how he managed to fire the shot."

Hank leaned over and snatched another beer. Passively he stared at the label and didn't open the bottle. "Of course, neighbors heard the shots and the police were called. It was without a doubt the messiest crime scene old Hearn Landry and his two bumbling deputies had ever come across. Landry said it looked like someone had smeared cherry pie all over the bedroom wall. And it only got worse two days later when the firehouse kid never showed up for his shift. Again, Sheriff Landry went out on the hunt and found the kid in his kitchen, blown to bits by the same gun."

Alan ran a shaking hand through his hair. His ulcer was bucking in his stomach like an angry bronco. Either the beer or Hank's story—or the combination of the two—had agitated it.

"Kolpeck was the medical examiner. He did the autopsies on all three bodies. Sophie Moreland was forty-eight or so when she died. Kolpeck said he couldn't believe it. He said she was as fit and youthful as someone half that age." Hank cranked the cap off his beer and took a swig.

While Alan wasn't paying attention, they'd finished the entire six-pack and, judging by the repositioning of the moon in the night sky, had been out here talking in the yard for quite some time.

"So you see, the lake is not something to be used carelessly. It takes just as much as it gives. There is a price to pay, and there have been those who have paid dearly. You and your wife are young and healthy. There's no need to go down the wrong path, so to speak." The timbre of Hank's voice lowered. "My suggestion is to stay away from the lake."

A light came on at the far end of the house: the bedroom window.

"You said at first you assumed Sophie had found the lake from hiking through the woods," Alan said, turning back to Hank. "But you don't think that now, do you?"

Hank sighed and seemed to genuinely consider the question. When he spoke, his voice was lower. "I honestly don't know. Maybe they *did* accidentally stumble upon it while out walking through the woods, maybe looking for a good spot to have a picnic."

Alan could tell Hank was only talking in half-truths now. "No," he said. "You don't believe that."

Hank chuckled and rubbed his bad knee. "Let's just say I've come to believe in a lot of things, all right? Things about man . . . and things about nature. Maybe sometimes nature has a way of intervening. Maybe that lake wanted the Morelands to find it because just like it *gives* it also needs to *take*."

"You're telling me the lake . . . what? Called out to them? Summoned them?"

"I don't know what I'm saying."

"This is getting harder and harder to swallow. Seriously."

"I'm not asking you to swallow anything. I'm only asking you to heed my warning and forget about what's on the other end of that dirt path. Might be a time when you'll find that it's worth the gamble, just like with the Morris boy. But for now, live your life and forget about it."

Alan glanced at the lighted bedroom window again. Briefly, Heather's silhouette washed across the shade.

"Do you have a few more minutes?" Hank said.

"I guess so. What's up?"

"Come with me," Hank said, standing. "I want to show you something."

# CHAPTER NINE

Alan let Jerry Lee into the house, then followed Hank across the street. A light rain had started to fall, and periodic flashes of silvery lightning fractured the sky. He expected to see Sheriff Landry's cruiser parked up the street, masked in darkness, but the street was empty, the pavement a milky blue in the pale moonlight. Somewhere in the distance, a dog barked.

They went around to the back of the Gerski house. All the lights were off except for the flickering blue strobe of a television in one of the upstairs windows. There were the porch steps leading to the kitchen and, below them, the concrete stairs to the basement door. He followed Hank down the concrete steps to the basement.

"Just be quiet," Hank said before opening the basement door. "Catherine's asleep."

Inside, Hank ran one hand along the wall and flicked on the lights. His Orioles paraphernalia came to life. Hank crossed over to a set of wicker doors in the far wall. He opened them, exposing a black, rectangular maw. Instantly, Alan smelled mildew and water damage. Hank rubbed one finger beneath his nose, then dipped into the darkness of the room.

Alan followed a few steps behind and winced as Hank tugged on an exposed bulb housed in the ceiling. Harsh light threw shadows in every direction.

It was an unfinished room, the walls gray cinder blocks, the floor a slab of unpainted concrete. A heating unit stood in one cobwebbed corner, surrounded by pyramids of cardboard boxes, folded aluminum beach chairs, plastic yellow recycling bins, a ten-gallon fish tank with a lightning bolt crack across one panel of glass, and a pair of enormous stereo speakers circa 1975. A picnic table umbrella was propped at an angle like a makeshift lean-to.

"It's like the Batcave," Alan muttered.

Hank crouched down before another mound of cardboard boxes and slid them away from the wall. Folded up behind the boxes and leaning against the cinder blocks was a wheelchair—a relic left over from Hank's old leg injury, Alan surmised. Hanging behind the wheelchair from a peg in the wall was Hank's old Orioles uniform, zipped up in an airtight bag.

Hank sifted through the contents of one of the boxes. When he found what he was looking for, he withdrew it from the box. It was a vinyl-covered photo album with some sparkly unicorn stickers on the front cover. Hank pulled it into his lap, sat down with some difficulty due, Alan assumed, to his bum leg, and scooted against the wall.

"Here," Hank said. "Come have a look."

Alan sat beside him on the floor and peered at the album in Hank's lap as he opened it.

Alan's first thought was that Hank and Lydia had had a second child who died of some horrible childhood illness. The child in the photographs, whose sex was indeterminable due to a lack of hair and whose attire consisted solely of white linen hospital gowns, stared out of one photograph with large, beseeching, doe-like eyes. A network of tubes streamed from one of the child's arms and vanished out of frame. Alan noticed a slightly out of focus dialysis machine in the background. It had been taken in a hospital room.

As Hank flipped through the pages, the photographs became more and more depressing. Alan silently prayed he'd stop before reaching the end of the album, because who knew what the final pictures would show? After all, this child was no longer with them . . .

"Leukemia," Hank said. His voice was sober, his hand turning the pages of the album admirably steady.

It was a little girl, Alan realized. In one photo she was propped up in a hospital bed, her pale, hairless scalp covered in a pink straw hat adorned with silk flowers. Her smile was heart-wrenchingly beautiful.

"Hank, I'm sorry." His voice was inconsequential. "I'm so, so sorry. She was . . . beautiful. What was her name?"

His hand paused in the middle of turning one of the pages. "That's Catherine."

Alan felt the world waver and tremble all around him.

"She was diagnosed with childhood leukemia when she was a baby. These pictures were taken in Baltimore before we came here. She suffered for years. We *all* suffered."

Another picture showed Catherine in a wheelchair—the very same wheelchair that was now leaning against the wall beneath Hank's baseball uniform. She was clutching a fistful of balloons and grinning at the camera. It was the same toothy grin her father had. Something folded in half inside Alan's chest.

"Got a whole box of pictures," Hank said, jerking a thumb at the open cardboard box but not pulling his gaze from the photo album. "I told you I'd been in that lake exactly seven times, including today with the Morris kid. Those six other times were with Catherine." He traced one of the photos. "Just like you, I didn't believe at first. And just like you, they wanted to keep it a secret from us when we first moved here. But I guess Catherine stole a couple of hearts—you know how kids are good at that, right?—and the next thing I know, Don is having a few beers on my back porch with me one night, same as I was having them with you tonight. He says, 'Let's go for a walk,' and I follow him across your yard—your uncle was living there at the time—and into the woods.

"We go down that path, those strange white stones seeming to light the way, and by the time we get to the lake he's told me pretty much what I've told you tonight. All of it. Of course, that was before what happened with the Morelands, so there was less concern and less understanding of what the lake could do—both good *and* bad." A teardrop fell on one of the photos. Hank wiped it away with his thumb.

"The Morris kid was fixed right up—one, two, three,"

Hank said. "It was different with Catherine. It took six trips to the lake over a three-month period. It was no different than a regular medical treatment, actually. No different than the chemotherapy. The healing was slower with Catherine. Like I said, there's no explanation for why it works the way it does." His voice had deepened, his eyes lost in reverie. "Guess there doesn't need to be an explanation." He closed the photo album and leaned his head against the cinder-block wall.

Alan remained motionless beside him. His mind was suddenly racing; he couldn't erase the images in the photographs from his head, couldn't shake them loose. He couldn't stop thinking of Heather, either, and the two dead babies they'd left behind.

"I'm showing you this because it's important you believe. And it's important you respect the lake's power." Hank swiveled his head toward Alan. Their noses were practically touching. Alan could smell Hank's aftershave and the cigarettes he'd smoked on his breath. "Stay away from the lake, Alan. For every story like Catherine's, there's a story like the Morelands'. It's not good for everyone. And it's best just to stay away."

Alan crept through the dark hallway and turned on the night-light in the bathroom. It was barely enough light by which to brush his teeth and wash his face. His ulcer was working overtime now, ever since he'd left Hank's house, and he leaned against the sink basin and held his breath for several seconds. One-handed, he located his antacid tablets in the medicine cabinet and dry-swallowed three of them.

Trembling, he staggered into the hallway to the bedroom. Heather was snoring gently and buried beneath a mound of blankets despite the heat. Alan stripped out of his clothes and climbed in beside her. She did not move, did not make a sound. Rolling over, he embraced her and slid closer to her back.

He could not shake the photographs of Catherine Gerski from his mind. Whenever he closed his eyes, her smiling, hairless moon face would look up at him from a wheelchair or hospital bed. And as he drifted off into restless sleep, he swore he could actually *smell* the clinical, medicinal staleness of empty hospital corridors, soured bed linen, and the fetid odor of inevitable death. Overhead lights fizzing and popping in their fixtures. A steel sink basin speckled with pinkish spatters of vomit. Each empty mattress—

*(blood there's blood on the mattress there's blood)*

—still bearing the impression of the person who'd died on it. People vanishing into death. All of a sudden, he was snuggling into Heather's soft, soap-smelling hair in their tiny bed in their tiny Manhattan apartment, whispering into her ear, *They'll always be here. They'll always be with us. Both of them. The mermaid and the sailor.* So foolish in his consolation.

Babies. Dead babies. What was a baby? How could babies die? *They don't die; they just get lost.* Stupid, inconsequential, inconsolable words. They called it *losing the baby*, so where were they now? To where have their material parts dispersed? Had they returned to the earth, their physical bodies the topsoil of fresh flower beds, their essence in the bloom of a new rose? Or had their spirit and essence retreated inside Heather? Or perhaps they had simply dispersed into the atmosphere. And they would always be running with the bulls in Pamplona and in the passion of young lovers and in the shrill of guitar solos and in the magnetic ebb and flow of the tides and the nerve-damaged throb of every old man's headache.

*Might be a time when you'll find that it's worth the gamble, just like with the Morris boy. But for now, live your life and forget about it.*

When his eyes opened, he was disoriented. His face was still buried in Heather's hair, which he'd dampened with tears. She was sleeping soundly. The clock on the nightstand read 2:18 a.m. Something had prodded him from fitful sleep—some notion, some realization. Something he'd forgotten about—or, more accurately, hadn't realized—until just now . . .

Swinging his legs onto the floor, Alan eased himself out of bed and staggered in his nakedness back into the bathroom. He closed the door and then, bypassing the nightlight, switched on the bathroom fixtures. Four spherical halogen bulbs burned brightly above the mirror. He winced like a vampire. The antacid tablets from earlier had done nothing to soothe his angry stomach.

Once his eyes adjusted to the light, he peered closely at his reflection. Sweat was already dampening his brow and sliding in ticklish rivulets down his ribs. He touched the skin above his right eyebrow with a finger that vibrated like a tuning fork. Touched the skin, prodded the skin. It had been this way all week yet only now did he actually *notice*, actually *realize*—

The gash on his forehead—the one he'd contracted after his foolish stumble on the dirt path that first day—was gone.

It had been gone since the morning after he'd touched two fingers to the surface of the lake.

# BOOK TWO
## ATAGA'HI—THE LAKE

# CHAPTER TEN

The headline proclaimed, MURDER-SUICIDE SHAKES UP SMALL TOWN, and the tagline read, LOCAL MAN KILLS WIFE, SELF.

Alan had located the article easily enough online. He sat now at his computer, which he'd set up in the back room of the house that functioned as a makeshift office, a cup of hot coffee beside the keyboard. A Google search of Owen Moreland's name along with the word *murder* provided a number of hits, the most promising being archived newspaper articles. Alan had to punch in his credit card number and purchase a subscription for twenty bucks in order to access the archives, but his curiosity bested any frugality he might have normally displayed.

The article was accompanied by a full-color photo of the Moreland house on Cedar Avenue, decorated in yellow police tape. Just reading the headline and looking at the photo of the house caused a hollow feeling to permeate Alan's body.

It wasn't as if he had doubted Hank's story—despite what he was and wasn't ready to believe about the lake, he knew Hank wouldn't lie to him about something as horrific as what had happened with the Morelands—but seeing it here in front of him was like being awakened by a loud, resonating gong directly behind his head.

He read the article, digesting all the words. The information was not much different than what Hank had relayed to him, except for the fact that there was no mention of the young fireman Sophie Moreland had been involved with, since his body, according to Hank's chronology, wasn't discovered until a couple of days later. That was when the police were able to piece it all together. The reporter made no attempt at hypothesizing a motive behind the slaying, despite Hank's inference that much of Groom County knew of Sophie Moreland's infidelity. The reporter's conclusion was simpler than the mere search for motive: it was a horrible, frightening tragedy that defied explanation and had come to mar their peaceful, perfect little community.

After reading the article twice, Alan felt an inkling of disappointment. He'd been hoping to find a photograph of Owen Moreland. Surprisingly, there was none with the article.

Alan jumped ahead to the newspaper of the following week where the conclusion to the Owen's story was detailed once again on the front page. The body of Wade Balfour, a twenty-nine-year-old firefighter, was discovered shot to death in his duplex outside of town. This time the reporter was less equitable; the love triangle was more than just hinted. The article closed with a few quotes from neighbors of the Morelands about Wade and Sophie's affair.

There was still no photograph of Owen Moreland.

Easing back in his chair, he cringed as the ulcer began to sizzle in his stomach. Then something occurred to him.

Instead of searching for Owen's name and *murder*, he did another Google search for *Owen Moreland* and *pharmacist*.

The results were limited, but the first website looked promising. It had Owen's name and job title in the heading along with an address on Market Street downtown. Alan clicked on the link and waited as the page loaded.

Information about the pharmacy and a photograph appeared on the screen. Thin, white face, rimless glasses, narrow cheekbones, and surprisingly pleasant, squinty eyes beneath a mop of unruly black curls, Owen Moreland grinned at him.

"There you are." He sipped some coffee. "Went a little berserk, did you, buddy?"

From down the hall, Jerry Lee began barking.

He scrolled through the website, but that was the only photo of Owen Moreland. Jesus Christ, he looked like a nice enough guy. Friendly, even. Alan clicked back to the newspaper article and looked at the photo of the house on Cedar Avenue with the crisscrossing of police tape running up and down the porch. Where was Cedar Avenue? The town wasn't that big.

Jerry Lee continued to bark incessantly from the other end of the house. Alan knew Heather was napping—she'd been napping a lot since the move, sometimes straight until nighttime—and it would take nothing short of a nuclear blast to wake her from her medicated coma.

"Goddamn it, Jerry Lee." He stomped into the living

room to find the dog staring out the patio doors. "Come here!"

The dog turned and gave him a cursory once-over, then looked back out the doors. Something in the yard had attracted his attention.

"What are you doing?" he said, coming up behind the dog and yanking him away from the doors by the collar. Alan peered out. He could see nothing.

At his heels, Jerry Lee growled deep in his throat.

"Sit," Alan said, opening the sliding glass door. "Stay."

Jerry Lee whimpered but obeyed.

Alan stepped into the yard. A strong wind bowled down from the mountains and bent the tips of the tallest pines. A steady *shhhh* echoed throughout the valley. Casting a wary glance at the terminal, rain-pregnant thunderclouds, Alan poked a cigarette between his lips and surveyed the yard. Behind the glass patio doors, he could still hear Jerry Lee growling.

"Hello? Anybody out here?" Feeling instantly like an idiot for talking to himself . . .

The wind shook the trees along the edge of the property. He looked up to see pine boughs crisscrossing each other in the wind over the mouth of the hollow. For a split second he thought of the peculiar brand of dreams he'd been having ever since he moved into his uncle's house—the dreams of Jimmy Carmichael standing in this very yard or his father staggering along the wooded dirt path, naked and pale and rotting with each step he took, his heels leaving bloodied hollows in the packed earth.

Something cried out behind him. It was the sound of an infant in sudden pain. He spun around and saw a mangy gray cat struggling through a mesh of nettles. It glared up at him, its yellow eyes wide and fearful, then it opened its mouth and emanated a yowl that caused the hairs to stand up on the back of his neck.

"So you're the one causing all the commotion. Get the fuck out of here."

It lifted one paw and, with the disdain of the terminally wretched, hissed at him.

"Okay. Real nice. Take off, partner."

But the cat was caught in the nettles. It tried to push itself forward, but the netting of weeds was too tightly meshed, snaring the beast. The cat's ears settled against the back of its head as it sank low to the ground. It practically disappeared in the tall grass.

"All right. But you're pushing your luck, buddy, you know that?" He went over to the cat and bent down, petting its back with the knuckles of one hand as it pressed itself even closer to the ground. It continued hissing at him, its ears plastered to its head.

From behind the glass patio doors, Jerry Lee paced wildly.

"Calm down," he said to the cat. The last thing he wanted was for it to swipe at him and open up his—

*(wrist)*

—flesh. "Keep it cool, buster."

A bright green nylon band appeared within the mottled gray fur around its neck. Alan ripped away the weeds and nettles just as a light pattering of rain began to fall.

The cat purred deep in its throat—the sound of a small motorboat. Alan expected it to tear off across the yard and disappear beneath the underbrush, but it didn't. Still low to the ground, the cat crept toward him and hid in Alan's shadow, distempered by the sudden patter of rain and frightened by Jerry Lee, who was barking again.

Alan slid one hand beneath the cat and scooped it up. The cat meowed in protest. Petting its head, he stood and held it close to his body as a peal of thunder ripped across the sky. The creature stirred in his grasp. Mewled.

"All right, buddy."

The bit of green nylon around its neck was a collar. A medallion hung from the front. The cat hissed at him when he tried to grab the medallion, so he opted to rotate the collar around its neck until the little circular medallion came into view, all the while making soothing cooing noises close to the animal's ear.

PATSY
83 Strand Street
Groom County, NC

"Where the hell's Strand Street?" He scratched behind the cat's ears, and it rewarded him with a calm, motorboat purr. He could feel its heartbeat gradually slowing against the palm of his hand. "Are you one of my neighbors or some stray sniffing out garbage and attacking squirrels?"

It nestled against his hand, still purring.

Blood came away on his fingers.

"What the hell . . . ?" Hunting around through its thick

fur, he located a shallow wound along its ribs. The flesh looked tender and raw; the puckered wound itself had gelled over with coagulated blood. "What happened to you, huh? Get in a scrape with one of Hank's fabled Smoky Mountain grizzlies?"

The cat hissed.

"Hey, now, I'm just fucking with you. Come on. Let's find your home."

Addresses meant nothing to him—he didn't know anyone's address in town except for the few folks he'd come to know on his own street—but he had recalled seeing a sign for Strand Street past the first intersection. Still cradling the cat, he walked to the intersection and turned onto Strand Street. He watched the numbers on the mailboxes tick down until he came upon eighty-three. It was a split-level with pea-green siding and an oval glass in the center of the front door.

"Is this where you belong, you fucker?" Alan said, rubbing the cat's spine, careful to avoid the area of injury. He could feel the notches of its backbone through its fur. "You need to stay out of my yard before you send Jerry Lee into conniptions."

He mounted the front steps and knocked on the door. He could hear movement, quick and furtive, in the house, and through the distorted oval of glass on the door he thought he saw shadows swimming deep within. But when no one came to the door he knocked a second time. The storm was growing closer, creeping down from the mountains, and the cat was not happy about it; the thing squirmed in Alan's arms and tried to nuzzle its head beneath his left armpit in an attempt to keep dry.

"Cool it, will ya?" he scolded.

The door opened and his blood froze.

Cory Morris stood there, wearing a gray hooded sweatshirt and baggy jeans cuffed at the ankles. His sandy hair was swept across his eyes. He looked at Alan with little interest. "Hey," he said. His tone was dry. His eyes never left Alan's. "How come you got Patsy?"

Somehow, as if through divine intervention, Alan found his voice. "Uh . . . Patsy was wandering around in my yard." He pictured the boy lying in the middle of the street, not moving. "Thought he might be lost . . ."

"He's a she," said Cory.

"Sorry."

"That's why she's named Patsy." Cory took the cat out of his arms. The boy's hand briefly grazed his, and he felt an icy shiver trail down his spine and spill like ice water into his thighs. His testicles crawled up into the cavity of his pelvis.

The damned cat hissed and actually took a swipe at Cory with one paw.

*He's not right. Even the fucking cat can tell.*

"Yes?" said a woman coming up behind the boy. She placed a hand on Cory's shoulder and stared at Alan with skepticism.

"Your cat," he stammered. "I thought . . . I thought you might be wondering where he's been."

"Cat's a she," Cory said again, frowning, as his mother pushed him out of the doorway.

"Well, she's got a cut on her right side. She's bleeding a little."

"Thank you," the woman said curtly. She was the same woman who had been crying in the court while her son ran to her, dripping wet from the lake, his shirt stained with fading blood.

"How's he . . . how's he doing, anyway?" He couldn't help but say it. "The car accident and everything . . ."

"Cory's fine. Not a scratch on him. It wasn't a big deal. Thank you for asking." She sounded exhausted and phony.

*Wasn't a big deal? She was hysterical in the street.*

From within the house, Alan could hear the cat mewling as if it were being tortured. *It senses something's wrong. Maybe that's why the smart son of a bitch ran away and wound up in my yard.*

"Thank you," she added, "for bringing Patsy back. We were worried."

"She's a house cat," Cory said, reappearing beside his mother in the doorway. He stared at Alan, one hand raking through Patsy's ash-colored fur. Some of the fur was greasy and slick with blood. Cory got his hand in it but didn't seem to notice or care.

"No problem." He swallowed what felt like a mouthful of gravel. "Glad I could help. Anyway, I need to get home. Just wanted . . . I just wanted to bring back your cat."

The woman nodded and slowly closed the door.

Alan shambled off the porch and glanced over his shoulder before he reached the street.

Cory stared out at him from the oval of glass in the door.


As the sky broke open and filled the world with rain, Alan made the unfortunate decision to shortcut between the houses on Strand Street. He had a pretty good sense of direction and a vague idea of where his own house was situated on the other side of the woods, so he wasn't too concerned until fifteen minutes went by and he was still bumbling around amongst the trees. He stomped down kudzu and brushed heavy pine branches out of his face, then paused at one point, disoriented. The pending rain chased a grayish ground fog down from the mountains and into the woods; it clung low to the ground, obscuring potentially dangerous pitfalls and broken limbs that jutted from the ground like pygmy spears.

He should have emptied out into his yard by now. Was it possible he'd gotten completely turned around, that maybe he had been walking in circles for the past fifteen minutes?

A clash of thunder boomed directly overhead, and the rain hammered down harder. Even the dense canopy of trees was not enough to assuage the sudden and vicious downpour. Rain sluiced through the trees, icy needles stinging his face. His shirt was instantly soaked, hair plastered down over his forehead. He walked in a rough circle, seeing nothing but dense woods all around him.

Alan turned around and, defeated, staggered back in the direction he had come . . . although nothing looked familiar to him anymore. The rain had already created wide, muddy puddles on the ground, and his sneakers were soaking wet. Then his foot struck something solid and immobile hidden beneath the curtain of fog. Unable to see through the fog, he crouched, the thighs of his jeans already soaked clean through with rain. He ran one shaky hand along the ground. His fingers fell upon something soft and yielding.

A series of branches jutting up through the fog rocked a few inches from his face. He pressed down harder on the object, and the branches rocked again. That was when he realized they weren't branches at all but the tapered points of a rack of deer antlers. His fingers were pressing into its head, sinking into the short, tan hair that covered its stiffened, lifeless body.

He sprung backward, losing his balance and driving his ass through a swirling puddle of mud. Groaning, he looked at his hand and saw the fingers that had prodded the dead animal were black with blood. He swiped his fingers down his shirt and used the hefty limb of a nearby tree to hoist his dripping wet ass out of the puddle. His knees were weak, and he suddenly had to piss like a goddamn Thoroughbred.

The woods opened up another fifteen minutes later—roughly around the time he'd resigned to the fact that he was going to die out here—and he stumbled into his own backyard. Inside, he kicked off his shoes and stood in a widening puddle in the living room.

Sleepily, Jerry Lee raised his head off his paws from where he snoozed beside the couch.

"Yeah." Alan snickered. "Don't get up. I'm fine, thanks."

Peeling off his wet shirt, he crept down the hall toward the bathroom. Dumping the shirt in the sink, he fished a clean towel from the closet. His stomach clenching and unclenching like a fist, he opened the medicine cabinet and located the misoprostol tablets. But before he could even crack the top of the bottle, the pain in his gut exploded. It felt like someone was driving a red-hot poker up through his rectum and pressing it against the lining of his stomach. He took a deep breath, held it, and waited for the pain to subside. His eyes closed tight, he opened the medicine bottle and shook a nonspecific number of tablets into his hand. He dry-swallowed them, and they tasted like hunks of chalk going down.

Out in the hallway, he froze when he saw Heather standing in the doorway to the office at the end of the hall, peering into the room.

"Babe?" he called.

She didn't respond.

"Honey?" He came up behind her and gently touched one shoulder.

She did not acknowledge his presence.

"You okay?" he said.

"Oh." As if he'd woken her from sleepwalking. "It's you."

"Got caught out in the rain." He followed her gaze across the room. She was staring at the computer monitor. He'd left Owen Moreland's pharmacy web page up, the bespectacled, sallow-faced man grinning from the screen. Something about that grin bothered Alan much more now than it originally had.

"That's him," Heather said.

"Who?"

She turned and headed down the hall toward the bedroom.

"Who?" he repeated. The timbre of his voice climbed a notch. "Who, Heather?"

"The barefoot hunter," she said and disappeared into the bedroom, shutting the door behind her.

# CHAPTER ELEVEN

Fever claimed him.

There was a sense of spilling over from one hallucination to another. Unanchored, disembodied, Alan ghosted like antimatter through the house. He transitioned from shaking apart as if in a deep freeze to sweating like a hostage, soaking the bedclothes as glistening globes of sweat burst from his skin. At one point, he dreamt he was floating on the ceiling looking down at himself asleep in bed. Another time, he opened his eyes to find his hands pressed against the bedroom window as he gazed into the yard. Sheriff Landry stood out there staring at him, the shadow cast by the brim of his hat blackening his face.

There was one moment in time when, in his dream, he crept from bed and floated down the hallway. He heard the faint phantom sound of someone talking in a low voice. He could make out a fleeing shadow against one wall. The whole house seemed to be canting to one side, the floors off balance like a ship attempting to shake its crew into the sea. His hands on the walls for support, he made his way into the living room. There, the voice became slightly more audible, and he knew with intuitive certainty that it was Heather.

In this fever dream, Alan felt like the ghost in someone else's reality. He could feel the cold, brutal air in the living room, and he wondered only vaguely where it was coming from. Standing there, he saw the back of Heather's head as she sat on the couch. He was accosted by the bizarre notion that this was happening to someone else he didn't know, a stranger in a different part of the country who had been having nightmares about a different lake, and the notion frightened him. Still watching the back of Heather's head, Alan felt himself go to her, listening to her words . . . and then realized she wasn't actually *talking* but, rather, she was *singing*. It was the way he imagined she would one day sing to their children.

**Hush, little baby, don't say a word**
**Mama's gonna buy you a big black bird**
**And if that bird does gobble you down**
**Daddy's gonna bury you right in the ground**
**And if that ground does spit you back**
**Mama's gonna have her a heart attack . . .**

But the words were all wrong. Horribly wrong.

Alan placed a hand on Heather's shoulder. Her voice stopped cold. He looked down over her shoulder, down at her lap . . . where she cradled not a baby but a mound of filthy black feathers. The thing squirmed in her arms, and its black talons clawed at the air. Its hooked buzzard's beak, sharp as a bull's horn, snapped as if on a hinge. A shrill, throaty cry ruptured from its throat. The buzzard's eyes were tiny and yellow but grotesquely human, pinned to either side of a textured, curving, reptilian head that was hideously phallic in appearance.

The bird expelled a burp of blackish-green liquid from its lower half, which spattered across Heather's bare arm. The smell was instantaneous: overflowing sewer pipes and dead, decaying things. Heather didn't notice, although he could see the splatter of shit begin to smoke and sizzle, burning through the flesh of her arm.

Heather turned her face up at him. Her eyes were hollow pits, her mouth a ridge of busted, blackened teeth. "Mama's gonna have herself a heart attack, Alan," she sang.

In another dream, he stood in the dark above Heather while she slept in bed. He had one hand on her belly. The dream was so lucid he could feel the warmth of her skin, the blood pumping through her veins. Then floorboards creaked out in the hallway.

With the unhinged pacing of a drunken trek, he was suddenly in the hallway, though the sensation of Heather's belly still lingered against the palm of his hand. He was trembling, burning up on the inside while his flesh froze in the cold. Why was it so cold? A cloud of vapor blossomed from his lips and crystallized in the air before his face. Unable to move, he could only stand in the hallway in his pajama pants and undershirt, his heart strumming like a live wire.

The cold air came in through the front door, which stood open at the end of the hall. He floated out onto the porch and his father was there, sitting on the steps in the dark, his face a pool of black ink. Only the glowing red ember of his cigarette was visible.

"We're better off without her," his father said. It was his voice, truly and completely, straight from the grave. He was talking about Alan's mother . . . though, for one gut-sinking second he thought he was talking about Heather. "Good riddance. You and me, we're better off."

"You're not here," Alan said. "I'm dreaming."

His father grunted. "So? You got some lip on you, talking to me like that." Groaning, he rose from the porch steps with exaggerated slowness. "Come on."

"Where?"

But his father didn't answer. He staggered down the steps and shambled like Boris Karloff around the side of the house.

Alan refused to follow . . . yet blinked and found himself standing in the backyard nonetheless. The cold wind whipped at his pajama bottoms and caused hard little knobs of flesh to rise on his arms.

His father stood at the far end of the yard, a pale white specter against the black curtain of trees. He was naked, the all-too-visible *Y* of his autopsy incision carved into the doughy flesh of his torso. His genitals had retreated into the bushy nest of his pubic hair. His face was colorless rubber stretched taut across his skull. As Alan watched, his father turned and faded into the trees.

Then he was there, following him down the dirt path

that cut through the woods, the moonlight fractured into laser beams coming down through the trees. The ghostly visage of his father floated ahead of him. He crossed through slats of moonlight and took on a translucence that allowed Alan to glimpse the spidery black shapes of the junipers through the shimmer of his flesh. The white guide stones seemed to radiate a dull, nacreous light. Things moved about in the woods on either side of him, some of them close enough that Alan could hear the guttural rasp of their respiration.

"Dad," he said.

His father paused. He rotated his head around and glared at Alan from over one bone-white shoulder, the tendons creaking with rigor mortis. But the figure was no longer Bill Hammerstun; slack, empty features hewn into myelin flesh, eyes as haunted as tombs, it was Owen Moreland who now led Alan down the path. There was a long gun slung over one shoulder, and he wore slacks with the legs cuffed, exposing his bare, muddy feet.

*He took his shoes and socks off so he could pull the trigger with his toe*, he thought.

"Come on, sport," Owen said, and his voice was still Alan's father's. "Just a little farther."

Alan closed his eyes and willed himself to wake up, wake up, wake up. But when he opened them he was already standing in the clearing at the end of the path, the ground fog unfurling and receding toward the trees to reveal the placid, moon-reflective waters of the lake. An icy wind rolled down from the high hills where lodgepole pines studded the loam all the way to the mountains. Giant birds dripped like tar from the branches of the tall trees.

Piloted by whatever inexplicable force commands such dreams, Alan's legs carried him through the wet grass to the edge of the lake. The water, black as countless midnights, housed his reflection with specular clarity.

"There are ghosts here," Owen said, suddenly right next to him. "This is a haunted place."

"I want to wake up."

"You're not sleeping."

Alan looked down. There was blood on his hands. "I'm dreaming," he insisted. "I want to wake up."

"It's deepest at the center," said Owen. "I've never touched the bottom. Don't know if anyone ever has. Don't even know if there *is* a bottom."

"No," Alan croaked, dropping to his knees and plunging his hands into the icy water to wash the blood off. A shudder barreled through his bones.

Owen's reflection in the lake dispersed into fragments of dust—

*"I want to wake—"*

Hands against his back propelled him forward. He crashed through the surface of the lake as if smashing through glass—

*(there are ghosts here this is a haunted place)*

—and sat up in bed, naked and sweating. His heartbeat was so furious it was painful. He raised his hands to his face and could see, even in the dimness of predawn, there was no blood on them.

While his breathing slowed, he eased beneath the blankets and curled himself around Heather, sliding an arm between her belly and the push of her breasts. He was shaking all over, his bones rattling like an old shopping cart. Pushing his face into her hair, he forced his eyes to close and waited for his breathing to regain some semblance of normalcy.

# CHAPTER TWELVE

Alan awoke on the third day, and it was like Christ rising from the dead. His illness had vacated his body like a spirit. Muscles rubbery, eyes nearly blind and squinting, he was an infant shuttled straight from the womb.

Heather was watching television in the living room, the sound turned down so low it was barely audible. For a long time, Alan stared at the back of her head. He recalled the fever dream, where she cradled one of those filthy buzzards like a newborn baby against her breast. How it shat steaming black ribbons onto her arm, scorching the flesh.

He shuddered at the memory.

Heather turned and stared at him. She was gaunt, hollowed, a wax impression of herself. She'd been steadily losing weight, too, and that frightened him. He had caught sight of her recently coming out of the shower, the twin blades of her shoulders like the plates of a stegosaurus poking through the taut white flesh. The bones of her hips had reminded him of spearheads, of bull horns.

"How are you feeling?" he asked her.

"I should be asking you."

"I'm okay."

"You've had a bad fever. You've talked nonsense every night in your sleep."

"Did I?"

"About birds. About your father." She frowned, and at least it was an expression. "Strange."

"Is there any coffee?"

"Some." She turned back to the television. "Oh," she called before he turned away, "I almost forgot. The sheriff came around looking for you the other day. I told him you were sick, and he left his business card. He said to call him when you felt better."

The news jarred him. Vaguely, he recalled pressing his hands against the bedroom window and peering out at Sheriff Landry as he stood in the yard. At the time he'd thought it had been a dream, but apparently it had actually happened.

"Did he say what he wanted?"

"No. I put the card on the refrigerator."

"Okay. Thanks."

In the kitchen he poured himself a cup of coffee from the cold pot, then reheated it in the microwave. Sure enough, Sheriff Landry's card was stuck to the refrigerator with a Garfield magnet.

In the intervening days since his conversation with Hank, Alan had done an impressive job convincing himself that what had been happening here in town—the Morris kid, Catherine's miraculous rebound from leukemia,

Owen Moreland—could be summed up by a simple series of coincidences. Sure, they were bizarre even as individual occurrences, and when they were all put together . . . well, it seemed more than strange. But the Morris kid's neck *hadn't* been broken; Catherine had simply beaten childhood leukemia; and Owen Moreland had found that his wife was banging another man so he killed them and then himself. Those things happened all the time. There was no need to attribute them to the power of some ancient Indian legend . . .

*And what about Heather recognizing the photo of Owen Moreland as the man she thought was a barefoot hunter standing in the yard?* a needling voice would occasionally prompt. *And how do you explain how quickly that cut healed on your face, Alan? How do you explain those things?*

He couldn't explain them.

He chose not to think about them.

*Jesus Christ.*

The vine, thick as a grown man's finger, was back, crawling up the wall from behind the refrigerator. The evening after Cory Morris had been taken down to the lake, Alan had pulled the refrigerator away from the wall and cut the vine out. The damn thing had been growing straight up through the floor, in the separation between the floor tiles and the molding, and clung to the drywall by a mucus-like coating. There had been the second vine that had looped around the coils at the back of the refrigerator, and Alan had cut that away, too. Now, seeing the enormous vine crawling up the wall so soon after cutting it away caused a cold spear to puncture his heart.

*How did you grow back so quickly, you bastard?*

The microwave beeped, startling him.

Alan went to the refrigerator and gripped it on either side. Jockeying it back and forth, he was able to pull it away from the wall several inches . . . but then it stopped. He squeezed alongside it and peered behind the refrigerator.

He counted seven separate vines, each one about the diameter of a pencil, branching off from the main stalk and curling around the coiled grate at the back of the refrigerator. They were taut, preventing the refrigerator from being pulled any farther away from the wall.

"Son of a bitch."

He bent and reached behind the unit, grabbed one of the vines, tugged at it. The fucker was strong and did not break. Moreover, his hand came away tacky with mucus. In all his life he'd never seen vines like these.

There were scissors in one of the kitchen drawers. He retrieved them and returned to the rear of the refrigerator. He pressed himself up against the wall and reached behind the refrigerator with the scissors. He snipped one of the vines with some difficulty, and the thing snapped and recoiled, one half retreating beneath the floor while the other half disappeared into the grillwork at the back of the refrigerator.

Dark purple, viscous fluid splashed the linoleum. Like blood.

Alan jerked his hand back, dropping the scissors as he did so. The scissors clattered to the floor and slid under the refrigerator.

"Perfect."

He felt like an utter fool.

Hesitantly, he reached behind the refrigerator and

pressed two fingers to the splotch of purplish fluid that had bled from the vine.

*No way. Could it be?*

It felt warm.

Again, he withdrew his arm as a cold wave passed through him. He got up and grabbed a butcher knife from the wooden block on the counter, then dipped back beside the refrigerator. He spent the next minute and a half sawing through the remaining six vines. Each one bled the same strange fluid and recoiled just as the first one had. By the time he finished, there was a sizable, blood-hued puddle on the floor behind the unit.

The microwave beeped again, reminding him his coffee was still inside.

He stood and gathered some paper towels, which he used to wipe the fluid off the floor.

*All of it . . . warm . . .*

Then he balled up the used paper towels and stashed them at the bottom of the trash can. After pushing the refrigerator back into place, he retrieved his coffee from the microwave and opened the refrigerator for the milk.

He dropped his mug on the floor, spilling the coffee and breaking off the handle.

The vines had grown straight through the back of the refrigerator, the greenish tentacles encircling the half-gallon jug of milk, a bottle of ketchup, a plate of chicken, a container of orange juice, various other items. One of the vines curled down to the bottom shelf and actually held a banana suspended in midair. It was like looking at some tropical, carnivorous plant.

Alan staggered back, skidding in the spilled coffee and

nearly spilling himself to the floor. If Heather had heard him drop the coffee mug from the living room, she didn't bother to come see what the commotion was all about.

He quickly cleaned up the coffee and the broken bits of mug, tossed them in the trash, then turned to address the vines inside the refrigerator with the same knife he'd used to cut them away from the back of the unit. However, after a moment of consideration, he realized he didn't want to leave any of that food in there, so he gathered the items, vines and all, and dumped everything into the trash. Dark purple fluid, tacky as syrup, had congealed on the top shelf. He wiped it down with a dishcloth, which he also tossed into the trash. Then, upon further consideration, he tied the trash bag and took it out to the curb.

The sheriff's cruiser was parked across the street.

"Looks like you're feeling better." Hearn Landry crossed the street, hitching up his gun belt in the most stereotypical of manners. "Heard you were a tad under the weather."

"Oh," said Alan. "Hello."

Landry tipped his hat back. "Is today trash day?"

Alan ignored the question. "My wife said you came by to see me the other day."

"Sweet little thing, your wife," Landry said. Though he probably meant nothing by it, he exuded a lecherous undercurrent that made Alan want to take a swing at him. "She been sick, too?"

Alan felt his left eyelid twitch. "No."

"Didn't catch your bug, did she?" Landry grinned, showing Alan all his teeth.

"Was there something you needed, Sheriff?"

Landry spat a brown gob onto the pavement. "You're Phillip's nephew, ain't that right?"

"I was. Up until he died."

"Took some kind of teaching position at the community college?"

"I teach English lit."

Sheriff Landry made a noise back in his throat that suggested he didn't think too highly of English literature. Alan didn't think the sheriff would know English lit if it bit him in the ass.

"My kid Bart's going there in the fall," Landry said, rubbing his squared-off jaw with one meaty paw. "Kid's as dumb as a brick shit house. He gets that from his mother."

Alan laughed. He couldn't help it. "Christ. Please don't tell me you came here to ensure your son's successful completion of my class."

"Huh? What?" Landry looked genuinely surprised. "Hell, no. I don't give a shit if that little bucket head fails out or becomes the goddamn dean of admissions. I was just making small talk with you, that's all. That ain't why I'm here."

"Then why are you here?"

"To make sure we got an understanding."

"What understanding is that?"

Grinning, Sheriff Landry snorted and held both his hands out in an imitation of surrender. He spat a second gob onto the pavement where it nearly sizzled in the heat. "I don't wanna play any games. I ain't big on games, Professor. You spoke with that fella Gerski across the street?" Landry jerked a thumb over his shoulder in the vicinity of Hank's house.

"Is this about the lake? Yeah, we talked." Thinking: *Jesus holy Christ, this whole goddamn town has shit the bed. What a bunch of lunatics.*

"He set you straight?" Landry said.

Alan frowned. "Straight?"

Landry took an imposing step forward. "You saw something that day with the Morris kid. Maybe you shouldn't have seen it, but you did, and what's done is done. We got a pretty nice town here—peaceful, a great place to raise a family—and I get bitter thinking about new folks coming into town and ruining that for the rest of us. You get what I'm saying?"

"Listen, Hank Gerski told me everything. I get it; I understand. Frankly, I think you people are fucking nuts, but that's your problem." Alan shoved his hands into his pockets and felt like an obstinate child. "No, I won't go near your precious lake. But you gotta make me a promise, too."

"Hmm. What's that?"

"That you quit spying on my fucking house. Creeps me out."

At first, Landry didn't react. Then, astoundingly, a wide grin nearly split his face in half. He looked like he had a comb stuck in his mouth. "Well, hell," he practically crooned. "That's all I wanted to hear." He tipped his hat and readjusted his belt. "You and your pretty wife have a good day now, okay?"

Without waiting for a response, Landry turned and

sauntered back to his car. He climbed inside with a huff and slowly rolled down the street. The son of a bitch even bleated his horn twice and waved as he went by.

Later that night, wide awake in bed and staring at the rectangle of moonlight on the far wall, Alan could not find sleep. Something was stirring in the back of his mind, something he couldn't quite put his finger on. Fleeting and unresolved, like glimpsing the tail end of a snake before it disappears down a hole in the ground . . .

Outside, bare branches clawed against the windowpane. He saw—or imagined he saw—something large arc past the panel of moonlight. He was reminded of his dream from the night before, following his father—or had it been Owen Moreland?—through the woods and how the buzzards melted and dripped from the trees. Here in the dark and supposed safety of his bedroom, Landry's warning reverberated in his head. Alan peeled his gaze from the window.

*Landry . . .*

He sat up in bed and swung his legs to the floor, prodded once again by the glimpse of that snake sliding down the hole. Without turning on any lights, he walked to the bathroom. A laundry hamper stood beneath the towel rack.

Landry's visit wasn't a dream. What else—

*(you're not sleeping)*

—wasn't a dream?

The hamper was filled with clothes. He scavenged past the top layer and dug around near the bottom. After a moment his fingers closed upon a heavy, balled-up bit of material. He felt his bowels clench. Like a fisherman reeling in a catch, he pulled the clothing out of the hamper, flashes of memory returning to him now—

*(you're not sleeping)*

—and knew what this article of clothing was before he actually saw it: his pajama pants. The ones he had been wearing in the dream where he pursued his father's corpse to the lake.

Pajama pants.

Wet.

# CHAPTER THIRTEEN

The vines grew around the handle of the sliding patio door, prohibiting it from opening. Hottest day this summer, and Alan found himself out in the yard sawing at the thick cables of vines with a hacksaw. The rapidity with which they grew was astounding. Like the ones that had grown in the kitchen behind the refrigerator, these also bled that syrupy purple ink onto the patio. Unlike the ones in the kitchen, these were even thicker and had begun sprouting the nubs of thorns along the stalk. By the time he finished cutting away the vines, the palms of his hands were inlaid with bloody pinpricks.

Swiping an arm across his sweaty brow, he took a step back and examined the rear of the house. More vines sprouted from the house's foundation and crept up the siding. They were tall enough to become entangled in the gutter. Some had made their way onto the roof where they actually grew beneath the roof shingles, prying them up.

Alan caught peripheral movement across the lawn by the trees, near the location of the dirt path. He looked and, to his horror, found one of the buzzards right there on the ground, its massive wings spread, the feathers sparse and diseased-looking, its body roughly the size of a Thanksgiving turkey.

It seemed to notice him the same instant he noticed it, because it abruptly cocked its grotesque, fleshy head almost comically at him and issued a throaty squawk that suggested the protestation of Alan's very existence. Then it dipped its head and drove its hooked beak into a mess of something on the ground. It made a move like a pneumatic drill hammering into the earth. Seconds later, when it brought its head up, a pinkish cord stretched from its beak to the mess of what now appeared to be a mound of mottled gray fur in the grass.

The buzzard jerked its head and the cord stretched with organic elasticity. One final jerk and the cord snapped wetly. It dangled like a fleshy dewlap until the bird, executing a series of mechanical neck bobs, swallowed the entire bit of flesh.

"Goddamn it. What is it with you damn things?" Alan gathered up a stone and chucked it at the cretin.

The ugly son of a bitch cawed at him, the sound causing his nerve endings to vibrate, but it did not move.

He selected a larger stone and fired it with better precision. This time he struck it on one of its wings, creating a sound like thumping an open palm against an empty milk jug.

The bird shrieked, not just in fright but in pain, and launched itself into the air with an awkward, ungainly ineloquence. It took off over the treetops, trailing in its wake a string of agitated cries.

Alan approached the mess of fur in the grass. Whatever it had been, it now lay splayed open, black tributaries of blood soaking into the soil.

Then he realized what it was. What gave it away was the little twinkling bronze medallion with the name Patsy etched onto it.

"Oh, Christ." His stomach rumbled. "Stupid cat. Should have listened to me and stayed home."

Not much of Patsy the Cat was intact. In fact, had it not been for the identification collar, he wouldn't have recognized it at all. *He's a she*, Cory Morris had said. Well, "he" or "she"—none of that mattered anymore. All nine lives had been expended.

Minutes later, he returned to the spot with a snow shovel and scooped up Patsy the Cat. He considered dumping the carcass just beyond the line of the pines until he envisioned one of those disgusting buzzards finding it and dragging it back onto the lawn. Goddamn birds.

Balancing the dead cat on the end of the shovel, he passed between the trees and down the dirt path in search of a suitable spot to dump the thing. He briefly considered wrapping it in a trash bag and taking it over to the Morris house in case they wanted to bury it or cremate it or whatever. But that idea was just a bit too creepy, so he went deeper into the woods.

As if the woods maintained a direct connection with all the horrible memories he kept bottled up inside him, he remembered his discussion with Dr. Chu, the psychiatrist who'd been on staff at the hospital where Heather had been admitted after opening her wrists. There had been a fish tank full of tropical fish on the credenza behind Chu's desk, and the whole office smelled of Pine-Sol. Dr. Chu had reclined in his chair, steepling his fingers beneath his nose, his black eyes narrowed in thought. Alan had sat across from him in an uncomfortable wooden chair, sweat prickling the nape of his neck.

"I've reviewed your wife's medical history," Dr. Lawrence Chu had said. "The two miscarriages, the therapy recommended by her ob-gyn. The test that came up inconclusive."

"What about them?" His heart fluttered like a hummingbird.

"It's my opinion your wife is suffering from severe depression. My recommendation is that she be kept under constant surveillance for a period of time which, of course, would include daily counseling sessions and the appropriate medical treatment she—"

"You're talking about putting her in a psych hospital?" His vision fractured. A potent heat billowed up from his shoes, up his legs, and filled his shirt and pants like a hot air balloon. "In a nuthouse?"

If Chu had been bothered by the term, he did not show it. His face remained expressionless. "I've already spoken with her. I'm on the fence whether or not I should petition her admission with or without your approval. Please understand, Mr. Hammerstun, that I by no means am trying to undermine—"

Alan held up one hand, cutting the doctor off. "Wait a minute. You can't do that. How can you do that?"

"Please allow me to finish."

"How can you *do* that?"

"I am on the fence, as I've said. Your wife is not combative or, for that matter, even physically active. With proper supervision and stronger antidepressants—"

"I'll watch her. I'll take a sabbatical from teaching and watch her until she's better. She's my wife. I'm not locking her up in some fucking institution."

Unaffected by his language, Dr. Chu retrieved a manila folder from within his desk, opened it, examined the documents inside. "I'm recommending two different antidepressants. I'm also recommending weekly therapy sessions. We have a wonderful staff in the psych ward."

"She won't need therapy. I'll watch her."

Dr. Chu had set the folder down on his desk. He'd folded his hands and leaned forward, closing the distance between them. "Your wife needs medication and she needs therapy. This is not her first attempt?"

Alan swallowed a heavy lump. "What do you mean?"

"There was another time? With pills?"

"She told you that?" His voice was small.

"If you wish to take your wife home, I suggest you agree to my recommendations. Otherwise, I will reconsider my position on that petition . . ."

He had uttered a strangled laugh that sounded more like a cough. "Okay," he had said, nodding like a fool at the doctor. "Okay, yeah. I get it. Let's do this. And let me get my wife back home."

Now, Alan shook his head and cleared it of the memory. Once again he was in the woods, a shovelful of dead cat along with him for the ride.

Pausing on the dirt path, he blinked and glanced around. Lost in his memories, he'd walked deep into the woods, maybe halfway down the path. On either side, the scrub brush and ivy were dense. Like tossing a shovelful of snow, he flipped the dead cat over the embankment into the brambles. It fell through the underbrush and was swallowed up by the forest.

Something crashed through the trees behind him. Something big.

He whirled around, dropped the shovel, and stared through the web of trees. It was impossible to see through the dense trees, their intertwined, leafy branches as impermeable as meshwork. He caught a whiff of something fecal, its potency amplified by the sudden breeze that bowled it through the woods toward his nose.

"Hello?" he called. His voice echoed as if he were shouting over a canyon. "Somebody out there?"

No one answered.

Sweat-slicked, he shivered nonetheless. He thought of the dead buck he'd stumbled across that day he got caught in the downpour. Surely this forest was chock-full of deer—and bears, foxes, wild game, and scores of other animals he probably didn't know existed in this part of the world. Bobcats? Gazelles? Hank's mountain grizzlies?

Eerily, Hank's voice returned to him now, from the conversation they'd had that night on Alan's back patio. He could hear him almost verbatim: *Woods surrounding the lake are said to be haunted, too, but that's just superstition. Maybe the Indians used to believe that—and maybe those woods were special back when they used them—but I've never seen anything out of the ordinary in there.*

"Fuck this," Alan muttered.

He turned around on the path toward home, but he must have gotten confused because when the trees parted and he stepped out into the clearing, he was looking at the glassy, silver surface of the lake. Somehow—stupidly—he'd walked in the wrong direction.

Here in the daylight the lake looked less ominous than it had at night. Even the energy that had been in the air like an electrical charge on the day the neighborhood men carried Cory Morris was gone. It was just a tiny, serene lake, like something out of a dream.

Across the lake and in the daylight, the giant trees stood empty of the horrible birds. Alan tried to recall if they'd been present on that day Cory Morris had been submerged in the water, but he couldn't remember. That day had been too hectic to remember anything specific that didn't have to do directly with the injured Morris boy.

Crossing the field, he tossed down the shovel and stopped at the edge of the water. A shiver zigzagged through him as he recalled the dream that perhaps hadn't been a dream. While the wet pajama pants at the bottom of the laundry hamper had been proof that he'd gone into the water, his recollection of the details of the event were no doubt contaminated by fever. He remembered his father being there, which was impossible, of course. And Owen Moreland had been there, too, which was equally impossible.

A fever-driven case of somnambulism was responsible for that late night jaunt and the swim that evidently followed. Likewise, it had been his fever-addled brain that created the hallucinations of his father and Owen Moreland—his subconscious prodded to the surface by a temperature of 102. He'd come to accept all those things and counted himself damned lucky he hadn't drowned while sleepwalking that night.

The stifling heat caused sweat to burst from his skin. The heat in his belly was even greater—the ulcer, eating him from the inside out.

Alan began climbing out of his clothes.

Moments later, the reflection staring up at Alan from the placid surface of the lake was completely naked. Had he been asked prior to this occasion, he would have said with finality that standing naked outdoors would have instilled him with a near crippling sense of humiliation bordering on fear. However, standing here now with his bare feet in the thick grass and the midday heat beating down on his bare shoulders, he felt oddly serene. Lulled, even. And the calmness that embraced him also spread through him like blood.

The ulcer burned at the base of his stomach. It was a bright strobe of electrical current; it was a smoldering hunk of coal burning through the lining of his belly.

He took a deep breath and dove into the water.

# CHAPTER FOURTEEN

Still wet from the lake, Alan entered his yard. The sun was directly overhead now; it beat down on him with unforgiving potency. He felt like a solo performer spotlighted onstage. The heat felt good. Despite the rising summer temperatures, the lake water was as cold as an ice bath. Alan found it invigorating.

He shook his head and ran his fingers through his damp hair. It had already begun to dry in the heat.

He went to the sliding patio doors. Paused. Stared. He had one hand outstretched, reaching for the door handle, frozen in the air as if in a photograph.

A single vine, thin as spaghetti, had wound its way around the handle.

His heart seemed to freeze in his chest.

Noise off to his left. He jerked his head in that direction and felt his blood turn to ice when he saw Cory Morris standing at the edge of the yard, partially obscured in the shade of nearby trees. Even from this distance, he could see the beads of sweat rolling down the boy's plump face and the darkened stains spreading out from the armpits of his T-shirt.

The boy's hands were covered in blood.

"Hey," Alan said, attempting to yell. The word came out in a weak croak, barely audible even to himself. Then, louder: "Hey! Did you do that to your cat?"

The boy turned and headed up the street.

"Cory!" he called after him. "Cory Morris!"

The boy vanished up the street.

# CHAPTER FIFTEEN

"Haven't heard from you in a while," Hank said. "You avoiding me or something?"

"Of course not." Alan had been hacking away at vines when Hank had come up behind him, a six-pack of beers cradled in one arm. Now, Alan paused and wiped the sweat from his brow. He was shirtless, and the warmth of the sun felt good on his back and shoulders. "I've just been busy trying to get the house in order. Once school starts, I won't have this kind of time anymore."

"Your hands are bleeding."

He glanced down. It looked like he'd grabbed a pincushion with both hands. He hadn't noticed until Hank brought it to his attention.

"Some mean-looking vines." Hank set the six-pack on the picnic table and selected a bottle for himself, popped the top. He offered one to Alan but he declined. "Might be better to wait for winter when they dry up and die. Might be easier to cut them. Would save your hands, too."

"Thanks but I'm good." Alan was using hedge clippers on some of the thinner vines. He went back to work, all too conscious of Hank's eyes on him.

"How's Heather? Lydia says she hasn't seen her in a while."

"She's fine."

"Been working out?"

"Heather?"

Hank chuckled. "No, dummy. You."

Alan shrugged and did not look up from his work. "Not really. I've been putting in a lot of hours working in the yard, that's all."

"Yeah," he said. "You look good. Strong, I mean."

He'd dropped five pounds over the past week and had started exercising, not because he had any designs to look better but because he had found himself with an overabundance of energy that seemed to come from out of nowhere. He'd even gone running one morning with Mr. Pasternak, who'd been more than happy to share his company at first. But as they crossed the five-mile mark, up by Swain Street at the edge of town, and rounded the roadway to return to town, Pasternak's cheeriness was replaced by a quiet suspicion. It was the one and only time Alan had run with the man.

Over the past week, his jaunt to the lake had turned into a daily occurrence. He would rise just as the sun was breaking over the evergreens, the sky still dark and crowded with stars in the west, and pull on a pair of sweatpants, a sweatshirt, sneakers. With a bath towel folded under one arm, he'd follow the path to the lake where he'd strip and swim for forty-five minutes, sometimes an hour.

The water was always freezing at first, shocking his system

and tightening his muscles. But by the time he swam halfway to the other side of the lake, the water was lukewarm—or maybe he'd just become accustomed to it—and his muscles grew loose and strong. The only part of the lake that never seemed to warm up was the center, where a channel of icy water seemed to funnel straight up from the bottom.

After his swim, he'd return to the house just as daylight fully claimed the sky and cook some breakfast—bacon, eggs, toast, apple slices sprinkled with cinnamon—the smell of which typically roused Heather from bed just as he was buttering the toast. In that week, his ulcer had vanished, his eyesight grew sharper, and he felt healthier and stronger than he had in years. Strangest of all, it appeared his tattoos had begun to fade . . . the color slowly drawing out of them, the skin itself feeling smoother and tauter.

In fact, the only negative side effect was goddamn Jerry Lee. The old retriever seemed disquieted by Alan's presence lately. Once, when Alan had reached out to pet him, the dog had sunk to his haunches and emanated a low, distempered growl. Too shocked to reprimand the dog, Alan had just watched as Jerry Lee crept away. Jerry Lee's odd behavior had caused him to think of Patsy the Cat and how the beast had swiped and hissed at Cory Morris as the boy held her against his chest. (Jerry Lee spent the following nights sleeping on the bedroom floor on Heather's side of the bed instead of Alan's—something the dog had never done in the past.)

"Lydia wants to know if you guys can come over for dinner tonight. We're thinking about tossing some burgers on the grill."

"I don't know. Kinda busy."

"All day?" Hank took a swig of beer. "You'll be doing this straight through dinner?"

Alan stopped, tossing the hedge clippers into the grass. He was breathing heavy, but he felt good, felt invigorated, and his muscles were hardly sore. He estimated he'd been out here for nearly five hours since morning.

"Listen," Hank said, looking more at his beer bottle than at Alan. "Can I ask you something?"

"Ask away." Though he felt a slight tremor shudder through his body. He was certain Hank was going to ask him if he'd been going to the lake.

Hank cleared his throat and looked like he was turning over many thoughts in his head. "Did I, uh . . . Jesus . . ." He rubbed furiously at his forehead.

"What?" Alan said. "What is it?" *Just spit it out, will you?*

Hank's words came out in a hurried waterfall: "Did I freak you out with all that talk about the lake and Catherine and everything else? Man, see, I didn't want you to think I was crazy or that maybe . . . I don't know . . . maybe I turned you off, turned you away by all that talk."

*Jesus Christ, is that what this is? The son of a bitch is worried I don't want to be his friend anymore?* It took all his strength to stifle a bitter laugh.

"Shit, that's not what's going on here." Alan thought he sounded genuine; it pleased him to hear how smoothly the words came out of his mouth. "It's summer. I'm trying to get all this work done on the house before I start teaching in the fall. It's nothing personal."

"You swear?"

"I swear."

"Christ." Hank's shoulders slumped, and a crooked smile broke out across his features. He looked pitiably relieved. "I've been worrying that you wanted nothing to do with me anymore."

"Don't be silly." Thinking, *Yes, be silly.*

"Well," he said, brightening up now, "that's a relief. Beer?"

"Sure." Alan took one from the six-pack, unscrewed the cap, and chugged half of it without coming up for air. He hadn't realized just how dehydrated he was until the beer hit his throat and worked its way down. His head craned back as he drank, he caught sight of one of those horrid birds perched on the pinnacle of the roof. He nearly gagged. "Jesus."

"What?" Hank said.

Alan looked around in the grass for a large stone to chuck at it. "On the roof. One of those filthy fuckers."

"What're you talkin' about?"

"The bird."

He found a stone roughly the size of a baseball in the grass and grabbed it.

"I don't see anything," Hank said, looking up at the roof while shielding his eyes from the sun.

Arm already cocked back, gripping the stone, Alan froze as he stared at the roof.

The goddamn buzzard was gone.

Later that evening Alan was overcome by compulsion. The town was small so it didn't take him too much time driving around to locate Cedar Avenue.

The old Moreland house was vacant, its windows boarded up, its yard wildly overgrown and nearly tropical in its disarray. A teepee of unclaimed newspapers sat in the center of the gravel driveway. The mailbox had been busted from its perch; it rested in the tall grass with a dent in its side, its door partially open like some animal that had died and gone to rot. But what collected Alan's attention were the two shapes perched on the stone rise of the chimney like gargoyles—the buzzards. Grotesquely oversized, they were hunched up against one another while balancing on the narrow ledge of the chimney, inky against a deepening darkness of an oncoming dusk.

Alan pulled the car alongside the shoulder of the road and turned off the engine. The homes along Cedar Avenue were staggered a good distance apart, the property lines designated by spindly evergreens. Digging around in the glove compartment, he located a flashlight. It would be fully dark soon. As he stepped out of the car, he felt secure in the fact that no one could see him behind the trees and in the encroaching darkness. Across the street was a small recreational park that was empty on this late evening, the swings sawing back and forth in the breeze as if ridden by ghosts. Beyond the park stretched many acres of low corn. He kept the flashlight off for the time being.

There was a single two-by-four nailed across the front door. A large, angry-looking padlock hung from the doorknob. The doorframe was splintered and rotting, a large spear-shaped chunk missing from it; Alan imagined that it happened on the day Sheriff Landry kicked his way into the house after neighbors claimed to have heard gunshots. Scraggly weeds curled up through the slats in the porch, twining together like strands of DNA.

Two more carrion birds were perched in a nearby tree,

heavy enough to cause the branch to sag. A fifth bird eyed him from the porch railing.

They were all over the place, creeping out of the lengthening shadows and clambering over the vacant house as if it were the carcass of an antelope in a prairie field. His good sense instructed him to get back in the car and go home. But there was something else—the same inexplicable, beckoning force that had prompted him to come out here in the first place—drawing him toward the house. It was a connection to something he couldn't quite explain . . .

Alan went around back. There was a cement patio and a redbrick barbecue pit filled with dead leaves. The drainpipe was pulled away from the house, jutting at an angle that reminded him of a broken bone breaking through skin.

Directly above him, sidestepping along the peak of the roof, one of the buzzards squawked at him. Both its wings were flared open, its feathers sparse and diseased-looking, trailing tendrils of graying cobwebs. Its scaly, dried sausage neck curled downward, its grotesque head bobbing with stupid inquiry. The creature's hideous hooked beak was adorned with what might have been the entrails of roadkill.

There was a sliding glass door here, also padlocked. Cupping his hands around his eyes, Alan pressed his face against the glass, which was pebbled with brownish gunk, but there were blinds pulled shut on the other side of the door, preventing him from seeing inside. Anyway, there were no lights on in the house.

Again, overhead, the bird shrieked. The sound—much like a sour note drawn out on a violin—stirred the hairs on his arms to attention. A second bird, nearly prehistoric in appearance, joined it, clawing down the canted roof on talons as sharp as knives. The sound its claws made on the roof was like the scraping of stones across cement.

The door was padlocked, but the panel behind it on the inside of the sliding track—the glass panel that made up the back section of the two-sectioned door—was pulled about an inch away from the doorframe. The glass was grimy enough for traction; Alan pressed both hands against the glass and slid it away from the doorframe toward the padlocked section. It slid a few more inches, the blinds swinging into each other on the other side of the glass like wind chimes, and then was arrested by something jammed up in the door track. Alan gripped the back of the door and tried to force it farther along the track. At first it didn't budge, but then something surrendered with a hollow snap, and the rear door slid open the rest of the way.

He stepped into the house, passing through the slats of venetian blinds like a performer through a stage curtain. A stagnant, tomb-like oppression overwhelmed him. It was air that hadn't been breathed—hadn't been recycled—in a long, long time.

It was dark enough inside to prompt Alan to click on the flashlight. The floors were carpeted, and there were darker spots where the carpet hadn't faded, presumably where furniture, long since removed, had once stood. But the living room had been cleared out, gutted, hollowed. No evidence that life had ever been here. The two-by-fours nailed over the windows limited the amount of light coming into the room, and what light *did* manage to seep in through the spaces in the boards was of the bluish, spectral variety.

Keeping the flashlight beam low to the floor, Alan

walked the length of the living room, his shoes silent on the carpet. There was something that looked like an oversized plastic trash bag tacked to the front door. He could see where pieces of the doorframe had been splintered. Another plastic bag, thick as tarpaulin, was draped like a runner from the front door and down the length of the main hallway. Industrial tape held it to the carpet.

This was where Owen shot his wife, he realized. When she came through the door, this was where Owen Moreland blew Sophie Moreland's head apart with a shotgun. Alan could almost see it, clear as day, in his head. Had the mess not been cleaned up? Had they merely covered it with plastic? Or was it impossible to get the bloodstains and pieces of brain out?

Alan shuddered.

He crossed the foyer and headed down the hallway to the stairwell. The carpeting stopped, giving way to bleached planks of blond hardwood. A credenza that looked like Dracula's coffin stood against one wall. Off to his right, he saw kitchen chairs stacked into a pyramid in the kitchen. It reminded Alan of that scene from the movie *Poltergeist*.

Something bizarre caught his eye. One wall was comprised of wood paneling, circa 1975, and Alan ran the flashlight along it. Someone had carved the same two words over and over again into the shallow wood. There were still shavings on the floor.

# devil's stone

Repeated without variation. A litany, a mantra. He touched the carvings, ran his fingernails into the grooves. Devil's

Stone. What did it mean?

Continuing to run the flashlight up and down the wall, he found further carvings, and these caused a tight ball to clench in his guts. They weren't words, though he recognized them immediately. They were symbols. The same hieroglyphs that were carved on the white stones along the path that ran through the woods to the lake: wavy lines, crenellations, upside-down triangles.

Too easily he could picture an insane Owen Moreland carving the symbols and the mystic words into the wood paneling while waiting for his wife to return to the house just to blow her brains out with his shotgun. Had he carved them before killing the young firefighter, or had he returned from the scene of that massacre, his mind already broken, and started whittling away in the wall? Whatever the case, the notion creeped him out.

Upstairs, it sounded like someone stepping on creaking floorboards.

Alan cocked his head, listening.

*There are ghosts here.*

He ascended the stairs, piloted still by that inexplicable drive, and froze in his tracks as a low, scrabbling sound emanated from the opposite end of the hallway—a sound like a piece of heavy furniture sliding across hardwood floors, digging grooves in the floorboards.

Someone was in the house.

He was certain of it.

"Owen?" His voice came out in a pathetic croak. Yet what frightened him more than the sound of his own voice was the fact that he'd thought to call out for a dead man.

Was he really expecting an answer? Did he really *want* one?

Again: the sound of heavy dragging. It was coming from the last door at the end of the hall. The door was closed; a sliver of white moonlight glowed at its bottom. It was just like—

*(the bathroom it's the bathroom and Heather is in the bathroom and I push through the door and there she is floating in pink water or she is on the bathtub's edge shaking the bottle of pills and they sound like a rattlesnake like maracas like slot machines and the clinking of metal bracelets and she is on the edge of the bathtub and her face is dead her face is lifeless there is nothing left inside her nothing there is nothing and when she speaks she is no longer herself no longer my wife because her barrenness has turned her into nothing into nothing into nothing)*

"Hello? Is somebody here?" he intoned, if only to quash his own discomforting thoughts. Despite the mugginess of the air, an icy chill straddled him.

Somehow, he reached the end of the hallway and touched the doorknob of the closed door.

It was ice-cold.

*She's going to be in here,* he told himself, abruptly trembling with fear. *You will open the door and find your old bathroom on the other side, the bathroom from the apartment in Manhattan. And Heather will be sitting on the edge of the tub. If you listen, Professor, you can hear the shaking-shaking-shaking of the pills . . .*

*(you never left you're still there you never left and this is all a dream a nightmare)*

He opened the door, a scream catching in his throat.

But it wasn't a bathroom. It was a bedroom. Empty. The

room had been cleaned out, leaving behind only the galvanized metal skeleton of a bed frame. Moonlight poured in through one of the windows—the boards had been pried away from the window frame and the glass pane had been smashed, leaving a scatter of jagged shards on the hardwood floor. There was more plastic tarpaulin, taped in sections to one whole wall and covering a good section of the floor . . . though much of it had been peeled back by the swarthy, hunched creatures that now populated the room.

The flashlight beam shook as Alan trained it on the creatures. They were buzzards, three great big fat ones, all of which turned and jabbed him with their reptilian stares, each one looking as big as a pterodactyl. The sound he had heard—the scraping of what sounded like heavy furniture along the floor—was the sound of their talons scrambling for purchase on the floorboards.

*God . . .*

One of the birds had a section of the tarpaulin in its bull-horn beak and was in the process of peeling it away from the Sheetrock, exposing a mud-colored, avant-garde spatter of what Alan instantly knew to be dried blood on the wall. The bird froze as Alan let the door swing open and targeted the creature with the flashlight.

One of its companions bleated at him—a sound more appropriate for a sheep than a bird—and extended its wings to their full span.

Dry-mouthed and terrified, Alan threw himself against the doorframe. He nearly dropped the flashlight. Too afraid to run—powerless to move, in fact—he could only stare back at them. They filled the tiny room with a rank, rotting fruit smell that was reminiscent of public restrooms and overflowing sewers.

One of the birds scrabbled to the broken window, its claws hammering a tattoo along the lacquered wooden floor. It splayed its wings and hopped to the windowsill, stirring the motionless air. It seemed to contemplate its next move for a moment before launching itself out the smashed window. Another bird followed its lead, dropping like a lead weight from the moonlit gap in the wall.

Only the third bird remained—the one with the corner of tarp in its jaws. It jerked its head, peeling the plastic away from the drywall with a sickening snapping sound, revealing more and more of the bloody mess spread like dried black paste on the wall. Unlike its two companions, the creature did not seem perturbed by Alan's presence.

"Get the fuck out of here." The words came out in a groan. When the bird didn't respond to his command, he slammed one foot down hard on the floor. The sound echoed throughout the room and out into the hallway.

The bird stopped. It examined him closely with milk-soured eyes, beady as two chips of obsidian, and then dropped the section of tarpaulin from its beak. As if broken and unhinged, its lower jaw hung open, showing Alan the black, greasy funnel of its maw, piebald with whitish pustules. It was like a stage performer, the bead of Alan's flashlight spotlighting it where it stood.

Alan crouched and gathered up a shard of broken window-pane and hurled it at the beast. The shard wedged itself into the coarse feathers at its breast.

The thing wheezed like an accordion and flapped its wings, sending dust motes and cobwebs floating around the room. Then it rose off the floor, its scale-plated claws curled into rheumatic bear traps, and expelled itself out the window. Its wingspan was so great that tufts of hoary feathers were stripped from its wings during the evacuation. The feathers seesawed to the floor.

The palm of Alan's right hand was wet. He looked down to find a slender laceration oozing blood from the soft, pink mound of muscle just below his thumb. Carelessly, he'd cut it when picking up the shard of glass.

He entered the room and stood for a long time staring at the smear of black blood on the drywall, exposed now beneath the partially shorn length of tarpaulin. Why hadn't this been cleaned up? Why just paper over the mess with plastic and leave it sit here? No wonder the house was still vacant.

Or had he answered his own question? Not having the house on the market would ensure no new families could move into town, which in turn would ensure that the secret of the lake would be kept as such: a town secret. Yet if that were the case, how come something similar hadn't been done to prevent Heather and him from moving into his dead uncle's place?

*Because the house was left to me in his will*, Alan thought. *We didn't just pick up and move here.*

Alone in the room, Alan played the flashlight's beam across the walls and floor. More of the same bizarre sigils were here on the wall, too, only these were painted in a dark substance that Alan recognized as dried blood. The upside-down triangle, the wavy lines. All of them. Again, the words *Devil's Stone* appeared, also painted in blood in great big block letters on the drywall.

*That's Owen's wife's blood*, he thought. Somehow he knew this without question. *Sophie Moreland. He blew her face apart, then painted those symbols and words on the walls with her blood. Where else would he have gotten the blood?*

There were new words here, too—a triptych that meant absolutely nothing to him. He had to take a step closer to examine the words better, just to make sure he was reading them correctly:

YOUNG
CALF
RIBS

Amazingly, he thought he would break out in nervous laughter. Young calf ribs? Was this . . . was Owen Moreland talking some sort of ritualistic blood sacrifice?

*Owen Moreland is not talking to you at all,* Bill Hammerstun spoke up at the back of his son's head. *Owen Moreland is dead, fool.*

Out of nowhere, anger welled up inside Alan. Was he really so blind? Had this been one setup after another, all part of the town's devious intentions of keeping its secret hidden from outsiders? Had they gotten to Owen Moreland just as they had gotten to him? They had tried to frighten Owen away from the powers of the lake the same way Hank had tried to frighten and intimidate him. It was a show, all of it—from Sheriff Landry's midnight cruises up and down the street to Hank's little conversation that night on Alan's patio. Jesus Christ, was the whole goddamn town *fucking* with him?

*What right do they have? How dare they decide who uses the lake and who doesn't.*

There was a dried brown bloodstain on the floor. For

the first time, he realized the bloodstain on the floor was *moving*, was swarming with living insects. Maggots. Black summer flies.

Shining the flashlight down on his hand, he noticed the cut below his thumb had already healed.

# CHAPTER SIXTEEN

It did not require much investigation to discover what the Devil's Stone was: an old Cherokee reservation on the other side of the Great Smoky Mountains. It was printed clearly on one of the maps Alan had purchased at a 7-Eleven, along with a clutch of Slim Jims and a bottle of Mountain Dew. A cursory Internet search provided some photographs and a brief history of the Cherokee people.

Alan awoke early the following morning before the sun had time to fully rise and, after his accustomed swim in the lake, returned home where he showered under a hot spray. He felt strong, healthy. His ulcer was now a thing of the past, and his tattoos had almost completely faded. Despite the heat, he took to wearing long-sleeved shirts outside, so as not to attract attention from Hank or any of the other neighbors who might come sniffing around.

By the time he crept out of the house that afternoon, Heather was still in bed, although she was not sleeping. She was staring at the ceiling, the thin sheet tangled about her feet, the slatted light of day seeping in through the blinds over the windows.

Jerry Lee was lying on the floor on Heather's side of the bed. The dog raised his head and watched Alan, who filled the doorway. Alan sensed a nonspecific distrust radiating from the dog. He ignored it.

"Be back in a little while, hon," he said from the doorway and left without waiting for a response.

As the mountains grew closer and closer and the farms and green fields became more expansive, Alan found himself lost . . . which was a regular riot, really, seeing how he'd been driving down a one-lane straightaway through a tract of unblemished countryside for what felt like an eternity. There were no houses, no shops, no signs of humanity save for the sequence of telephone poles strung along the side of the road, their lines bowing and notched with tiny black birds.

Eventually, the roadway turned to dirt. It crossed up into the mountains, then went through a narrow pass. Jagged bluffs rose on either side of the car, dousing him in shadow and cutting him off from the rest of the planet. On the other side of the mountain pass, he could see a farmhouse and, above the low trees, a grain silo. He rolled the Toyota over two sets of railroad tracks and came to a four-way stop. Small clapboard houses in various states of disrepair slouched against one another. Across the intersection was a feed store with soaped-over windows and a jumble of unattended bicycles on the side of the road. In the distance, the spires of a church spiraled up into the gray sky.

According to the map, this was Devil's Stone. There were no street signs so he could only hope the map was correct. He let the car idle at the shoulder while he surveyed his surroundings. Dark-skinned men smoking black cigars eyeballed him from sagging porches. A pack of mangy, emaciated dogs loped across the street. The one bringing up the rear of the pack—some piebald mixed breed with a wolfish face—paused and stared him down before taking off after its companions. Overhead, a hawk wheeled lazily in the gunmetal sky.

It was three o'clock when Alan pulled into the parking lot of a low, basalt-block building with neon beer signs in the tinted windows. Inside, heavy-shouldered men sat hunched like vultures over a lacquered bar top gripping pints of piss-colored ale. A wall-mounted jukebox with an LED display rolled out some country number, all fiddles, steel guitars, and other melancholic instruments.

Alan claimed a barstool and ordered a Budweiser on draft. The guy behind the bar, who looked like the descendant of angry pirates, slid the pint glass in front of him without so much as a grunt.

He wondered what the hell he was doing here. Not just in this seedy bar but on this reservation. His curiosity had been piqued by the words carved into the walls at the Moreland house, but he wasn't quite sure why he'd felt the need to follow them, like a map leading to buried treasure. What had Owen Moreland known about Devil's Stone that had prompted him to carve the words over and over into his wall? Also, what about the other words? The calf ribs and such? What did those mean?

"You lost?" The words came out slurred from a dark-skinned man in a deer hide vest and dark, braided hair.

"Excuse me?"

"Are you lost?" Despite the question, the man didn't appear to be combative, only genuinely curious. Perhaps a little concerned even.

"No," Alan said. "Not really. I was just out for a drive and thought I'd stop in for a beer."

"A drive? Out here?" The man sounded incredulous. Then his eyes narrowed. "Are you a fed?"

"A fed?"

"A federal agent," the man clarified. "Sometimes we get FBI or guys from the Interior Department come down this way."

"No. I'm a college professor."

"Looks like you're thinking real hard about something is why I asked." The man drank some of his beer, then wiped his mouth with his sleeve. "Sometimes I think I can read minds."

"Is that right?"

"My grandmother, she was a mind reader."

"That's interesting."

"She was very good." Again, the man narrowed his eyes and looked Alan over. "You sure you're not lost?"

"This is Devil's Stone, right?"

"Is that what you're looking for?"

He considered. "I don't know what I'm looking for."

"Sure," said the man. "The town is. Devil's Stone, I mean. Named after the stone itself."

Alan blinked. "What stone?"

"The one at the crest of Packer's Pass. The, uh . . ." The man looked around the barroom, rubbing his rough chin. After a moment, he pointed through the wall of the joint in the vague direction of northwest. "Up that way. Packer's Pass begins after the school and the train tracks."

"What is it?"

"A rocky plateau. Part of the foothills. Christ, I haven't been up there since I was a kid."

A bright little ember sparked to life in Alan's stomach. *Packer's Pass*, he thought. *The Devil's Stone.*

Then his heart froze and his blood ran cold. Bill Hammerstun and Jimmy Carmichael sat at the other end of the bar, pints of beer in their hands. They were staring straight at Alan though he couldn't make out their eyes, darkened under the shadows of their heavy, sloping brows. Alan jerked his arm and nearly spilled his beer.

"Hey," said the old Indian beside him. "You okay, buddy?"

As he watched, he could see a rivulet of black blood seep out of the gunshot wound in his father's temple. It dribbled down the side of his pasty face and dripped into his beer, staining the foamy head a dark crimson.

A tremor quaked through Alan's body.

"Hey, pal." The Indian placed a hand on Alan's shoulder. "You look like pea soup."

Alan laughed nervously. He was flushed and could feel the sweat trickling down his ribs. When he looked back at the opposite end of the bar, the two men were still there, but they were no longer Bill Hammerstun and Jimmy Carmichael. Just two dark-skinned men in hats, their faces turned down toward

RONALD MALFI

their beers. The foamy beer head was no longer crimson.

*Holy fuck, am I losing my mind now?*

"Yeah, I'm okay." He managed a chuckle and forced himself to appear calm. "I just thought I saw my dead father sitting over there. Scared the piss out of me for a second."

The man grinned, exposing teeth that looked like baked beans. "Aw, hell. I see my dead father all the time. Come on, partner. Let me buy you a beer."


Packer's Pass was a narrow, undisciplined twist of corrugated dirt roadway shrouded by overhanging trees that eased upward along a slight incline through the woods. The trees were healthy and lush, the boles of the slanting oaks silvered by the sun. There were no houses along this route, though Alan spotted rusted, discarded bed frames and the shells of burned-out automobiles through the trees that reminded him of stories about sacred grounds where elephants go to die. Something small and quick darted through the underbrush, a blur of mottled fur.

The old Indian from the bar had informed him that Packer's Pass had gotten its name several years ago after a few campers had gone missing in the nearby woods. A search was conducted, and the only thing the searchers had found was one of the camper's backpacks halfway up the hillside along the dirt road. The pack had been shredded into ribbons, presumably by a mountain lion or bear, the items within strewn indiscriminately around the forest floor. The locals believed the campers were attacked by something much more sinister—something they referred to as *Adahy*, which, the old Indian explained, translated roughly to "He Who Lives in the Woods."

None of the campers were ever seen again.

The roadway grew bumpier before it flattened out, opening up onto a small clearing toward the back of which sat a whitewashed shack with a sloping, weather-ruined roof. The windowpanes were blind with muck, and sod grew on the porch planking. Birds nested in the eaves, and ivy climbed the crumbling white bricks of a sagging chimney. A 1958 Chevrolet, colorless and defeated by rust, its chrome bumper and gapped grille pitted to a spotty red brown, sat beside the house. Its busted headlamps were like the empty eye sockets of a skull.

Alan slowed the Toyota to a crawl and rolled down his window. He could smell smoke in the air but could see none. Peering at the house, he was confident it was deserted. He braked and let the car idle, his hands clenching and unclenching on the steering wheel. He was about to turn around and drive back down the dirt road when he noticed what looked like a grave marker—an ovoid slab of granite—protruding from what appeared to be a weedy, overgrown flower bed at the front of the house. Carved into the stone and quite visible even from the car was an upside-down triangle.

His throat felt itchy.

Movement behind one of the grime-covered windows caught his attention. He jerked his head in its direction but could see nothing more. Surely no one still lived here. Surely no one—

The front door opened. A woman in a pastel housedress

and drooping nylons appeared. Her face was a withered mask of deep bloodhound wrinkles. She shuffled toward the edge of the porch with a pained, rheumatic slowness and folded meaty arms over her heavy breasts. Her hair was a silver nest atop her head; cobweb tendrils of loose hair fluttered like pennants in the breeze.

Alan climbed out of the Toyota and raised one hand in a gesture of both affability and complete disclosure. His intentions, he wanted to show her, were of the nonconfrontational variety. "Hi," he called, taking a few steps through the tall grass. Twigs and dead leaves crunched beneath his sneakers. "I'm sorry. I might be lost . . ."

The woman produced a slender brown cigarillo from the pocket of her housecoat. She lit it with a match and puffed dirty rings into the air. "You're looking for George," she said. Her voice was scabrous, grating.

"George? You must have me confused with someone else." He pointed to the stone with the upside-down triangle on it. "I wanted to ask you about that symbol."

"You're the college professor," she said. The tip of her cigarillo flared red. "George has been waiting for you."


The inside of the house looked no better than the outside. The walls were unpainted slatted panels, and what daylight managed to penetrate the filthy windowpanes took on a fatty, tallow hue. Roots and vines spilled down through rents in the ceiling like jumbles of intestines. The tiny kitchen area—designated as such by the small icebox trailing an extension cord and the laminate countertop overflowing with soiled dishes—smelled of oils and astringents. On the stove, something burped and boiled in a large pot.

The meaty woman with the bristling silver bun of hair motioned him inside and pulled out a chair for him around a rough-hewn wooden table. Still smoking and without uttering another word, she went directly to the icebox and withdrew a Mason jar of a greenish, soupy viscous liquid while Alan sat down at the table. He heard a television on somewhere in the house, what sounded like an afternoon game show. Leaning back in the chair, the kitchen floorboards creaking beneath his weight, he peered down a shallow hallway cluttered with stacks of newspapers into the room at the end of the hall. A tattered mauve sofa and an Elvis lamp were visible. Animal hides hung from the walls like tapestries.

Alan prodded a groove in the tabletop with his thumbnail. "How do you know who I am? Who's George?"

The words hung in the air as if caught up in the smoke from her cigarillo. She went to a can of Maxwell House and scooped out a spoonful of white powder.

Nails clacked on the linoleum. A sad-looking hound poked its head into the kitchen and surveyed Alan with the reddened, rheumy eyes of an alcoholic.

"How do you know who I am?" he repeated.

This time, the woman glared at him from over one large shoulder. Her eyes were milky and gray, the sclera marbled with blood vessels. Again, she refused to answer.

"That stone marker in the yard," he said, taking a different approach. "The one that looks like a tombstone. What is it?"

"A barrier and a warning."

"For what?"

The woman dumped the spoonful of white powder into the Mason jar, then stirred the concoction. The greenish liquid turned cloudy. She brought the mixture across the kitchen and set it on the table.

In the doorway, the hound rested on its front paws, the velvety folds of flesh above its eyes cocking alternately.

"Here," she said. "Drink this."

Alan watched the powdered sediment settle at the bottom of the Mason jar. "You're kidding me, right?"

In tattered felt slippers, the woman shuffled back over to the stove. With a large wooden spoon, she stirred the bubbling, pungent contents of the pot.

"Excuse me." His voice wavered. Looking at the Mason jar of green liquid made him queasy. And despite his morning swim in the lake, he suddenly felt fatigued. Even his ulcer was starting to return; he could feel the magma sunburst roiling in his lower intestine. "Excuse me but I'm not drinking this. Who's George? Is he even here? Ma'am?"

She clacked the wooden spoon against the rim of the pot. A chunky paste the color of flesh dripped from the end of the spoon. Alan tried hard not to imagine what was boiling away in that pot. "George is up in the mountains, where he's been going every afternoon for the past couple of months. He will not be back until dusk."

"Until . . . dusk?" He didn't understand. "Then what am I doing—?"

"You will go to him. He has been waiting."

"He's been up there waiting all day for me?"

"No," she said. "Waiting for the past couple of months."

"Up in the mountains," he muttered, more to himself than the big-shouldered woman.

"That is why you must drink."

"Why?"

"Because you are not of the People. The land here does not want you to pass through, even if you must, even as it is George's will." She pointed at the Mason jar with the wooden spoon. Some of the pinkish slop dripped from the end and splattered on the dirty tile floor. "That's why you drink. It will keep you safe."

"Safe from what?"

"From what you might find in the woods and in the mountains. Or from what might find you."

"I'm not drinking anything. I don't even know who George is or why he might be expecting me."

"He has seen a vision," said the old woman. "And when George YoungCalfRibs sees a vision, it comes true."

*George YoungCalfRibs . . .*

It was a *name*. Hearing it chilled him to the bones.

"Hold on," he managed, his tongue suddenly thick in his mouth. "Wait a minute . . ."

"George waits. You must drink."

Alan turned back to the Mason jar. The stuff looked thick; it would not go down easily. Not to mention what it might taste like . . . what might be *in* it . . .

Perhaps stupidly, he grabbed the jar and brought it to his mouth without giving it further thought. Conscious not to inhale, he opened his mouth and gulped down the gelatinous liquid in three aching swallows.

Surprisingly, the stuff was tasteless. There was a dry,

powdery quality to it as well. The sediment at the bottom of the jar oozed into his mouth like a clump of wet sand where—to his surprise and relief—it disintegrated almost instantly.

He set the jar down and gasped. His mouth tasted of menthol. "That wasn't—," he began, then cringed as his ulcer roared to fiery life. Briefly, fireworks exploded before his eyes.

The old Indian witch cackled, then set down the wooden spoon on the stovetop. She went to a narrow closet door beside the icebox. The door squealed open, eliciting a curious look from the sloppy-eyed hound.

"Jesus," he wheezed, staring down at his hands as his vision cleared. Sweat broke out along the back of his neck, clammy and warm. "What was in that, anyway?"

From the closet the woman withdrew a long, tapered alpenstock with a silver handgrip. She hobbled toward him, pointing with the staff toward the opaque windows. "The walking stick will guide you through the woods and up through the valley. Out behind the house you will find a path of fine white stone flanked with yellow flowers. Take the path to the river but do not cross it." Her sour eyes cut to slits, and her voice took on an enigmatic quality. "This is very important—*do not cross the river.* Follow it north. Use the sun as your guide. Your journey will end once you reach the Devil's Stone."

This was all too much, all too quick. *Am I here? Is this really happening?* Alan had the strong desire to get back in his car and drive the hell home. But even before he managed to stand up from the chair, he knew he would not be going home. Not until he spoke with George YoungCalfRibs.

The old woman handed him the walking stick. It was heavier than it looked.

"If you hear things moving around you in the forest—and you will—," she added, "do not look at them. If they speak to you, do not answer them."

"What are they?" He could not mask the awe in his voice.

"They are spirits of those who have been lost. It may also be the *Tsul Kalu*, the slant-eyed and sloping giants coming up from the Shining Rock just to see the white-faced man who passes. They all mean you harm. But if you heed me, schoolteacher, then you have nothing to fear." She squinted beyond the grime-caked windows and out at the midday sun. "Go now. You need to be back from the mountain before nightfall."

The old woman all but shoved him toward the front door. As she opened the door, the squeal of its hinges alerted the dog, who raised its head from its paws and stared at Alan with casual detachment.

"Go," she said again as he stepped onto the rickety porch. "George waits."

He thought she might watch him as he went around the back of the house in search of the path, but she didn't; the front door slammed with enough force to splinter the frame, leaving him all alone on the porch.

At the back of the house, wind chimes made of hollowed bamboo shoots hung from the eaves, their sound as forlorn as a sailor's lament. Alan spied the path right away—a crushed gravel walkway bordered on either side by yellow bellflowers that ran straight from the rear of the house into a copse of black firs. Beyond, the sky was battleship gray, the sun a bulb of molten glass.

The walking stick in hand, he proceeded down the path and through the thicket. The forest rushed up to meet him almost out of nowhere. Nettles twined around his ankles. He paused only once to look back, spying the slouching, whitewashed shack framed within a clutch of cottonwoods and evergreens.

The crushed gravel path cut straight through the forest with hardly a twist or undulation. Around him, however, the forest seemed to swell and rise, flanking him like a canyon of juniper, at the bottom of which ran the path. The old woman's warnings still resonating in his head, he remained alert for the presence of others—for footfalls in the dead leaves and rustling in the nearby trees—but he couldn't hear or see anyone. He was utterly alone.

Not for the first time, the notion that he was being set up returned to him. Was it possible this whole thing was yet one more peg in Sheriff Landry's attempt to warn him away from the healing lake? As he walked, crunching the tiny bits of gravel beneath the tapered metal tip of the walking stick, he tried to put all the events that had led him here back into place: Hank telling him the story about the Morelands; the sigils and words carved into the walls of the Moreland house, which hadn't been cleaned up since the incident, as if it sat waiting for him to arrive. Was it possible this was just another staged event in a long line of them? Something to scare him away, keep him quiet and obedient?

*You don't believe that, sport,* a voice spoke up in his head. It sounded strangely like Jimmy Carmichael's. *You don't believe this is a setup any more than you believe you can fly.*

It was impossible to estimate how long it took him to reach the end of the path, but by the time he crossed out of the woods and into a rocky, lichen-slick ravine, the sun had repositioned itself in the sky. Silver threads burned through gaps in the cumulus. Digging the staff into the earth and hoisting himself out of the ravine and to the crest of an embankment, he felt his exhaustion weighing down on him like a physical thing—a feeling he hadn't known since he'd started going to the lake each morning. The ulcer kept a steady pulse against the lining of his stomach.

*See? There is no power in that lake. I've been exercising, swimming, and that's why I've been feeling better,* he told himself. *There is no power there. I'm walking through a dream. And I only feel sick now because of that concoction the old woman made me drink. Or maybe it's this forest, this place. The path itself. Or just being here on this reservation.*

Could he keep denying the effects the lake had on him? Could he continue being so forcefully, willfully blind?

*What are you afraid of?* Jimmy Carmichael wanted to know.

Below, the vista was breathtaking. Alan paused to soak it all in. An impossibly lush, impossibly green panorama of sloping countryside loped on toward the purple foothills, bisected by a dazzling, fire-lit river. Weeping willows, their long, tendril-like fingers stroking the grass, rose in pods, their arrangement so perfectly symmetrical it looked preordained. He was closer now to the mountain range than he had thought; he could see the fir-studded peaks and valleys, the shadowed cols and canyons in sharp relief, the broken shale and loose talus heaped in mounds within the crevices of the foothills. The spectrum of color was infinite.

Continuing down the other side of the embankment toward the river, he was overcome by the distinct impression that he was no longer in North Carolina—and not just into the next state but somewhere far, far off, as if following the path had somehow transported him to an alternate plane in an alternate time. Any minute, wild buffalo could overtake the distant fields, pumping their powerful legs and kicking up dry plumes of dust, and he wouldn't have been surprised. This was a special place. The air tasted cleaner, smelled fresher and untouched by mankind. How could a city like New York reside on the same planet—in the same universe—as this remote and hidden place?

Alan saddled up to the river, which was more like a large stream and quite shallow. He noticed smooth brown stones on the floor of the river, and the water looked crisp and clean. The muscles in his thighs aching and his heart strumming like a guitar string in his chest, he followed the left bank of the river through the valley. Overhead, clouds intersected and turned the color of soot. Distant thunder rumbled.

He followed the river until it cut sharply down a steep slope—steep enough to create a small waterfall and, below, a whirlpool of choppy white foam. Pausing here, Alan stretched his calves on a nearby boulder and popped the tendons in his back. It seemed as though his tattoos had once again regained their potency, the sharpness of their color and design standing out against his white flesh.

*It's all in my head. A trick of the daylight.*

The storm was creeping down the mountains and would be here shortly. Shielding the sun with one hand, Alan peered in the approximate direction of north. His gaze settled on the silhouette of a twin-horned crag, black against the overcast sky: the Devil's Stone, surely. Dark smoke twisted up from behind the stone and vanished into the air.

Continuing in the direction of the Devil's Stone, he approached from what he estimated to be the southern side, the pillar of smoke growing thicker in the storm-pregnant sky. Indeed, the stone looked like a face—no, a skull—sprouting twin goat horns. Two cavernous pits recessed into the stone like vacant eye sockets, each one the size of a man-hole cover.

Alan walked around the side of the stone and found George YoungCalfRibs sitting on the ground before a smoldering fumarole.

# CHAPTER SEVENTEEN

The Indian motioned for Alan to sit opposite him on the other side of the fire pit. Fiery orange light issued from the pit and cast deep shadows across George YoungCalfRibs's sharp features. Alan could tell he was old, but the Indian's actual age was impossible to determine. He wore a buckskin shirt, denims, and a bone breastplate. His hair was raven and threaded with silver wisps. Two inky black feathers protruded from behind his right ear.

Setting aside the walking stick, Alan sat down and folded his legs under him. The heat from the hole in the ground struck him with dizzying effect, the smoke making his eyes water.

George YoungCalfRibs's somber eyes pierced through to his soul. Alan couldn't move, couldn't blink, couldn't look away. Skin like burlap, the knuckles of his big hands like the turns in a hangman's noose, the old man cleared his throat. Alan could hear a dry rattling deep in his lungs.

*Death rattle*, he thought. *Illness.*

"I dreamt of your arrival for six moons without break," George YoungCalfRibs said in a whiskied voice. "Since then, I have been coming out here to the valley and the Devil's Stone, guided under the protection of the warrior *Tsul Kalu*, waiting for the day of your arrival. I'm glad it is today." He grimaced without pretense. The lines of his mouth were like cracks in ice. "I'm tired and the summer days are long."

"I found your name written in blood on the wall of a vacant house," Alan said, his own voice sounding paper-thin. "A house where something horrible happened." He wiped sweat off his brow. "How did you know I'd come? It couldn't just be from . . . from a dream . . ."

"There are some future events that have already been written. It is up to us only to act them out. You coming here is just such an event." There was a pile of pinecones beside the old man. He picked one up and tossed it into the fire pit. The firelight intensified, and more smoke spiraled up into a sky that seemed to be darkening prematurely. "Of course, not all events are predestined. We have the power to make our own decisions."

"Why am I here?"

"Because you do not know all there is to know about the lake."

"You've been to the lake?"

"It was many years ago and only once. I traveled with my father, and we found the hidden clearing. There were no houses to mar the land back then, and much of the countryside was forest straight out to the foothills. The deer were plentiful, and we watched them drink from the lake, strong and healthy."

"Did you go in the lake?"

"No." The old man's voice was sharp. "That day, the lake was not for us."

"What do you mean?"

"It was not the right moment for us to use it. We had not been allowed. We could only observe it and respect its power."

"Its power to heal—that's real, isn't it?" It wasn't until the words were out of his mouth did he find he actually believed them. Despite the heat from the fire, the notion sent a shiver up his spine.

A hawk circling overhead cried out. Startled, Alan looked up and watched it soar through the burning cumulus clouds.

"Your question does not require an answer," said the old Indian, his onyx eyes holding him in their stare. "You are well aware of what the lake is capable of, I think." And there was more than just suspicion in his tone.

Suddenly, Alan felt as open as a textbook. "Then why am I here?"

"You are here to learn the things you *don't* know." He tossed another pinecone into the fire. It blazed, belching out a billow of dark smoke, then simmered back down. "I have attempted to explain this once before, to change the direction of one's path. Unfortunately," he said, with a slight agitation of his hand, "I was too late. I'm hoping I am not too late with you."

*Owen*, Alan thought. *He's talking about Owen Moreland. That's why those words and symbols were on the walls.*

*But Owen hadn't listened, had he?*

"Tell me what I need to know," Alan said.

"It is called the *Ataga'hi*. It was meant as a gift to the animals in order for them to heal themselves after being struck by a hunter's arrow or cut by man's blade. For a long time, the lake remained hidden from man until it was made visible to the People from Yowa, the Great Spirit. It healed the sick and the lame and gave spiritual and emotional peace to those possessed by evil thoughts. It was to be used and treated with respect.

"But countless winters of abuse and selfishness—of man's greed and raping of the land—have soured the waters and the forest whose job it is to hide and protect the lake. Our people stopped going to the lake long ago when we saw how it had been corrupted. But others—*your* people, people not of the land—continued to go. Then, years later, they built houses and streets of pavement, lampposts and ballparks and industry, which not only further soured the land but angered it, too. It has been poisoned."

"What are you saying?"

George YoungCalfRibs leaned forward over the fire pit, the flames casting his face in a demented orange hue. "It has become a bad place." His tone was simple, matter-of-fact. "It no longer hides and offers rejuvenation to those worthy enough to find it. Now it calls to whoever is careless enough to seek it out. That is its revenge on the ones who have soured its waters and poisoned its land."

He thought of Owen and Sophie Moreland, of course. He thought, too, of Hank's bum leg that refused to heal no matter how many times he went into the lake.

But then there was Catherine whose leukemia had been seemingly cured by the lake. And there was Cory whose neck had surely been broken. How many others had secured their own personal miracles on its shore?

*It fixed my ulcer and made me stronger*, he thought.

Alan stammered, "It does good things, too. I've heard stories; I've seen firsthand what it can—"

George YoungCalfRibs held up one hand, silencing him. "Don't be fooled. There are still healing powers in the lake. But even those powers are shrouded by the black cloud of evil."

Hearing the word *evil* succeeded in shaking George YoungCalfRibs's sermon into the realm of science fiction. Alan uttered a wavering laugh and shook his head before he realized what he was doing. He hadn't meant it to sound obstinate and disrespectful, but there was no denying that it did. Immediately, he apologized.

"Your laughter is a sad response, considering you are currently in a most dangerous position." He paused, heavy eyes locked on Alan once again. "You . . . and your wife."

His mention of Heather shook him to his core. All lightheartedness evaporated from him like steam. "What about my wife?" It came out as a wheeze, a whisper.

"The lake is like a magnet," he said simply. "Your house is the closest thing to it. It's too close to the forest and sits on the soured land. Your house rots with you and your wife in it. Rots like carrion."

He thought instantly of the hideous buzzards—the carrion birds—and how they'd started occupying the trees in the yard, creeping closer and closer to the house like vultures circling over a coyote dying in the desert.

"Vines keep it tethered to the soil," the Indian said, "like a balloon. They are channels, conduits, for the transfer of power."

"The vines," Alan muttered.

"You can cut them away but they grow back. They come up through the earth. They are the lifeblood, the beating veins, of that house now."

Alan's mouth went dry.

"And those symbols," George YoungCalfRibs continued. "Carved into the stones."

"Yes. What are they? What do they mean?"

"They are the eyes of the Great Spirit. A man who approaches the path is judged and either permitted admittance or turned away. His soul is judged to see if he is ready. If he is not ready, the symbols say one thing. If he is right and just—if he is truly ready—the symbols will say so."

"How do I know what they say? How do I read the symbols?"

"That is of no importance to you." Another pinecone tossed into the fumarole—*whoosh.*

"But the upside-down triangle," Alan went on. "The same symbol you had carved back at the house on that slab of stone in the yard—"

"It means stop and don't go any farther. It means turn around and don't look back."

What had the old Indian woman said when he'd asked her about the upside-down triangular sigil on the stone marker in her yard? What had she called it? *A barrier and a warning.*

"But what if somebody was to approach the lake from a different direction and not from the path? Like if someone happens upon it coming through the woods from a different—"

"There is no other way to approach the lake." George YoungCalfRibs's voice was curt.

Alan thought of the night he spent bumbling around in the rain in an attempt to shortcut through the woods, the rain coming down in torrents through the trees and creating a muddy, pine-needled stew of the ground. That afternoon, he'd been certain he was heading in the right direction and that his shortcut would surely cross the dirt path or that he might empty out into the clearing itself. But that had not happened; he'd simply meandered around the fog-dense woods, becoming more and more disoriented with each passing minute, until he'd finally stumbled into his own backyard.

*There is no other way to approach the lake . . .*

"The symbols can no longer be trusted," George continued. "They are in disharmony with the land."

"I don't understand. What is it you want? Why have I come here? Somehow—in some way I can't begin to understand—you knew I'd come here . . . but for what purpose? What is it you have to tell me?"

"Leave that house immediately," he told him. "Burn it to the ground so no one else can live there after you. Do it before it's too late."

"Too late for *what*?"

"Things are already set in motion." He cast his gaze toward the sky. "You must leave me now. Head back before night falls."

"But I've got so many questions—"

"You must go before it grows fully dark. Leave me."

"Please." It came out as a reluctant whimper.

George YoungCalfRibs did not speak further. Keeping his eyes trained on the darkening sky, he commenced with a chanting tessitura that stirred the hairs on the back of Alan's neck to attention.

With the assistance of the old woman's walking stick, Alan rose and hiked back around the Devil's Stone, pausing to cast a final glance at George YoungCalfRibs. The old Indian remained chanting and staring at the storm-pregnant clouds, his profile illuminated with a flickering glow from the fumarole's firelight.

It began to turn towards night as he followed the river down the valley and toward the veil of trees, the sky a twilight blanket of glittering jewels at his back. The temperature had dropped considerably, and the sweat from his excursion down from the Devil's Stone froze on his skin as he hiked, chilling him.

When he reached the woods, the half-moon was already up in the eastern sky cradled in a nimbus of wispy gray clouds. He pushed on quickly through the woods, focusing on the crunch of dead leaves beneath his feet underscored by the solid, periodic *clink* of the metal-tipped walking stick striking the occasional stone.

George YoungCalfRibs's words echoed in his skull, and the image of him crouched over the firelight with his black eyes and red skin like an old catcher's mitt burned into his mind. *Things are already set in motion*, he'd said just before telling him to leave.

What did that mean, exactly? Did he somehow know Alan had been going to the lake? Surely, if he possessed the preternatural foresight to anticipate Alan's arrival, then something as simple as reading his mind perhaps would not be beyond him. And was it reading his mind, or had his arrival here today been more than enough to give him away? After all, had he not been going to the lake—had he not spoken of the symbols and found the Indian's name written in blood in the old Moreland house—he wouldn't have sought him out.

*Sure, I just gave myself away. Son of a bitch.*

From somewhere startlingly close by, someone spoke a single word—*hey* or *wait*—to him in the darkness.

Alan's sneakers skidded in the dirt. He stood as stiff as a board, his heart suddenly crashing against his ribs. The voice—it had been a man's voice; he was certain—did not come again.

The old woman's warning rushed back at him, with all the fury of a passing locomotive: *If you hear things moving around you in the forest—and you will—do not look at them. If they speak to you, do not answer them.*

Despite this warning, Alan found himself about to call out to the darkness in response to the mysterious voice. He even opened his mouth, the words about to spill from his throat, when something off to the right of the path caught his eye: a shape, a shadow. A *second* shadow, one right behind *his own* shadow, stretched along the underbrush in the pale glow of moonlight. Alan held his breath.

*They are spirits of those who have been lost. It may also be the* Tsul Kalu, *the slant-eyed and sloping giants coming up from the Shining Rock just to see the white-faced man who passes.*

Closing his eyes, he managed two or three shaky breaths. He shut his mouth, reopened his eyes, and continued down the path. Trying desperately not to glance back at the shadow he knew was following him, he heard a second set of footfalls only a few paces behind him, crunching through the underbrush. He tried to convince himself that it was an animal—a possum or even a fox—and that the word he thought he'd heard was nothing but a mind trick.

*But the shadow? The shadow following me in the shape of a man?*

Of course. Yet maybe it was the old Indian himself, returning from the Devil's Stone.

*Sure*, he thought. *Sure.*

Yet he couldn't bring himself to turn around and look. Knew he *shouldn't* look . . .

After a while, the second set of footsteps faded away. When Alan finally summoned enough courage to look, his shadow was the only one that followed him through the woods. As quickly and silently as his visitor had arrived, he'd left.

The half-moon was directly ahead of him and opposite the mountains when he reached the old woman's clapboard house. A pale-colored light issued through one of the grimy windows, casting a white-yellow square on the slouching porch. A tendril of smoke corkscrewed up from the stone chimney.

He set the walking stick against the stone marker with the three-sided sigil on it. Then he climbed into the Toyota and took two deep breaths, for some inexplicable reason anticipating the engine failing the moment he turned the key in the ignition. When it started up, he silently thanked God while wondering why he'd been so worried. Spinning the wheel, he bounded around the property and headed toward the rutted roadway and away from the old woman's house.

Not wanting to catch a glimpse of anything in the woods on either side of him as he drove, he kept the headlights off until he was back on the main road. It was probably the smartest decision he'd made in weeks.

# CHAPTER EIGHTEEN

Hours later, Alan arrived home to find the house dark and the air pungent with the scent of burning coffee. He called Heather's name, as it wasn't late enough for her to be in bed yet (unless she hadn't gotten out all day), but she didn't answer.

In the kitchen, he found a pot of coffee trembling and boiling over on the stove. It was an old stovetop percolator, some ancient relic that had been passed down through Heather's family until it found its way into their home. Muddy coffee belched out of the spigot and splattered against the stovetop.

He clicked off the burner and walked down the hallway, calling Heather's name again. A sliver of light issued from beneath the partially closed bedroom door at the end of the hall. Something turned over in his stomach—

—*that rattlesnake sound, that shaking of maracas behind a closed bathroom door*—

—and he rushed to the door, flung it open—

"Hon," he managed, freezing in the doorway.

Heather was sitting cross-legged on the bed wearing sweatpants and a too-tight T-shirt that made her breasts look fuller. Kleenexes were balled in her lap. She looked up at him, her face blotchy and red, her eyes brimming with tears. Her lower lip trembled. "I'm sorry," she said, her voice just barely above a whisper. "I'm sorry for ruining your whole life."

He could only stand there, not moving. "What is it?"

"I can't give you what you want."

"I want you."

She smiled wanly.

"You're scaring me," he said.

"I'm sorry. I'm so sorry. So sorry, Alan. I'm sorry."

He cringed inwardly each time she said it.

"So, so sorry . . ."

"Did you do anything?" he asked. He'd hidden all the pills in the house, including her Ativan, but she still could have found some. Or maybe she'd done something else. He silently cursed himself. There were household cleaners under the goddamn kitchen sink that he only thought about just now. "Did you . . . take anything?"

"I just want to sleep." Heather eased down on her side, the bed groaning beneath her.

"Answer me." His voice was dry, hollow. "Did you take any pills?"

"No."

"Did you take anything else?"

"No. Yes." She laughed. It was a horrid sound. "I took a detour."

"What are you talking about?"

"Off the path. A detour."

For one terrible second, he thought she was talking about the path that cut through the woods and led to the lake. For some reason, the idea of Heather walking down that path and finding the lake horrified him. But when she spoke again, he was somewhat relieved to find that she was speaking metaphorically.

"We had one path chosen for us, one life," she went on, "and I turned around and went another way. My body did it. I didn't want it to but my body did it. I'm sorry."

"It's nothing to be sorry about." Alan couldn't move from the doorway; he could only stare at the curve of her back as she lay on the mattress, not facing him.

"So, so sorry . . ."

Trembling, he went down the hall and into the kitchen. He stood for a long while in front of the telephone on the wall. He contemplated calling information, telling them he wanted the phone number for Dr. Lawrence Chu, that he was ready to have Heather committed. He even reached out for the receiver. His hand shook.

Acid funneled up his esophagus and scorched his throat. Instead of picking up the phone, he opened the window and pulled a chair next to it. He sat and lit a Marlboro, exhaling smoke out the window. The air coming in smelled cool and untouched: the fragrance of midsummer. He smoked the Marlboro down to the filter and when he was done lit a second one and repeated the process.

*What now, sport?* said his father. *What happens now?*

"Quiet," he whispered, silencing him.

When Alan finished his third cigarette, he shut the window and went to the bathroom where he washed his face and hands and took a misoprostol tablet for his ulcer.

In the bedroom, Heather was still reclining on a mound of pillows. She had turned on the CD player in his absence, Ryan Adams singing "Mockingbird" in a cool voice. Her face was colorless and slack, her eyes recessed into deep pockets. Her gaze conveyed the lethargy and surrender of someone frighteningly near death. Strands of dark hair hung around her face like trailing cobwebs.

"My head hurts," she said and rolled back over, turning away from him.

He crawled into bed behind her, spooning her. Soon his eyes spilled water on the pillow where he rested his head. Holding her tightly, he wondered if she could feel his heart beating through her body, pounding with fear in the midst of their embrace.


Alan awoke sometime in the middle of the night just as the laughter of dead children faded into the ether. He sensed them somewhere above him, floating like vapor, swirling around his sleeping body. In his semiconsciousness, he even waved a hand in the darkness above him, stirring dust motes in the bands of moonlight that spilled through the slats in the blinds.

He thought, *This is where things fall apart. This is the part where the monster comes shrieking—scales and fangs, claws and horned appendages—to the surface.*

He had been dreaming of Cradle Lake.

And something George YoungCalfRibs had said . . .

Lying there. Thinking in a fog of silence.

Eventually, he rose from bed as the first rays of sunlight cracked the sky. By accident, his naked foot came down on a pair of Heather's panties that had been summarily discarded on the floor. He thought of inchworm snatches of gelatin tissue buckled, quivering, atop a mattress stained with blood. How many crazy things were there in this world? How many sick fucking things that chased away a peaceful night's sleep?

In boxer shorts and a Metallica T-shirt, he staggered down the hallway like an extra in a George A. Romero film. At the end of the hall, he stood shivering in a panel of light—a streetlamp coming in through the front windows. This side of the house was still shrouded in nighttime. His stomach boiled; sweat sprung from his pores and cascaded in torrents down the slopes and concavities of his body. He went into the kitchen.

Something the old Indian had said . . .

*For a long time, the lake remained hidden from man until it was made visible to the People from Yowa, the Great Spirit. It healed the sick and the lame and gave spiritual and emotional peace to those possessed by evil thoughts. It was to be used and treated with respect . . .*

Alan went to the refrigerator and opened the door, wincing at the interior light and half-expecting to see those hideous vines in there again. But there were no vines.

*It healed the sick and the lame and gave spiritual and emotional peace to those possessed by evil thoughts.*

He removed a gallon jug of water from the fridge,

uncapped it, guzzled. It chilled his entire body and exploded in a gush in his stomach—ice water versus the boiling belly ulcer. The ultimate death match. Taking the jug to the sink, he emptied the remainder of its contents down the drain.

*She, too, is possessed by evil thoughts*, Alan told himself, picturing the bottle of pills and the way Heather had lain in that bathtub, her wrists opened up, the water a pinkish hue.

*She, too, is—*

He jerked his head and stared out into the black soup of shadows that comprised the living room. Someone was standing before one of the windows, his silhouette perfectly outlined against the windowpane.

"Who's there?" His mind raced. Feeling foolish, he nonetheless said, "Dad?"

The shape moved across the living room, vanishing as it crossed the sections of wall between the lighted windows. A moment later, Alan heard the knob on the front door turn. The door opened, a sliver of vertical dawn creeping along the frame.

Still carrying the empty water jug, Alan went to the front door. He kicked on a pair of worn slippers. When he stepped onto the porch, the cold, early morning wind made him overly aware of every inch of exposed flesh on his body. Hugging himself with one arm, he walked to the back of the house. The moon was a shimmering diode in the ether while the sun hinted at its arrival beyond the distant trees in the east.

Owen Moreland stood in front of the entrance to the path. He was dressed in a gray sweatshirt splattered with blood as dark as motor oil, and there was a nonspecific *unfurling* to one corner of his cranium, as if the skin there had doubled in size, burst, and peeled back like the petals of a wilting flower. Muddy blood dribbled from the wound in streaks down his pallid face. "Hey, Professor, happy trails."

*I'm dreaming. This isn't real.*

Owen turned and slipped between the trees, down the path.

After a moment, Alan followed. Part of him believed he was dreaming. Another part knew with unrivaled certainty he was awake. When he reached the lake, Owen had disappeared. The ground fog dissipated off the lake's surface revealing a mirror-like placidity that reflected perfectly the full image of the moon. Shimmering, twinkling, spectral . . .

"Happy trails," Owen said, suddenly grinning directly in front of him.

Owen's teeth had been blown from his mouth, his lower jaw a dangling, broken party favor streaming with fibrils of coagulated sinew and ink-black gore. His face split down the center, his eyes bulging off to the sides on expanding, flattened stalks like the eyes of a hammerhead shark. A gush of blood rushed forth through the vertical precipice that split his face in two, pumping like a geyser. Icy blood splashed against Alan's own face; it felt like a million shards of glass spearing into his flesh.

Alan didn't scream.

There was nothing left inside him at the moment.

Bending at the edge of the lake and moving as if still asleep, Alan filled the plastic jug.

# CHAPTER NINETEEN

When Alan came through the front door, he was wet, shivering, and cold. He knew instantly without remembering any of it that he had been in the lake. He was a somnambulist, a fevered perambulator with no recollection of his past, no portent of his future.

Jerry Lee was in the foyer, whimpering at the sight of Alan standing in the doorway, dripping water onto the carpet.

"Bad dog," Alan muttered, grinning.

Jerry Lee retreated into the shadows and hid beneath a credenza.

Kicking off his sopping wet slippers and dropping his soaked T-shirt and boxer shorts to the floor, Alan crept quietly to the bathroom. The water jug was heavy, filled to the top. He set it on the edge of the bathroom sink and breathed in and out, in and out, in and out. The muscles in his chest flexed in the bathroom mirror.

He urinated for what felt like one complete revolution

of the earth. In his hands, holding himself, he felt different. He looked down. Easily discernible was the lengthening of a fleshy hood creeping toward the tip of his penis. He was flaccid and the skin was loose . . . but there was more of it now than there had ever been.

*It's growing back, every last cut off part of me.*

His ancient boyhood scars had healed, too. Two days ago, his molars had expelled the blackened pellets of his fillings into the sink while he'd brushed his teeth. And now, as insane as it seemed, his foreskin was growing back . . .

He shook off but stood over the toilet for what felt like two eternities.

Then, from habit, he rummaged through the medicine cabinet for his ulcer medication. However, upon locating the little white plastic tub of pills, he realized he was no longer tormented by the ulcer. It had vanished. Gone.

Still naked, he went into the bedroom. To his surprise, Heather was awake but not up, lying on her side and watching the pinkish sunrise coming through the pursed slats in the blinds. Alan stood for some time in the doorway, unwilling to move. He heard the incessant, nearly mocking drone of an invisible ticking clock—huge in his head, the Big fucking Ben of psychosomatic timepieces.

She didn't ask where he'd been. She didn't even look at him.

(He recalled snapshot images of a timeless New York—autumn trees and colors like smeared and oily paint on a palette. The smell of coffee strong in late morning, the windows open and the noises of the city pulled into the apartment as if by invisible strings. Jerry Lee barking at the passing taxis while he urinated on a sickly looking tree surrounded by a wire-mesh sleeve out along the curb. Heather, long before the miscarriages, long before the heartache, laughing in silent reverie at things she remembered from her childhood, the beautiful memories beautiful people carry with them . . .)

*Broken* was the word that came to him now.

"Hey," he said. It was like speaking into a drainpipe. "Are you going to stay in bed all day?"

"I don't feel well."

"Can I get you something?"

She shook her head.

"Water?" he said.

Again, she shook her head.

"I'll get you water," he said anyway.

As if walking through a dream, he went into the kitchen and retrieved a glass from the cupboard, which he filled with water from the jug he'd left on the bathroom sink. Back in the bedroom, he crouched down beside Heather until they were at eye level. Her stare was lifeless, listless, as if she could see right through him.

*Do you remember that summer when we went to Atlantic City for the weekend, just on a whim, and got drunk while we won nine hundred dollars playing the reds and blacks on roulette, and how we wanted you to sing at the karaoke bar— remember the karaoke bar?—but there was such a long line that we gave up and drank some more? Remember the girl named Amanda we met and how the three of us got drunk on overpriced whiskey, then went to the ocean in the middle of the night? We tore off our underwear and threw them into the sea, all of us. And we laughed. In the morning you looked like death and said you were never going to drink again in your life, but by noon we were sipping mimosas at the bar and grill along the boardwalk and you touched my hand from across the table and your big eyes looked at me and you said, "This is it, Alan. This is what it's all about," and you smiled so prettily, mermaid, and, Jesus fuck, that was before the nightmare, Heather, and I want that back, I want that back, I want that back . . .*

"Here." He had to grab one of her hands and physically wrap it around the glass of water. "Drink it. You'll feel better."

"I don't want it."

"Heather," he said, his voice grave, "*drink* it."

Without speaking another word, she brought the glass to her lips and drank.

"I don't blame you for any of this." The words came from his mouth but they were someone else's; surely he wasn't speaking now, wasn't in control of his body, his voice. His mind was elsewhere. He was on autopilot. "I've never blamed you for any of this."

Heather finished the water and clung to the glass. Her eyes were moist but still void of life.

Alan ran one hand across her head, smoothing back her sweaty hair. He could smell the depression coming off her in waves. She seemed to be burning up with fever. "I've been meaning—"

In the kitchen, the telephone trilled.

He rubbed her hair. Rubbed her hair. He rubbed her hair.

Ringing . . .

Eventually, he walked to the kitchen to answer the phone. Sunlight beamed through the windows and pooled on the linoleum. Birds were already singing in the trees. He stood there, naked and cold, with the receiver to his ear. "Yeah?"

He thought he could hear breathing.

"Is someone there?"

But whoever it was had already hung up; the dial tone rang on like a mournful call.

He hung up the phone and went to the window, parted the curtain, peered at the street. All the houses looked silent. Still asleep. The world could crumble and fall apart in the blink of an eye. He scanned for Hearn Landry's police car but saw no sign of it.

By the time he returned to the bedroom, Heather was asleep once again. She snored lightly, her chest and belly rising and falling with ease. Alan pulled the sheets and bedspread over her and adjusted the pillows behind her head without waking her. Then he retrieved the empty glass from her hand and set it on the nightstand.

In her sleep, Heather clutched at the air. As if she didn't want to let the glass go.

As if clinging to things that were not there.

# BOOK THREE
# THE GREAT SPIRIT OF
# THE EARTH

# CHAPTER TWENTY

By the time classes started in the fall, Heather Hammerstun had changed. She gained some of her natural weight back and looked healthier, brighter. She had made contact with an art history professor from Alan's college, and she began painting again. By mid-September, looking spry and youthful and dedicated, she was put in touch with a gallery in the next town over, the owner of which agreed to have her work three days a week, leaving the rest of her time free to paint.

The lines that had creased her mouth and eyes for far too long had vanished seemingly overnight, along with the scars on her wrists. In fact, there was no evidence of the scars whatsoever. She never brought up the horrible events they'd left behind in New York—those events never even seemed to cross her mind anymore, Alan noticed. And he certainly did not bring them up. Soon those things had happened to some other couple, doppelgangers whose ties had been severed. The Hammerstuns were haunted no longer.

They went for long walks in Groom Park, where they picnicked on potato salad and read James Merrill, Sartre, Dylan Thomas in the fading warmth of the season. Heather *laughed*—it became this all-encompassing charm that he held on to in his own subconscious tightly at first, for fear he would lose it. But he slowly loosened the reins when the charm continued to sparkle. He began to trust it again. *You will always be here.* There was faith in that, new as it was for a man like Alan Hammerstun to finally find hope in faith. *Laughed.* He found her hypnotizing again, as he had on the day they'd married.

Of course, Heather noticed the changes in herself, too—those changes that were simply unavoidable. He heard her utter a sharp, surprised laugh one afternoon. He rushed to her only to find her leaning over the bathroom sink toward the mirror, so close her nose was practically pressed against the glass. She was tugging on her earlobes.

"This," she'd said, "is so completely bizarre."

He asked her what was so bizarre.

"Look," she told him, still tugging on her earlobes. "My ears aren't pierced anymore. How the heck do you think that happened?"

He'd said he didn't know, and she had shrugged it off . . . though he could tell the notion stuck with her for some time.

And things got even more peculiar one evening when she experienced mild discomfort, then bled during sex. She cleaned up as best she could in the bathroom, both confused and embarrassed, while swearing it was too early for her period. (Alan could only remain motionless in bed, wondering if her hymen had grown back.)

But these things, as puzzling as they must have been to his wife, were inconsequential in the face of her release from her depression. If they bothered her, she did not say. If she thought about them throughout the day, Alan could not tell.

Moreover, Heather didn't mention the changes that were so evident in *him:* the rejuvenation of his foreskin, the childhood scars that had vanished into nothingness. Even his faded tattoos were unremarkable to her (though some nights after lovemaking she traced the ghostly remembrances of where those tattoos used to be. But she never asked what happened to them, never seemed curious in the least. Alan wondered if that was somehow part of the magic of the lake—to heal but to conceal as well.)

*Happy trails.*

On the darkest nights, Alan could hear Jimmy Carmichael's words whispered in his ear like the day in the morgue when he stood over his father's body. He could smell the man's stale sweat, overpowering cologne, and sour breath.

*Happy trails, sport.*

The singular bad event that happened in September was the death of Jerry Lee. The golden retriever's clock had finally wound down. Heather was morose for two days following the dog's death, though it was a different sort of sadness than the one that had claimed her for so long.

Alan was equally saddened, although he had grown distant with the dog in the weeks prior to its passing. Jerry Lee had become distempered and nervous. Different somehow. Frequently, the dog would urinate in the house, which Alan understood many old dogs did. But sometimes Jerry Lee would growl at Alan and twice had even snapped at him with what Alan surmised was an intention to draw blood. Alan wondered if the freedom of the country was too much for the dog—Jerry Lee had been a city dog all his life, and the scent of the open countryside and the dog's distant, feral brethren had awoken in it some previously dormant sense of wildness. For a while, Alan even contemplated putting the dog down. He loved Jerry Lee but didn't want the beast lunging at him or Heather, of course, and he feared it was only a matter of time before that happened.

He took Jerry Lee to a vet in town, a kindly older gentleman named Grouse, who examined the dog as thoroughly as a NASCAR mechanic.

"He's old but healthy," Grouse had said, patting the dog's side. "I see no need to put this dog down. What, exactly, is the problem?"

"He gets angry," Alan said. "Feral. He doesn't like me or my wife touching him."

"Well," Grouse said, still patting the dog, a quizzical look on his grandfatherly features, "he seems perfectly fine to me. And he's a healthy, healthy boy."

Yet despite Grouse's assessment that Jerry Lee was a healthy, healthy boy, the dog had continued to slip. One night he remained staring out the patio doors at the darkened backyard. Occasionally, a pathetic whine would rise from the beast, melancholic like a foghorn, and Alan would go to the doors and peer out into the yard. But he never saw anything. When Alan went to grab Jerry Lee's collar to haul him away from the doors, the dog growled deep in the back of his throat—a sound like an outboard motor on a johnboat. That night, Jerry Lee remained by the patio doors, staring out at God knew what, and never joined Alan and

Heather in the bedroom.

"He's getting old," he'd told Heather one morning over breakfast. "Dogs are just like people. When they get old, their faculties go."

Heather nodded but looked unconvinced.

"What?" he said. "What is it?"

"I don't know." Her brows were knitted together. "It's just . . . it's something else." She looked at him. Hard. "Like . . ."

"Like?"

"Like he doesn't trust us anymore."

Later that afternoon, Jerry Lee took umbrage with a particular spot on the floor in the center of the living room. The dog raked his nails along the hardwood and growled.

Alan examined the spot but couldn't see anything wrong with it. "What is it?"

The dog only whimpered and looked back at the spot on the floor.

"What's under there?" Heather had asked, coming up behind him.

Alan shrugged. "Nothing. Just the crawl space."

"Maybe an animal died down there?"

"Possibly."

"Or maybe . . ." But her voice trailed off.

"What?" he prompted.

It was her turn to shrug. "Maybe it's something just *under* the floor. Like, almost at the surface."

Alan had frowned. "What are you talking about?"

"Never mind." She couldn't explain what she was talking about, she told him.

Jerry Lee died just a few days after the visit to the vet.

Alan had awoken earlier than usual on that Sunday morning to the sound of heavy tapping somewhere off in the house. He crawled out of bed, slipped on a pair of sweatpants and a T-shirt (he and Heather had taken to sleeping in the nude lately and engaging in rigorous and lengthy bouts of lovemaking that left them both exhausted and glowing), and went into the living room. To his horror, he found Jerry Lee dead against the glass patio doors. The tapping sound he had heard was one of the buzzards, bigger than a housecat, sitting on the other side of the glass. The hideous creature was absently knocking its curved, bone-colored beak against it.

"Shit." He'd stared down at Jerry Lee for a long time. The dog's eyes were open and glazed over, filmy in their sightlessness. With one fist, Alan pounded on the glass until the buzzard spread its wings and bounded off through the tall grass. When it reached the line of trees at the edge of the property, it climbed into the air and nested in one of the high branches. It kept watch on the Hammerstun house like a gargoyle.

Jerry Lee's body had already grown stiff with rigor mortis. Alan wrapped the dog in an old afghan quilt and carried it to the Toyota. He placed Jerry Lee in the trunk and after breakfast took him to Dr. Grouse who promised a proper disposal of the animal.

"There's a cemetery out back and up the hill," Grouse had informed him. "It's not very expensive, and many folks like the idea of having their—"

"No," Alan had said curtly. "Thanks, anyway."

And he'd left.

• • •

Alan found teaching at the community college easy, though unrewarding, and he skated through his days without difficulty. For the first time in a long while, he was excited about returning home at the end of each day. Sometimes Heather would be there, preparing dinner and wearing a nice new dress, looking fit and glowing. Other nights, when she stayed late at the gallery, he would arrive home before her and prepare his own version of dinner—things overly burned, undercooked, or overzealously seasoned—which they would eat late once Heather had come home. Then they'd watch television over a bottle of wine before adjourning to the bedroom for another session of furious lovemaking. Some nights, they didn't even make it to the bedroom.

Alan curtailed his daily jaunts to the lake as the summer turned to fall. Soon he would go only once a week to refill a jug of water. He never told Heather about it; moreover, his treks to the lake would always happen in the earliest hours of the morning, even before the sun had time to rise, so he began doubting the authenticity of these trips himself. If it hadn't been for the fresh jug of water in the refrigerator, he would have written it off as a series of lucid dreams.

He had no more run-ins with Sheriff Hearn Landry, although he did get Landry's son, Bart, in one of his classes. Young Bart Landry was dim, petulant, meaty, and possessed the protruding brow of a caveman coupled with the slack, detached look of a country imbecile. As the elder Landry had promised, his son was a poor student, but at least he wasn't disruptive.

Hank had taken his family to Florida around the end

of summer, just before school started for Catherine, so he wasn't around when Jerry Lee died. Upon his return, he was saddened at the news. He joined Alan on his back patio one cool, fall evening for some beers. Fireflies strummed in the air. After talking about the dog for a while, Hank commented on what he had seen to be a sudden change in Alan's wife.

Alan frowned. "What do you mean?"

They were seated around the picnic table, the day turning into night all around them. Hank set his beer on the table and didn't meet Alan's eyes. "Can I ask you a . . . a personal question, man?" he said eventually.

"I guess so."

"What happened to Heather?"

"I don't know what you mean."

Hank pressed his lips together and still would not meet Alan's eyes. Picking at the label of his beer bottle, he said, "Her wrists. Both Lydia and I noticed it the day you moved in. She was . . . all bandaged up." Finally, he looked up. Hank's eyes were glassy. "Is she okay?"

"She is now, yes."

"Is it too much for me to ask why her wrists were bandaged like that?"

Alan's mouth tasted suddenly dry. "Why do you think?" he said evenly. It was like talking through a dream.

Hank raised his eyebrows and looked abruptly uncomfortable. He picked more furiously at the label on his beer bottle. "I mean, someone who's got their, uh, their wrists bandaged up like that . . . well . . ."

"Go ahead," Alan pressed. He knew he was being cruel

but didn't care. "Say it. Say what you're thinking."

"Suicide." Hank practically *breathed* the word. Somehow he'd managed to rob it of substance, which was exactly what Alan thought he'd intended to do. "Did she . . . try to kill herself?"

After swallowing a lump of spit that felt like a chunk of obsidian, Alan said, "Yes."

"Why?"

"Things happened back in New York."

Silence simmered between the two men for a beat. Then Hank asked what kind of things.

"Things," Alan said flatly, "that upset her. Obviously."

"Hey." Hank raised one hand. "Listen, I get it. I'm sorry. I didn't mean to pry."

Alan shrugged, chugged some beer.

"Look, man," Hank went on, "I like to think we're friends, right?"

Alan nodded.

"If there was something you and your wife, you know . . . needed . . . I'd like to think you'd ask me for help."

"There's nothing we need."

"Because I'd help if I could."

"There's nothing we *need*."

"Yeah, right." Hank sighed. "Not anymore. Everything seems fine now."

A hot ember ignited deep inside Alan's gut. "What's that supposed to mean?"

"It's just that Heather seems to have done a complete one-eighty." Hank shrugged, as if this whole discussion had become unimportant to him. "A month ago she was walking around like a zombie, breaking down, crying to Lydia, staying in the house for days without coming out. Christ, I don't know what I'm saying. It's just . . . if something was going *on*, you'd tell me. I mean, wouldn't you?"

Alan exhaled what felt like steam through his flared nostrils. After gathering his composure, he said, "And just what do you think is going on?"

Hank visibly recoiled. He turned away from Alan and looked beyond the trees at the distant mountains. They were the color of cobalt in the deepening night. When he brought his beer to his mouth, his hand shook.

They talked no more about it that evening.

In the darkness, Alan came awake with a sudden jerk. He had no idea what time it was—late evening or early dawn—and he struggled to sit up in bed, the sheets beneath him dampened with sweat. In fact, his whole body glistened beneath a sheet of perspiration. His respiration was ragged, coming in hyperventilated gasps.

*There's someone else in here with us*, he thought, frightened.

There was a sound—sharp and quick, like a distant bark. Like someone moving a chair across the kitchen floor. For a split second, he attributed the noise to Jerry Lee banging around in the dark. But then he remembered the dog was no longer alive and that it was only Heather and him in the house.

*And someone else . . . someone else in here with us . . .*

He held his breath and listened for the sound again.

*It's not in the kitchen*, he thought, the hairs on his arms teasing upward. *Someone is here, right here in the bedroom with us. Jesus Christ, I can feel it.*

"Heather . . . Heather . . ." Whispering like a ghost.

Heather slept peacefully and did not stir. Her skin looked like candle wax in the light coming in through the window.

Then there it was again: a definite *thump* at the other end of the house. It was the sound of something—of some-one—barking a shin on a piece of furniture, sending it skidding across the floor.

*Someone's in the house.*

When he was ten years old, two thugs had kicked in a window on the ground floor of their Manhattan brown-stone while he and his father had slept. In threadbare Jockey shorts and a tight bowling league T-shirt, Bill Hammers-tun appeared in the doorway of Alan's bedroom, a baseball bat held in both hands. Alan remained in bed, the blankets pulled up to his neck, and didn't move. His father went down the creaking stairwell, and Alan heard shouting and scrambling around downstairs. He heard someone cry out in pain and something shatter like glass on linoleum. The next morning, his father went to Fifty-First Street and bought a handgun from one of his pool hall cronies.

Alan thought of that now as he climbed out of bed and crept into the hallway. The house was dark, the hallway awash in shadows so thick they could have been vortexes to other dimensions. He owned no gun and, unlike his father, held no baseball bat at the ready. Running one hand along the wall, he felt around for a light switch that was not there.

In the kitchen, he flipped on the lights and winced at the overbearing glare of the ceiling fixtures. The kitchen chairs appeared to be in perfect order around the table. Nothing seemed out of place.

"Owen?" he whispered. It took a lot out of him to say that name aloud—as if he was confessing some horrendous atrocity he'd committed . . . or admitting to his own slipping sanity. His recollection of following Owen to the lake had been relegated to another feverish dream . . . yet standing here now, he wasn't quite so sure . . .

Unwashed plates were stacked in the sink like ancient stone tablets. Water dripped incessantly from the faucet. The ceiling lights fizzed and flickered but remained on.

He tried to feel relief but it was tough to summon it. He had been so goddamn certain . . .

*I still am. I can still feel it. There is a third presence in this house. We are not alone.*

He grabbed a carving knife from the butcher block and, wielding it before him, continued into the dark pool of the living room. Every footstep creaked. He paused, expecting to see the silhouette of Owen Moreland in front of one of the windows again, but he didn't.

Held his breath.

Counted to twenty.

*Jesus Christ, I can* feel *it.*

His heart was strumming steadily in his chest now. His nude body was slick with sweat.

Turning on all the lights, he searched the house for any intruders. Of course, he found no one, yet the feeling that he and Heather weren't alone did not leave him. In fact, the more he searched and came up empty, the more certain he was that someone was *hiding* from him.

"Goddamn it." A mouse's whisper.

Back in the kitchen, he replaced the knife in the butcher block. The knife's handle had imprinted itself on the palm of his right hand—he'd been squeezing it so tightly. He went around shutting off all the lights, then headed down the hall toward the bedroom—

—*when someone grabbed his ankle.*

He shrieked and stumbled backward in the dark, crashing against the opposite wall. The sound was like artillery fire in his head. He jerked his knee toward his chest . . . *and could feel something tugging back, tightening around his ankle, not wanting to let him go . . .*

"Alan!" Heather flipped on the hall light and stood naked in the sudden blaze. She stared down at him. "What happened?"

"Something—," he began but cut himself off. Breathing heavily, he propped himself up on his hands and looked down at his right ankle. "Oh, Jesus . . ."

A thin vine was wound around his right ankle. Alan's eyes followed it across the floor where it disappeared between the molding and the drywall. A strand no bigger than a length of spaghetti but strong as hell. A nervous laugh tickled the base of his throat.

Standing above him now, Heather looked petrified. "Goddamn it, what the hell are you doing?"

"It's nothing." Laughing louder now, like a madman. "I swear." He unwound the vine from his ankle. It came away willingly enough. Then he wrapped it around his fist and tugged it until it sprung free of the wall. Unlike the thicker vines, this one left no purplish fluid behind when it broke.

Heather crouched beside him, ran a hand through his sweaty hair. "You scared the shit out of me."

"I thought I heard someone in the house."

"Did you check?"

"Yeah. No one's here. Must have been a bad dream." Although he still didn't believe it.

"Come on," she said, hoisting him up off the floor. "Let's go back to bed."

But Alan slept fitfully. And when he awoke, it was late morning and he was still exhausted. He remained in bed for some time, running one hand along the empty spot on Heather's side of the bed, while watching the trees bend in the wind.

He got up, pulled on a pair of sweatpants and a ratty old Clutch T-shirt, and examined his arms. His tattoos were fully gone now, the skin perfectly unmarred. It was as if he'd never had them.

He walked into the hallway, anticipating the smell of frying bacon and coffee percolating on the stove. He smelled none of that.

The kitchen was empty. There was no food cooking, no coffeepot jouncing away on the burner.

The living room was equally empty. He checked the doors and they were all locked. So were the windows. Peering outside, he saw the Toyota still in the driveway.

"Heather?"

He returned to the hallway and froze. There were no windows in the main hall, so it was dark even in midday—just as it was now. The only glimpse of light came from beneath the closed bathroom door.

It was silly—everything was fine between them now—

but his heart began to race nevertheless. It felt like he stood there, unmoving, for the passage of countless millennia.

*Don't forget,* he reminded himself. *She fooled me once before. After the pills, she said she was okay and everything was fine for a while. Then, that night, with the bathroom door shut . . . the razor in the soap dish and the bloodstained bathwater . . .*

*(fooled me once before)*

"Hon?"

Alan went to the door, tried the knob. Locked.

Panic shook him. For an instant, he forgot *how* to open a door.

Knocked with a fist. Fucking *pounded.*

"Heather? Open the goddamn door! Heath—"

The door popped open. Heather stood on the other side, her face creased with concern. She was wearing a flimsy cotton nightdress and looked so small standing there in the harsh light of the bathroom. "What's wrong? Are you okay?"

He looked her up and down. He even grabbed her by the forearms. "Me? Christ, are *you* okay?"

"Were you calling me? I didn't hear you."

"What were you doing in there?"

A wide smile broke across her face. She looked instantly stunning. Something turned over in his chest seeing her smile like that. Then she hugged him. He returned the embrace, more than just puzzled, until he noticed the white stick and the open package on the bathroom countertop.

"Congratulations," she whispered in his ear. "You're gonna be a dad."

# CHAPTER TWENTY-ONE

Dr. Regina Crawford was tall, with short-cropped hair the color of polished silver and an edginess to her overall demeanor that called her sexuality immediately into question. But she was a frank and pleasant enough doctor who made Alan comfortable the moment he shook her hand.

"So you've had two miscarriages in the past," Dr. Crawford said, flipping through a chart.

They were crowded together in a tiny examination room, Alan sitting as straight as an arrow in a chair against the wall while Heather, still in her paper gown, sat on a reclining, cushioned table covered in butcher's paper. Crawford leaned against a counter that could have used a good scrubbing.

"The doctors could never actually tell us why," said Heather.

"How've you been feeling?" Crawford asked, motoring on.

"I've been feeling good. Strong."

"And eating?"

"I've been eating well. Alan has taken over the cooking duties, too, and I couldn't be more thankful. Sometimes the smell of food cooking makes me violently nauseous."

"And you've been keeping away from medical books?" Dr. Crawford cocked one slender black eyebrow. Her eyebrows appeared to have been drawn in with a grease pencil. "Been refraining from chitchat with other pregnant women to compare aches and pains and everything else?"

"Well," Heather said, "I've been reading some stuff on the Internet but nothing I—"

"Bah." Dr. Crawford held up one hand and scowled.

Heather grinned.

"Next thing you know, you'll be telling me you think you have malaria or rickets or X, Y, Z, whatever. If you want something to read, I can give you a list of materials."

"Oh," Heather said. "Okay."

"So," said Crawford, "you two want to have a look?"

After Heather had reclined on the table, Crawford switched on a TV monitor bolted to a stand and produced a cylindrical phallus, the tip of which she greased up with clear jelly. "This is going to feel about as comfortable as you might expect, honey, but try to bear with me."

"I've done these before," said Heather, and she shot Alan a glance.

He smiled and gave her a nod of approval.

The cylindrical phallus disappeared beneath Heather's paper gown. The black-and-white image on the TV monitor changed. Alan leaned forward in his seat. Something that looked like a clown's smiling, toothless mouth appeared.

"That's the cervix," Dr. Crawford said.

The image readjusted. What Alan was looking at now was the vague suggestion of a well, or the opening to a well, and nothing but empty space beyond it. Blackness. For one terrifying moment, he wondered what he'd do if Heather was wrong—if the pregnancy test had been wrong—and they weren't pregnant after all. What if the sonogram showed no baby, just an empty womb? What would the goddamn car ride home be like?

*No*, he thought. *I feel it. It's different now. It has to be. Because I couldn't take any more heartache . . .*

*(dead baby plastic biohazard bag blood dead)*

He noticed something clinging to the top of the well-like opening on the screen. It looked like a partially bent finger.

"There you go," Crawford said matter-of-factly. "There's your little peanut."

Alan leaned even closer. "Look at that . . ." To him, the relief sounded all too evident in his voice.

"And there," Crawford said, pointing to a fluttering diode on the screen, "is the heart. See?"

"Yes." Heather was crying. "Yes."

Crawford withdrew the horrible plastic phallus. There was bloody mucus on the tip. "I can print you off some photos."

"Thank you," Heather said. "That would be wonderful."

Crawford smiled with half her mouth. "Your due date is June 15."

Afterwards, they had lunch at a quaint bistro. They talked little about the baby, though Alan could tell from the glow in Heather's eyes that the baby was all she was thinking about. He had seen that glow before. He hoped things would end differently this time.

And he thought, *Maybe this time I will become a father. Maybe this time things will take—things will work out—and I will do all the fatherly things I've always thought I'd do, the things my own father didn't do for me.*

As they drove home, Heather found an alternative rock station on the radio and leaned back in the passenger seat as if she now ruled the world.

"Oh, God," Heather intoned, leaning forward in the passenger seat, straining the seat belt. "Will you *look* at those things?"

But Alan was already looking. He eased down on the brake until the car came to a stop midway up their driveway.

Buzzards were everywhere: in the grass, on the porch railing, the roof. The sheer number of them caused the gutters to sag. There must have been twenty-five, thirty of the fuckers.

"Where did they come from?" Heather rolled up her window, as if in fear the giant birds might swarm the car and try to get in. "They look like monsters."

"The woods." His throat was dry. "I've seen them before."

"There's so many."

"Wait in the car."

She clamped a hand around his wrist. "What are you doing?"

"I'm going to scare them off."

She wasn't even looking at him; still leaning forward in the seat, she was silently counting the birds that had gathered like a plague upon the house. There was even one perched at the top of the stone chimney. When it spread its wings it looked like something prehistoric. Heather gasped.

He opened the driver's door and stepped outside.

"But what are you gonna *do*?" Heather called after him.

"Just wait in the car," he said and shut the door.

Outside, all was eerily silent. Alan could smell burning leaves in the distance and the crisper scent of the trees on the wind. But there was another smell beneath those—a decaying, fecal odor that he knew was coming from the carrion birds. The ones closest to him in the tall grass, crouched like black-feathered tombstones, shuffled closer. They made shrill noises that sounded nearly mechanical. He noticed whitish-gray shit splattered in dried clumps on their feathers.

He waved his arms. "Beat it!"

Several of the birds on the rooftop spread their accordion wings and trilled like alarm clocks.

"Alan," Heather said, leaning over the driver's seat and speaking through the partially opened window, "should I honk the horn?"

He nodded.

She honked. Repeatedly.

The sound did nothing.

*Get the hell out of here, you filthy fuckers.*

He leaned in the window and pulled the keys from the ignition. Again, Heather asked him what he was doing but he didn't respond. He went immediately to the rear of the car and popped the trunk. Inside, beneath the spare, was an emergency roadside kit. He snatched it up and cracked open the lid. Sifting through jumper cables, a jack and tire iron, a fire-retardant blanket, and some first-aid equipment, he located what he was looking for: road flares. They looked like miniature sticks of dynamite.

Alan grabbed two and lit them. Purple fire exploded from the top of each stick, raining down like fireworks on his fisted hands. The sticks grew instantly hot.

He hurried around the front of the car, waving the flares like a madman. The birds nearest to him squawked and unfurled their shit-splattered wings. They were as large as dogs up close, their necks and heads like the curved rusted spigots of European fountains. He could see their eyes, too, and they were yellowed, bleary smears with dark pupils like chips of obsidian at the center.

"Go!" he shrieked. "Get out of here!"

The birds closest to him retreated into the tall grass toward the house. As he continued closing the distance, they flapped their great wings and rose off the ground in unison. On the porch, several of the vultures leered at him, their tapered, smoke-colored beaks hanging open as if on broken hinges.

Winding back his right arm, he flung one of the flares onto the porch.

The attack incited a cacophony of discordant cries from the creatures as they leapt almost *catlike* off the porch railing and into the grass. Again, their great wings unraveled and began pumping. They were ungainly and implausible looking, but they all somehow managed to climb into the air and take off over the nearest line of trees. For a second, the mass of them completely blotted out the sun.

"Jesus," he breathed, watching them go. His mouth tasted sour.

Only the one on the chimney remained. The thing was plucking at something on the roof—what Alan initially mistook for a snake. But when the buzzard raised its head, the length of the snakelike thing trailing from both corners of its beak, Alan knew unequivocally that the monstrous bird had one of those thick vines in its mouth.

For a moment he contemplated chucking the second flare at it. But then he thought about the roof catching on fire and hesitated.

Atop the chimney, the large bird eyed him—

*Son of a bitch, it's like the fucker's mocking me . . .*

—then spread its wings. Only it didn't fly away immediately. It remained perched there, its talons scratching the crumbling stone chimney, its eyes never leaving Alan. Startlingly, it emitted a high-pitched, strident cry that shook the marrow of Alan's bones. Then it flew off the chimney and disappeared over the trees.

*They're watching me. They're getting braver and more cavalier and they're coming for me. I know it. I can feel it.*

"Alan!" It was Heather, rushing up behind him. The sound of her voice so close caused him to jump. She grabbed his left wrist in two hands and pulled down on his arm. He saw the second flare drop out of his hand and onto the ground.

"Oh," he said: very small.

"Your hand . . ."

Indeed, the flare had scorched the skin—the soft flesh that ran between his thumb and index finger, as well as the back of his hand.

*Doesn't matter now*, he thought. *It'll be healed by tomorrow morning. Hell, maybe even by this evening.*

Heather stomped the flare dead in the grass. When she looked at him, there was a nonspecific compassion in her eyes he still wasn't accustomed to seeing. But it felt good.

"Come on," she said, wrapping an arm around him. "Let's get you inside."

# CHAPTER TWENTY-TWO

And then two nights later—

*His father stands at the foot of their bed, his naked flesh bluish gray in the pale light of the moon coming in through the bedroom windows. Even in the gloom Alan can make out the obscene autopsy scar. When his father turns his head and motions toward the bedroom door and the hallway beyond, Alan sees the bullet hole in his temple. It had been a clean, precise wound when he'd seen him all those years ago on the stainless steel table in the morgue, but now it continues to bleed oily black blood down the side of his father's face. It dribbles down his neck and segments into tributaries along the fleshy folds of his skin.*

*Alan sits up in bed, perspiring. He looks to Heather's side of the bed, and when he finds she is not there, panic rises in him like mercury. Stricken, he looks back at his father. The old man is still staring at the gaping black maw of the bedroom door-way. In the hallway beyond, Alan catches a glimpse of some-one—Heather!—shuffling past in the darkness.*

*He opens his mouth to call her name and finds he can-not speak. Something is blocking his windpipe. Suddenly, he cannot even breathe. His panic increases. There is . . . there is something in his* mouth . . .

*He coughs. An expulsion of black feathers wafts to the bed-sheets. Coughs again . . . and this time it's feathers and blood, lots of blood . . .*

(sick twist of tissue on the mattress dead babies)

*. . . and something else. Whatever it is that's clogging his windpipe, impeding his breathing . . .*

*He reaches into his mouth . . . and he can* feel *something all the way at the back of his throat. It's just barely out of reach. He manages to work his thumb and first finger farther back until he's able to pinch a corner of whatever it is. It feels odd, foreign.*

*At the foot of the bed, his father turns back to him and makes a* tsk-tsk *sound of disapproval.*

*Slowly, Alan pulls the item out of his throat. He can feel it coming loose, and the sensation makes him want to gag. But somehow he doesn't. He pulls it out, blood spilling in rivulets down his chin and pooling onto the sheets piled into his lap. It comes wetly and with a sucking sound. It is large and unwieldy. Impossible that this thing was in his throat just moments ago.*

Tsk-tsk, *says his father.*

*"What is it, Alan?" It's Heather. She has appeared behind his father, also naked, also with the autopsy incision running the length of her chest and abdomen. She looks hideously disfig-ured in the lightlessness. "What do you have?"*

*It is in his lap now, smeared with his own blood. Or at least he thinks it's his own blood.*

*"I don't . . . I don't . . ." But he cannot formulate a coherent sentence. Anyway, his throat is still store and stopped up with blood. He leans over and spits some out onto the floor.*

*It is a bag, a plastic bag. That is what he pulled from his throat. A large plastic bag with a biohazard symbol on it. And there is something inside. Though the bag is colorless, he cannot see what is inside because it's also filled with blood. But there is something inside.*

*It moves.*

And Alan sat up sharply, a scream caught in his throat.

Still panicking, he looked over and was instantly relieved to find Heather fast asleep beside him. Jerking his gaze toward the foot of the bed, he was equally relieved to see that his dead father was not standing there, dribbling blood and brain fluid onto the floor.

Still, something had awoken him, and he didn't think it had been the nightmare.

*There's someone else here, someone else in this house.*

Again, that sensation clung to him. He couldn't shake it yet did not understand how he knew it to be true.

*Right here in this house with us. Right here with us.*

Flipping the sheets off him, he climbed out of bed and tugged on a pair of jeans that were flung over the back of a nearby chair. Stepping into the hallway, he was cautious of every permeating sound. The floorboards groaned beneath his feet. Despite the dream, he was not thinking of his father. And despite the incident with the birds two days prior, he was not thinking about them, either.

Owen Moreland. He was thinking about Owen Moreland.

*Is that what you think?* said a voice at the back of his head. *That this house is haunted by the ghost of a guy who lived the fuck down the street? What the hell is wrong with you?*

Alan didn't know what the hell was wrong with him. He could only walk silently down the hallway, trailing one hand along the wall to keep his bearings.

As he had done on a previous night, he searched the house until he was satisfied that no one had broken in and that he and Heather were alone. Satisfied but not necessarily relieved. Something still ticked away inside him. It was a feral, instinctual feeling and he couldn't shake it.

Before heading back to the bedroom, Alan swore he heard a noise come from directly above his head. There was no upstairs level—it was a single-floor house—but when he looked up he found himself staring at a cutout square of Sheetrock in the ceiling.

*The attic,* he thought.

There was a small stepladder in the kitchen pantry, along with a Maglite. He carried the ladder and the flashlight back into the hall and set up the stepladder beneath the attic doorway. He ascended the ladder and placed one hand flat against the cutout square of Sheetrock. Pushing up, particles of dust drifted down into his hair and eyes as he opened the tiny door. Cold air breathed out.

He clicked on the flashlight and climbed to the top of the ladder until his head broached the opening in the hallway ceiling. He shone the flashlight's beam into the attic, panning the area slowly.

It took him almost a full thirty seconds to realize what he was looking at.

*Holy Christ . . .*

They looked like the tentacles of a prehistoric under-sea creature or possibly something from an H. P. Love-craft mythos. They spilled from rents in the ceiling, coiled around joists, and wound their way through knotholes in the exposed two-by-fours. He felt the cold night air issuing through the cracks they created in the roof, the smell of pine and the distant mountains as strong as horrible memories.

Dread overtook him.

*This is what I've been sensing in the house*, he thought. The hand holding the flashlight shook, causing the shadows to dance across the low attic beams. *Not another person but these goddamn vines. They're everywhere. It's an infestation.*

Alan crawled into the attic before he realized what he was doing. The moment he stood, his feet balanced on two separate two-by-fours between which yellowing insulation tufted out like mounds of dirty snow, he was aware of the proximity of the vines. Some were long enough to come down nearly to his shoulders. He was careful not to let them touch him. Just the thought of those vines getting tangled in his hair or caressing the side of his face disgusted him.

Fanning the flashlight's beam across the ceiling, he was overwhelmed by the sheer *violation* he felt in looking at the vines. They had come in under the shingles in the roof and had snaked down in twisting, wiry bundles. It was like standing inside an ancient and overgrown Mayan temple. At any moment, he expected the vines to come alive, to snake down his back and wrap themselves around his biceps, to wind around his ankles until he was hanging upside down from the rafters . . .

Something warm and wet splattered on his face. He shrieked and almost lost his footing on the beams. The flashlight dropped soundlessly into the mound of insulation, the beam thrown into a dark and distant corner between two joists.

Pawing at his face, his hand came away moist and sticky. Vaguely warm. He thought the fluid looked dark—like blood—but he couldn't be sure until he picked up the flashlight and shone the beam onto the palm of his hand: syrupy purple fluid. He then turned the beam on the ceiling, directly above his head, just as a second patter of liquid fell in his eyes.

Alan shuddered and swiped fingers across his eyelids. Above, the vines seemed to sway as if in a subtle breeze. Some were as thick as broomsticks, sprouting curved, angry-looking thorns. They hung down from what appeared to be a centralized network of vines clinging to the ceiling, like a nest of garden snakes. The syrupy purplish liquid dripped from the vines and splattered gooey patterns onto the exposed insulation along the floor. They reminded him of—

*(umbilical cords)*

—intestines.

Down in the kitchen, he washed his face and hands thoroughly, disgusted by the thought of that purplish slime on his flesh.

When he tried to go back to sleep, he found himself unable to calm down, thinking too much about the vines in the attic. Above the monotonous sounds of Heather's breathing beside him, he even swore he could hear the rustling of movement up there in the attic, separated by a thin panel of Sheetrock and some moldy insulation. *Moving*, he thought. *Alive.*

He spent the next two days in the attic, cutting away the vines and stuffing the cut lengths into trash bags. It was grueling work. The vines bled their amniotic fluid onto the two-by-fours and the insulation, as well as onto Alan himself, and the curled thorns, angry as fangs, bit into the palms of Alan's hands even through his work gloves.

Once he'd completed the task, he slammed a ladder against the side of the house and climbed onto the roof. Vines, thick as rubber hoses in some instances, crisscrossed the rooftop in a grid. He pried the vines away from the roof and let them spool down into the yard. Then he hammered the pried-up shingles back into place. The September sun beat down on him without forgiveness while he worked, and it caused sweat to spring out of his pores and soak his T-shirt.

When he'd finished, he dragged the trash bags out to the curb. There were over a dozen bags all told, and the palms of his hands now sweated blood.

Hearn Landry's cruiser was parked across the street in front of the Gerski house. Alan shaded the sun from his eyes with one hand and tried to see if Landry was sitting behind the wheel. The glare across the window was too great; he couldn't make out anything.

Overhead, one of the buzzards screamed.

# CHAPTER TWENTY-THREE

For the next three nights, Alan awoke doused in sweat, certain someone had been breathing down on him. Heart strumming, he sat up and looked around the darkened bedroom. But aside from Heather's soundless form beside him in bed, he was utterly alone.

# CHAPTER TWENTY-FOUR

Heather began telling people about her pregnancy toward the end of October. She called her parents in Tucson and her sister, Carol, in Fort Lauderdale. (These calls had been made before, though prematurely, and Alan had tried to talk Heather out of them this time as well. "It's not that I'm worried," he said, not wanting to worry her. "It's just that we should give it some more time before we start telling the world." Heather had frowned. His concern registered with her as skepticism, and she didn't like it. Finally, he relented.)

Her parents sent them a crib, which came in a giant box and required assembly. Alan surrendered his home office and moved the crib in there. He painted the room a uni-sex pale yellow, and Heather pasted Winnie the Pooh and Eeyore decals on the walls.

She told some of the neighbors, too, and Lydia threw her an impromptu baby shower the day before Halloween. Alan did not attend; he remained at the house, periodically climbing into the attic to make sure the vines hadn't started to grow back. Hank came by and knocked on the front door. Alan didn't answer and hoped Hank would think he was either out or taking a nap or something. Hank milled around the front porch for what Alan determined was an inordinate amount of time before heading back across the street. Alan watched him go from the vented panel in the attic.

He'd been suffering nightmares about octopus tentacles breaking through the bedroom ceiling and strangling both him and his wife as they slept, and he was unnerved at the prospect of the vines' regrowth. But they hadn't grown back in the attic. However, the one behind the refrigerator was a persistent son of a bitch that kept returning, trying his patience.

Several more vines—thin ones, like spaghetti—twisted up through the spaces between the old floorboards, behind a curio cabinet, or around the windowsills. One evening, as Alan walked through the darkened house searching for the intruder he knew did not exist, he reached for a light switch in the hall only to feel the fibrous, hairlike strands of the vines caress his fingertips. He flipped on the light and found two greenish tendrils curling out from behind the switch plate. When he removed the plate, he was astounded to see the vines had run up behind the drywall and coiled around the electrical wires.

This bothered him.

He did not like the idea of those vines being behind the walls.

*In* the walls.

• • •

Mischief night and a bunch of neighborhood kids toilet papered a number of houses on Alan's street. They whooped and hollered, and in the morning he noticed a few cars had been egged. Alan, who remained awake for most of the night listening to the noises of the settling house, heard it all. At one point, he said, "Heather?" and waited for her to respond. But she was sound asleep and he didn't speak again. Not that it mattered—he didn't know what he had wanted to say, anyway.

Heather set a bowl of Halloween candy by the front door. She was in good humor and looked bright and healthy. She took to singing to herself with increasing frequency, claiming that a mother's soft humming was good for the fetus. Alan didn't know about that, but it seemed to put her in a good mood, which then put him in a good mood.

They took turns answering the door, the TV in the living room showing the original black-and-white version of *Night of the Living Dead.* For the most part, the children came in groups, like pack animals, and they'd thrust their satchels out in front of them amidst a chorus of "Trick or treat!" while awaiting the inevitable distribution of candy.

Around eleven o'clock, another knock came to the front door.

Heather kissed Alan on the top of his head and said, "This one's yours. I'm going to bed. Don't be long."

He stood. "A little late for trick-or-treaters, don't you

think?"

"Whoever they are, give them the rest of the candy so we don't have it lying around the house, tempting me. I don't need to get any fatter than I'm already going to." She headed toward the bedroom.

Alan went to the door. But when he opened it, he stood looking at an empty porch. The front lights were on, casting yellowish pools onto the porch. Beyond, the trees looked like black pikes rising out of the loam. A harvest moon burned overhead.

He was about to turn around and lock up the house when he noticed a figure standing among the trees. The figure was small, almost definitely a child, dressed all in black with what appeared to be a hood pulled up over the head. Only the face was visible—ghostly white with dark pits for eyes. It appeared to hang in midair and float like a balloon.

Alan felt something curdle in his stomach. Occupied with clearing the vines from the house, he hadn't been down to the lake in a few days, and he could already feel his ulcer returning. "Who's there?"

The figure did not move. The ghost face was staring straight at him.

"I see you there. Who are you?"

The figure shuffled closer. The child's face was painted to resemble a skull—white greasepaint with black circles around the eyes and the suggestion of jawbones and teeth painted around the mouth.

And he knew instantly this child was Cory Morris.

"Cory," he said, and the name nearly stuck to the roof of his mouth. "That's you, isn't it?"

Cory did not answer.

"What do you want?"

The boy was holding what Alan at first mistook as a trick-or-treat bag. When the boy moved closer, the moonlight striking him through the branches of the trees, Alan could tell it was something else . . .

Cory turned his head awkwardly and looked to the right side of the yard, where the great swell of trees rose. Alan shuddered at the way the boy's head turned—he could not stop thinking of how he'd looked when Hank had scooped him up off the street, how he said his neck had been broken. Cory pointed beyond the trees.

Alan looked in that direction. At first he could see nothing, but just before he looked away, he thought he spotted another figure—this one as pale as bone—moving through the shallow veil of trees. Then the trees seemed to coalesce and shift in one united movement to the left. It was then that Alan realized he wasn't looking at trees at all but at something huge just *beyond* the trees. It seemed like his heart stopped.

Cory made a furtive movement, and Alan jerked his gaze back to the boy in time to see him chuck whatever he'd been holding onto the porch. The thing landed a mere few inches away from Alan's feet.

"Oh, Christ . . ."

Sickened . . .

Snakelike, tapered, hooked beak like that of a giant squid, it was the head and neck of one of the buzzards. It was nearly the size of a child's arm. It still purged black blood from the ragged tear at the base of its long, kielbasa-like neck.

Out in the yard, Cory turned and took off between the trees. He ran like a gazelle.

Alan tried to find his voice, to call after the kid, but there was nothing left in him. The shock of what lay at his feet—and from what he saw or *thought* he saw moving through the trees—had rendered him temporarily mute. He hurried inside, shut and locked the door, and remained panting in the foyer while he got hold of his bearings.

Then, knowing damn well he couldn't leave the buzzard's neck on the porch for Heather to find, he went into the kitchen where he found a trash bag, some paper towels, and a pair of gardening gloves. Back outside, he put the atrocity into the trash bag, then mopped up what blood had seeped onto the porch. All the while, he kept glancing at the line of trees across the front yard, expecting to see Cory's ghost face reemerge. But it never did.

*Does he think that greasepaint fooled me? Does he think I didn't know who he was, that I wouldn't recognize him? Little bastard. First thing tomorrow morning, I'm going to his house and having a word with his mother.*

But he knew he wouldn't.

He didn't want to see Cory Morris again.

The next morning, before leaving for class and while it was still dark, Alan swam in the lake. Then he refilled the water jug and carried it to the house, where he put it in the refrigerator.

By noon, his ulcer had vanished again.

# CHAPTER TWENTY-FIVE

"Let's have *Songs of Innocence and Experience* read by the time we come back from Thanksgiving break, okay?"

Low murmurs. His students were no longer paying attention. They had an extended weekend ahead of them, and God knew where their minds were. Alan knew from experience that this was the time of the semester when interests tended to wane the most. He thought William Blake's slim chapbook—which was mostly pictures, anyway—would serve as the perfect assignment. Even if they didn't read it over the break, it wouldn't take them long to catch up once they came back to class next week.

Alan looked at his watch. His day was over. He and Heather had an appointment with the ob-gyn once he got home, then tomorrow they'd agreed to join the Gerski family for Thanksgiving.

The students filed out of the classroom like zombies. Someone made a *whoop-whoop* call once they emptied out into the hallway, but the sound hardly registered with Alan. In the solace of an empty classroom, he packed up his briefcase and shoved his battered copy of Blake's *Songs of Innocence and Experience* into the pocket of his tweed sports coat, then headed for the door.

He went to the cafeteria where he got an apple and a bottle of water. While standing in line to pay, Morton Kent Boyle, the head of Alan's department, came up beside him.

Boyle was an annalistic literary pundit and Shakespeare aficionado who, if faculty innuendo was at all reliable, collected ex-wives like some people collect stamps. Most recently, Boyle had authored the highly acclaimed compendium *Guy Fawkes: Treason at the Feet of the House of Lords*, which enjoyed notoriety in the lobby display case of the humanities annex (and where a witty individual had managed to break into the display case and inscribe the addendum "Who Gives a Fawke?" across the book's dust jacket). He was short, stocky, with the lucid green eyes of a jungle cat beneath a gleaming hairless pate.

"Things going well, Hammerstun?"

"Yes, sir."

"We're going to change the date of next month's inservice. December is always a headache."

"Okay."

"Doing any traveling for Thanksgiving?"

"Just staying around the house."

"That's nice. We're schlepping the brood to Ohio to stay with Meg's parents for Turkey Day. We'll be doing the same damn thing for Christmas this year, too." Boyle jabbed a sausage-like finger at him. "You and your wife ever have kids, I suggest staying home for every holiday. Stay home as much as you can. Traveling is a nightmare."

Alan nodded. He hadn't told anyone at the college about the pregnancy.

"Do you have any idea what a pain in the ass it is to transport Christmas presents to goddamn Ohio? And of course the kids can't see them, so . . . well . . ."

As he paid for his food at the register, he felt Boyle's eyes on him.

"Been working out?"

"I'm sorry?"

Boyle pantomimed making a muscle. "Lifting weights or something?"

"Oh. I guess."

"You play golf?'

"No."

"You're in good shape," Boyle said, still eyeing him like a piece of meat. "You should come out with me and some of the other faculty. Play a few holes."

Alan grinned and said that would be nice, even though he'd never played golf in his life and didn't think it mattered what shape you were in to hit a ball with a stick, swill beer, and ride in a cart. "Have a nice Thanksgiving," he said and left.

He nursed the bottle of water on his way across the parking lot to his car. The sky had turned the color of sheet metal, and the distant clouds threatened rain.

He didn't notice Hearn Landry's police cruiser parked next to him until the sheriff stepped out of it, unassumingly dressed in a Carolina Panthers sweatshirt and jeans.

"Howdy, Professor." Landry had a wide smile on his face, and the remnants of his summer tan made him look like a burn victim.

"Oh. Hello."

"How's the semester going?"

"Fine."

"My kid Bart giving you any trouble?"

"Not at all. He's a good kid."

Landry made a noise deep in his throat that suggested he didn't believe him. "How about you? You doing okay?"

"Sure." Alan unlocked his car door.

"And your pretty wife?"

"Doing fine, thanks."

"Heard she's preggers."

Alan cringed. Hearn Landry was an unrefined son of a bitch, and he didn't much care for the lecherous tone in the sheriff's voice. Aside from that, it sounded like Landry was checking up on him. "That's right," he said nonetheless.

"Congratulations."

"Thank you."

Landry folded his arms and leaned against his cruiser. He stared hard at Alan.

Alan smirked. "Is there something else you wanted?"

"Not particularly."

"Is there . . . ?"

"What?"

"Is there something you . . . wanted?" Trying to give more weight to the question this time.

"Not particularly." Landry sounded like a record caught in a groove.

"You here to pick up Bart?"

"Nope."

"Just making the rounds, then?"

"Something like that."

"Your son's doing very well in my class, by the way."

"Bart's an idiot," said Landry. He looked down, examining his fingernails. "Don't know why he insisted on this college thing, to be honest. I got him a gig in Charleston all lined up, working for a construction company. He's a big kid. Get a lot of use out of them big arms of his."

Alan forced a smile. "I should go now."

"Sure." Landry waved a big bear paw in his direction. "Go on and do what you do."

"Are we cool?"

"As ice." Smiled. Shark teeth.

Without another word, Alan climbed into his car and started it up. He pulled out of the parking lot just as it occurred to him that Landry was parked in one of the faculty spaces. Alan watched him as he diminished in the rearview mirror.

Landry never moved.


By the time Alan pulled onto his street, he was in full-fledged paranoid mode. After leaving the college, he wondered if he was being followed. He continued checking his rearview mirror for signs of Landry's police car. Twice, he thought he saw dome lights weaving in and out of traffic, two or three cars behind him. To make sure, he took random turns at intersections and did not go straight home until he was satisfied he was either not being followed or that he'd given Landry the slip. He gunned the Toyota through a stale yellow light for good measure, leaving the mass of automobiles in his wake.

He even recalled the brief conversation he'd had with Morton Kent Boyle in line at the cafeteria; in retrospect, Boyle's comments about whether or not Alan had any plans to travel for the holidays seemed suspect. Was it possible the fastidious head of the English department was working with Landry? It all seemed ridiculous, but he could not calm his overactive mind.

Then as he pulled into his driveway, he saw Hank burning a pile of dead leaves on his front lawn across the street. Hank raised a hand, and Alan knocked a staccato beat out on the car horn, though he was sweating through his shirt as he did so.

Heather must have heard the honks and thought he was summoning her, for she came out of the house in a blouse that emphasized the slight bulging of her abdomen. She had started to show recently, and she had found enjoyment purchasing maternity clothes.

"Well," she said, climbing into the passenger seat, "that was sort of rude."

"I wasn't honking at you." He was still eyeballing Hank in the rearview mirror.

"What took you so long? We're gonna be late for the appointment."

Alan didn't tell her he'd taken the long way home on the off chance he was being followed by Landry. And in actively keeping such information at bay, he couldn't help but realize the absurdity of it, too. After all, what point was there in giving Landry the slip? The sheriff obviously knew where he lived. In that regard, why would Landry want to follow him in the first place?

*They're trying to get inside my head, mess up my thoughts.* He pulled out of the driveway too fast; the Toyota's undercarriage barked and Heather shot him a barely perceived glare. *They're trying to protect their precious fucking lake. And they're keeping tabs on me now, watching me around the clock like a goddamn prisoner.*

It angered him to think that he had to abide by their rules, their restrictions. Who were they to tell him he couldn't swim in a goddamn lake? What authority did they have over him?

*None.*

"I don't want to be late, but I still want to get there in one piece," Heather said, watching the car's speedometer climb.

"Sorry." He eased the Toyota to a slow gallop. His mind was reeling, and his knuckles were white as he squeezed the steering wheel. Taking deep breaths, he loosened his grip and ran the back of his hand across his sweaty brow.

Heather frowned. "Are you okay?"

"Yeah," he said, sounding forcibly calm to his own ears. "Why?"

"You seem nervous."

"Do I?"

"Are you worried about something?"

"No," he said. "Not at all."

"I've been feeling fine, you know." She rested her head on his shoulder.

He took the moment to glance in the rearview mirror to see if anyone was following him.

"Everything's gonna be okay this time. I can feel it."

"Me too," he lied. "I can feel it, too."

They arrived at the hospital with only a few minutes to spare. Alan let Heather out at the entrance, then parked in the garage. Riding the elevator to the third floor, he felt jittery and unlike himself. When the doors swished open and a rotund woman with a walker got on, he was quick to pop out of the elevator before realizing he was only on the second floor. He hurried down the corridor and took the fire stairs up one flight.

Heather was already with Dr. Regina Crawford when Alan arrived in the examination room.

"There's the proud papa," Dr. Crawford said, not looking up from the dials on the sonogram monitor.

Alan stepped toward the back of the room, his hands fumbling with each other in front of him. For some reason, his heart was slamming in his chest and he couldn't get himself to calm down. Sweat broke out along his chest, dampening his shirt. He couldn't remember the last time he'd been to the lake—two or three days ago?—and wondered if its effects were wearing off.

Dr. Crawford assisted Heather in lifting her blouse, exposing the pale white bulb of her belly. Dr. Crawford got a white towel and tucked it partway into the waistband of Heather's pants, then folded the section of towel over her groin. She took a tube the size of a canister of caulk and squirted bluish gel onto Heather's stomach.

"Cold," Heather said.

"Sorry, hon." Dr. Crawford put on a pair of rubber gloves. "Have we been feeling any movement?"

"I think so. It's hard to tell."

"You'll probably only feel the really extreme movements. All those small kicks and jabs will just feel like indigestion at this point."

"God knows I've been feeling *that*," Heather said and offered her doctor a crooked half smile.

"Okay, here we go," Dr. Crawford said, and the sonogram monitor blinked once, twice.

Alan held his breath.

*What is it?* Jimmy Carmichael's voice said from the back of his head. *What's got you so rattled, sport? Ain't you been heading down them happy trails, boyo?*

For a split second, he worried if the sonogram would find nothing—that there was no baby inside Heather . . .

*Stop it.*

Static, morphing shapes alternated on the screen. A tubular protrusion grew in size as Dr. Crawford manipulated the transducer across Heather's abdomen. On the monitor, the protrusion gave way to an ovoid chamber. The thing within the chamber moved with surprising forcefulness.

"Hold on," Dr. Crawford said, still manipulating the transducer. "Roll a bit on your side, so I can get a better view."

Heather rolled over with a groan.

Alan remained standing against the wall, his hands still fidgeting with each other.

In the center of the monitor sat the suggestion of a tiny cranium and the slender, tapered swipe of a small shoulder and arm. A foot, all five toes clearly visible—

*(in the bag)*

—on the screen.

"Oh, wow," Heather breathed.

As Dr. Crawford once again adjusted the transducer, the image on the screen rolled onto its side, bringing its profile briefly into relief.

Alan released an audible gasp.

A single oblong eyeball fitted above two narrow slits for nostrils . . . a mouth like a ragged slash through which he swore he could make out the suggestion of teeth filed into sharklike points . . .

Both Heather and Dr. Crawford turned to him.

He smiled at them weakly, then looked back to the monitor. The child's head turned away from him, presenting only the back of its skull. He could see the contours of the brain. A normal-shaped head. Alan blinked and convinced himself, by the stares of both his wife and the doctor, that he was seeing things, that his eyes were playing tricks on him and everything was fine.

Nonetheless, he had to ask. "How does everything look?"

"We seem to be coming along nicely," said Dr. Crawford. "We're going to take a few snapshots and measure the head, the hips, the leg bones. We can better narrow the due date based on the rate of growth."

Alan ran a hand along the back of his neck. His palm came away moist with perspiration.

After Dr. Crawford had taken the measurements and snapshots, she said, "Okay, folks. If we can get the little fellow to turn around again, we might be able to determine the sex—"

"No," Alan said, and it was nearly a bark.

Again, both Heather and Dr. Crawford turned to him.

"I mean, we haven't discussed whether or not we
to know," he quickly amended. But in reality, he didn't
want to see the baby turn again. He didn't want to see what
it looked like.

"Oh," Heather said.

Alan looked at her. "Is that okay?"

"Well," she said, "I guess it might be nice to be surprised."

"Yes," he said.

"Are you sure?" Dr. Crawford said. "Because if you
don't want to know now, you won't know until you deliver."

Heather's gaze volleyed between Alan and the doctor.

"I can have you both look away," Dr. Crawford suggested, "and I can take a peek myself. Then I'll write it
down on a piece of paper. If you change your minds at any
time, you'll have your answer in an envelope."

"Yes," Heather said. "Do that."

"Okay. Just roll over on your side some more, honey.
And I'll tell you when to look away from the screen. You
too, papa."

Alan turned away.

A minute went by before Dr. Crawford said, quietly and
to herself, "Okay, there we are." Then louder: "You folks can
turn back now." She replaced the transducer on its stand
beside the monitor and peeled off one rubber glove.

By the time they left Dr. Regina Crawford's office, Alan
was already beginning to feel somewhat better.

Heather was in high spirits. She held on to the envelope
Dr. Crawford had given them with the sex of the baby written inside, tempted to open it. In the end, she stuffed it into
her purse and turned the car radio up loud, singing with an

old Leonard Cohen song.

They stopped for dinner at an Italian restaurant outside of town and had a nice time. The food and ambiance calmed him, and by the time darkness settled over the town and they returned home, Alan was feeling pretty damn good.

Yet later that night he awoke in a panic. Sweating, breathing heavily, he was again overcome by the sensation that someone—or something—else was in the house with them. He flipped the sheets off and pulled on a pair of dungarees. Again, he searched the house but could find nothing. The vines had been a constant nuisance, but he had been fastidious about cutting them away each time they appeared, climbing a wall or winding through a space in the floorboards, and there were no more vines to be seen. He retrieved the stepladder from the pantry and climbed into the attic. But there were no more vines up there, either.

*The weather is getting colder,* he told himself, replacing the stepladder to the pantry. *The vines won't start growing again until the spring. They'll get brittle and die off when winter comes.*

Or so he hoped.

His ulcer was simmering in the pit of his stomach. Instead of climbing back into bed beside his wife, he laced up his sneakers and pulled on a hooded sweatshirt, then crept outside. It was dark, and a low cloud cover kept the stars from shining. The moon was visible in the distance, a scythe-shaped grin behind wisps of clouds. A flashlight would have been beneficial, but he didn't want to draw attention to himself. Anyone could be watching. Cautiously, he scanned the street for Landry's police car, but the street was empty, silent. No lights were on in the Gerski house.

He crossed the backyard. He could see the path clearly

now, as the leaves had fallen from the trees. He hesitated before entering the woods, recalling what Cory Morris had pointed out to him on Halloween night: the pale, fleeting visage of a man—or what looked to be a man—and that nondescript, lumbering *thing* he'd glimpsed moving through the trees. Was it the Great Spirit? What had George YoungCalfRibs called it? Yowa? Or possibly the thing that had taken those campers out on Packer's Pass, the thing the old Indian at the bar in Devil's Stone told him about? Alan couldn't recall the Cherokee name for it, but he remembered all too clearly the translation: He Who Lives in the Woods.

A chill traced down his spine.

Then a moment later, steeling his courage, he cut through the trees and started down the path.

# CHAPTER TWENTY-SIX

Thanksgiving Day at the Gerski house carried with it the subtle nuance of deception. Alan felt it the moment he and Heather came through the front door, a casserole dish in Heather's hands, a bottle of Chianti in his.

Catherine took the casserole dish from Heather and asked if she could touch Heather's stomach. Heather smiled and told her sure, and the girl caressed the side of Heather's abdomen with hesitant wonder. Then Heather and Catherine disappeared into the kitchen where Lydia was pulling the turkey out of the oven.

Hank invited him into the living room where he opened the bottle of wine and poured them both a glass. Hank made a brief toast and they clinked glasses. Alan recognized the Paul Desmond record that was playing on the stereo: *Late Lament*. It was one his father had listened to, his old man's taste in music perhaps his only redeeming quality.

"So," Hank said, "did you find out the sex of the baby yet?"

"No. We've decided to wait."

"Oh, well, okay." Hank grinned, his teeth already purpling from the Chianti. "You wanna step out back? I got a couple of cigars we could smoke."

He'd been trying to quit smoking in preparation for the baby, but it hadn't been going so well. *Fuck it*, he thought, following Hank to the backyard. There was plenty of time left for him to quit.

The sky was overcast. Great charcoal-colored clouds had settled upon the distant treetops like horizontal bands of smoke. The distinct scent of burning firewood hung in the air.

Hank unwrapped two cigars, cut them, and handed one to Alan, along with a butane lighter. Alan lit his cigar, then handed the lighter back to Hank, who lit his own, sucking on the end vehemently. Both men expelled plumes of grayish smoke into the still air, where it appeared to float away and join the distant clouds.

"You been feeling good?" Hank asked. "You look good."

"Sure," Alan said.

"About ready to be a dad?"

"Yeah, I think I am."

"Well," Hank said, examining his cigar between two fingers, "I guess you don't have much of a choice now, huh?" He chuckled but there was nothing humorous about it.

It was at that moment Alan sensed an undertone. His guard went up immediately.

"Listen," Hank said, "I've been meaning to bring up something, but I didn't want to do it in front of the women. I was hoping you and I would pick up where we left off—

you know, drinking beers together and what have you—but you've been pretty busy with Heather and the pregnancy, I guess. Which is understandable. No hard feelings is what I mean."

"What is it?" The cigar suddenly tasted bitter. "What did you want?"

Hank seemed uncomfortable. "Well, I mean, I don't want you to think I'm *accusing* you of anything. It's just . . . see, I've been thinking about some things and . . ."

"Spit it out."

Hank sucked on his lower lip. He wouldn't look Alan in the eyes. "Heather told Lydia you guys couldn't get pregnant."

A cold worm moved in Alan's stomach. "Did she? When?"

"Months ago. Before the pregnancy. Remember when I asked if Heather was all right? About . . . about the scars on her wrists? Well, Lydia talked to your wife just like I talked to you, and Heather told her about what happened in New York. She told her about the miscarriages and how you two couldn't have children. She told her about that night in the bathroom."

"Why are you talking to me about this?"

"Because now you're pregnant," Hank said flatly. "And those scars on her wrists? They're not there anymore."

Alan turned to go back inside. Hank snagged his arm, turned him back around. Instinctively, Alan swatted Hank's hand away, causing the man to take a step back and raise both hands in a show of surrender.

"I thought we were clear about the lake. What happened?"

*This is it*, he thought. *This is the deception. This is what he's been gunning for all along. It's not his lake.*

"I don't believe in your goddamn lake, and you have no right to stick your nose in my family's business," Alan said. "You or anybody else in this town. Do you understand?"

Hank sighed. He looked suddenly miserable. "I'd hoped *you* would understand."

"Who do you people think you are, anyway?"

"Alan . . ."

"No, tell me. What gives you the right to tell me what I can and can't do? What gives you permission to decide whether or not my wife and I have a child?"

"Please, man, it's not about anyone deciding anything. It's not about—"

"Oh, I know what it's about. It's about control. It's about keeping something for yourself and not wanting any-one else to benefit from it." Alan leaned closer to Hank and swore he could smell fear coming off the man in waves, the way a shark smells blood in the water. "Tell me something. Is the power of the lake limited? Are you afraid it'll get used up if too many people know it's there?"

"That's not it at all. I've told you why before; you didn't listen to me. You have no concept of what the lake is capable of if it's misused. There's a power here, a certain strength. And it's not just in the lake but in the land itself. All around us.

"See, after I learned about what happened to you guys in New York, I began to wonder if your uncle left you that house for a reason. You once told me you were surprised he even remembered you. So I started wondering if maybe the land called you and your wife here. Maybe it seeks out people who need it and uses them in return."

"That's insane," Alan growled.

"Maybe you think you're using the lake, but really the lake is using you."

"No." Alan tossed the cigar on the ground, crushed it out. Far off in the woods, something howled. "For whatever reason, you're just trying to scare me off."

"I wouldn't do that if there *wasn't* a reason." And in truth, there seemed to be genuine concern in Hank's voice and in his eyes. "Remember what I said about the Morelands? I said it was possible they found the lake hiking through the woods or going on a goddamn picnic or something? But you were right—I didn't believe that then, and I don't believe it now. They were *summoned.* Just like you."

"Cut it out. This isn't about the lake. This is about you and the town and your precious fucking secret. It's about you people wanting to feel superior to everyone else."

"Come on."

"I want you to leave my family alone."

"People are meant to get sick and grow old and die. Your skin is supposed to die and slough off and you grow more. Part of life is having pieces of you fade away, and if you keep—"

"Is that the same train of thought you had when you were dragging your kid down to the lake?"

The silence that crashed down upon them was instantly deafening.

Hank eventually broke it with a level, even voice. "I'm telling you this as a friend. I don't want to see you hurt yourself or your fam—"

"No."

Back inside the house, Alan called for Heather. She was

already seated at the dining room table, along with young Catherine. Lydia had set the turkey down in the center of the table and smiled at Alan. If the aggression on his face registered with her at all, she made no acknowledgment. She merely waved a hand at the empty seat beside Heather and, quite pleasantly, told Alan to sit down.

Hank came up behind him, put a tentative hand on his shoulder. Alan's initial reaction was to brush the man off, but he fought it, not wanting to cause a stir in front of the others.

"Let's have a seat and a nice meal," Hank practically breathed into his ear. "We've got a lot to be thankful for this year, huh?"

Alan still recognized the undercurrent to Hank's words. He controlled the urge to shove the man out of his face. Instead, he claimed his seat beside Heather, who smiled warmly at him and didn't seem to notice that he was burning up inside. She looked pretty, radiant even. The pregnancy was good for her. In the back of his mind, he tried to recall whether or not he'd filled up her water jug recently . . . but then chased the thought away as Hank sat opposite him at the table.

He knew it was ridiculous, but he felt almost as if Hank were reading his thoughts.


They left immediately after dinner, not even waiting for dessert. Alan rose from the table and confessed to having a terrible migraine. He told them he needed to get home and go straight to bed. He then looked at Heather, not wanting to ask her to come with him in front of the others but giving her a look that suggested she do so. Thankfully, she picked up on the look and stood as well. She apologized to Lydia until she and Alan were out the door.

One hand against the small of her back, he hurried her across the street toward their house. He looked over his shoulder and was not surprised in the least to see Hank watching them from one of the front windows.

Back home, he bolted the door and closed the curtains. Heather stood watching him from the foyer, her lightweight coat and shoes still on. When he zipped by her to peer out one of the windows she frowned and asked him what was wrong.

"I thought you had a headache," she said.

"I do. I'm going to take a shower, then go to bed."

"Do you want company?"

He caught his breath, counted silently to ten, and pried himself away from the window. When he turned to Heather, it took all the strength he had to summon a convincing smile. He kissed her cheek, then her mouth. She kissed him back and leaned forward into him. The soft mound of her belly pressed against him.

*This is my family*, he thought. *I have to protect my family at all costs. No matter what.*

No matter what.

"Let's skip the shower," he said, "and go straight to bed."

"Aw." She stuck out her lower lip. "I was looking forward to the shower part."


After lovemaking, they remained in bed as darkness pooled in through the bedroom windows. The smell of their sex hung like humidity in the air, and Alan could still taste his wife on his lips.

He was drifting off to sleep when Heather got up and went to the kitchen for a glass of water. He heard the distant dream sounds of clanging glasses and a running tap. They could have been in someone else's world. Then she climbed back into bed beside him, snuggling up to him and wrapping an arm around his abdomen. Caught in the semiconscious state between sleep and wakefulness, he smiled and thought he could hear himself murmuring nonsense. The thrust of Heather's belly pressed gently against his right hip.

Once sleep fully claimed him, he was shuttled off to the depths of some black forest where the trees stood as tall as skyscrapers and large, indistinct behemoths trod in the periphery of his vision. The sounds of the trees breaking as these monstrous entities cleared the way were as loud as car crashes; they clashed like a tympani. In the night sky, sigils comprised of iridescent lights burned in the place of stars, like bastardizations of the zodiac. As he looked at them they seemed to shift and move slightly, almost imperceptibly. When they moved, their shapes changed. He thought he could almost recognize what they were trying to turn into, their shapes and forms and figures. Nonsense turned into secrets turned back into nonsense.

Soon Alan was at the cusp of the lake. On the opposite shore, something large and unwieldy progressed through the trees. Thick trunks were felled, and birds took flight into a sky suddenly the color of a fading bruise. As the thing came out of the trees and approached the edge of the lake, Alan could see its hugeness . . . and he could actually *feel* how big it was as the air around him seemed to swell and waver in the creature's presence.

Panic overtook him, but his dream feet would not allow him to run. He stood at the cusp of the lake on his own side of the circular body of water, suddenly cognizant of the fact that he wasn't wearing any clothes. He stared at the other side of the lake as the creature appeared in full form beneath the iridescent zodiac in the sky.

It was tremendous, perhaps twenty stories high, and possessed the body of a moose capped with the S-shaped neck and tapered, hooked beak of a vulture. The neck was networked with thick vines—as thick as electrical cables, much thicker than the ones that had been plaguing the house all summer and fall—and they pulsed in synchronization with the massive creature's heartbeat.

And it was a heartbeat Alan could feel reverberating through the ground and up through the spongy black marrow of his bones.

The great creature lowered its hook-shaped head until it was hovering above the lake's surface. The giant beak was the size of a sailboat. The thing's eyes were black pits, the centers of which were alive with the flames of living fire. The longer Alan stared into those flames, the more certain he was that he could see himself screaming in the midst of that inferno . . .

At his feet, something snakelike sprouted from the wet soil and coiled speedily around his bare left ankle. Alan shrieked. He looked down and saw a vine like a garden hose winding up his thigh. Instead of thorns the vine sprouted tiny gray feathers. Dropping quickly to his knees, he groped for the vine . . . but the moment his hands struck it, the vine released him and retracted into the ground. For whatever reason, he felt a compulsion to go after it, and he dug one hand into the hole in the earth after the vine, straight down to his wrist. The soil beneath was moist and warm; feeling it caused something to snap at the base of his spine, and he felt his entire body shudder.

Across the lake, the behemoth roared, and the sound was like a thousand lawn mowers.

Then, suddenly, Alan was awake and back in bed. Only he wasn't propped up on his pillow, his head by the head-board. He was curled into a fetal position at the foot of the bed, his knees pulled to his chest, his entire body shaking from the power of the lingering nightmare. He attempted to sit up, but a bolt of pain rocketed through his body, momentarily paralyzing him.

His hand was still in the soil from his dream . . .

He glanced up to see his right hand disappearing between the thatch of pubic hair at the center of his wife's body, where her legs came together. It took him several seconds to discern exactly what he was looking at—exactly what he was doing—before he withdrew his hand in self-disgust. The sound of the withdrawal caused his stomach to lurch. He feared he might vomit.

At the head of the bed, Heather moaned in her sleep, her naked body pale blue in the moonlight filtering through the part in the curtains. The swollen rise of her belly reminded him of—

*(something large moving through the trees)*

—an enormous pearl.

Hastily, he sat upright. The fingers of his right hand were webbed with secreted fluid. Again, he thought he would retch, but he didn't want to wake up his wife.

Heather murmured beneath her breath and turned on her side. She did not seem aware of anything that had happened.

And what, exactly, had happened?

He didn't know. Disgusted with himself, he rolled off the bed and, naked, scampered silently down the hallway to the bathroom. There, he flicked on the lights and was horrified to find that the tacky fluid on his right hand was pinkish.

*Blood.*

Christ, what had he done?

Cranking the water on in the sink, he shoved both hands beneath the tepid stream and scrubbed them. When he glanced up at the ghost in the mirror, he could hardly recognize the cretin.

# CHAPTER TWENTY-SEVEN

It kept happening. On the third night, Alan couldn't repress his disgust: he made it down the hallway at a quick enough pace to neatly expel that evening's dinner into the toilet bowl. Even though Alan was careful to keep his retching noises as quiet as possible, he didn't think Heather would wake up. And she didn't. In fact, she didn't seem bothered by the violation at all.

After a week of such madness, he found himself needing to visit the lake daily, as he had done in the very beginning, because his lack of sleep and overall anxiety were weakening him. The water was even colder now with the drop in temperature, and by the second week of December, it was downright torturous. Yet he visited it religiously and filled Heather's water jug twice a week. He felt stronger and healthier almost immediately, just as he had before, but the lake unfortunately did very little to assuage his anxiety.

He hated going to work and couldn't wait until Christmas

break arrived. Any time he spent away from home, he was convinced that something horrible and invisible was sneaking in, coiling itself around the very heart of the house, and squeezing the life out of his family when they weren't even there to protect themselves. And he was the husband, the father-to-be. It was his job to protect them all.

His mind continued to return to the conversation he'd had with Hank on Thanksgiving Day. It was evident to him that Hank had been conspiring with Landry and God knew who else in town to keep him away from the lake.

Twice since Thanksgiving Day, Hank had stood on Alan's porch and knocked on the door for what seemed like an eternity. The second time, he hadn't left until he'd called out that he knew Alan was in there and he wished he'd talk to him. (Alan had remained in the back bedroom and hadn't responded; luckily, Heather had been in the shower at that point, otherwise he would have had some explaining to do.)

Another time, just moments after Alan had arrived home from work, he had seen Landry park his cruiser at Hank's house. Alan watched from the kitchen windows, suddenly on edge. Landry got out of the car, looking like a grizzly bear in his winter parka with the faux fur collar. Hank came out the front door and met Landry midway down the front lawn. They talked for a few moments, their faces almost intimately close to one another, plumes of vapor wafting from their mouths. Then Landry nodded and clapped Hank on the shoulder. Alan expected Landry to make his way over to his house, but the sheriff simply got back into his car, kicked it over, and motored on down the street. Hank had vanished inside his house without so much as a glance over his shoulder.

*Conspiring against me*, Alan had thought. *The whole messy lot of them.*

Yet despite his anger towards Hank, one thing the man had said to him Thanksgiving Day had lodged in Alan's mind. Something he couldn't readily shake because, at some point prior, he had started to think it, too. It was about how strange it was his uncle had left him this house after being absent for the bulk of his life, particularly when the old man had two very capable adult children. What exactly had Hank said? *So I started wondering if maybe the land called you and your wife here. Maybe it seeks out people who need it and uses them in return.*

Of course, on the surface, the notion was preposterous. The "land" hadn't written his uncle's goddamned will. And anyway, what logic was there in trying to scrutinize the actions of an ailing old man in the last throes of his life? Maybe Uncle Phillip had become estranged from his kids. Or maybe he hadn't wanted to burden them with the responsibility of the place.

*Maybe it seeks out people who need it and uses them in return . . .*

Was there something to that?

And each night, whether Alan found his hand halfway inside his wife or not while she slept, he would awake with the sudden and irrefutable conviction that someone else was in the house with them. He started sleeping with an old Louisville beside the bed, and he would creep like a lone warrior through the darkened house each night, searching for an intruder he knew was there but continued to somehow remain elusive. And every morning, though no evidence of the intruder could be found, he would notice fresh twists of vine spooling out of the wainscoting or from between floorboards. He tugged them out angrily and, at first, tossed them in the trash. Soon, however, he bought a bottle of lighter fluid and began burning them in a ceramic flowerpot in the yard.

It was December, goddamn it. How were the vines still growing?

One Saturday afternoon, Heather arrived home from Christmas shopping to discover that Alan had taken a hammer and broken through a section of drywall in the main hallway, between their bedroom and the bathroom. She stopped dead in her tracks, her arms laden with packages and shopping bags, and stared at Alan who was covered in fine white powder, his shirt off, his chest heaving with each exhausted exhalation.

"Jesus Christ. What are you doing?"

Alan reached into the wall and yanked out a tangle of knotted vines. "They're everywhere." He didn't tell her he had started hearing them move in the walls at night. *Intruders*, he thought.

"What *are* they?"

"Vines, I think." He considered. "I don't know."

"What's all over your chest?"

He looked down. Some of the purplish fluid had squirted onto him. Against the white powder from the drywall, it looked like blood.

"Vine juice, I suppose," he said eventually, and for some reason that very phrase made him want to bray laughter. But by that point Heather had already moved down the hall and into the kitchen.

If Heather had picked up on the things that were bothering him, he couldn't tell. In fact, she seemed to be oblivious to his plight; moreover, her mood seemed to become better and better as her pregnancy progressed. She bought things for the nursery and things for the baby. She sang in the shower and rubbed her augmented belly while they sat on the sofa at night, watching television.

She didn't even make any more comments about the section of wall Alan had cracked open in the hallway, which he eventually repaired at his leisure. And when he noticed vines sprouting up from other parts of the house and he took a hammer to those walls as well, Heather didn't so much as bat an eyelash.

Dinner one night. Soup and sandwiches. Something quick. The both of them.

"Can I ask you something?"

Heather looked up from her tomato soup. "Sure."

They were eating at the kitchen table, something they had started doing midway through the first trimester of the pregnancy. Heather had said it was important to start having meals at the table and not in front of the television for when the baby arrived.

"At night," Alan said. "Do you have . . . strange dreams?"

"Oh," she said. "They say that's normal."

He looked hard at her. "Normal?"

"It's my body going through chemical changes. There's really nothing out of the ordinary about it."

"What kind of dreams are they?"

"What do you mean?"

"What do you dream about?"

She shrugged. "I can't really remember. Why?"

It was his turn to try and sound casual. He didn't know if he did such a good job. "Do you ever dream that someone else is in the house with us?"

Heather laughed. The sound caused the hairs on the back of Alan's neck to stand at attention.

"What's so funny?" he said.

"Alan, honey," Heather said, setting her spoon down in her soup and running one hand over the mound of her belly, "there *is* someone else in the house with us."

And the notion rattled him. He'd been thinking of intruders and of vines snaking in through the cracks and crevices. He'd never considered the baby . . .

In his mind, Heather's voice, as ephemeral as a ghost's, rose and found him through the ether of his gray matter: *The first one was a mermaid. This one will be a sailor.*

"You look gloomy," his wife said, frighteningly matter-of-fact.

"I feel funny," he intoned, no longer hungry.

Heather smiled and began to sing, causing the cold finger of dread to trace down Alan's spine. "Hush, little baby, don't say a word . . . Mama's gonna buy you a big black bird . . ."

He told her to stop singing.

"Mama's gonna buy you a big black bird, Alan," she sang, then laughed again.

"Cut it out."

But Heather just kept laughing.

•  •  •

Later that night when Alan awoke with that same sensation of violation upon him—of the unseen intruder in his home—he first looked over to his wife.

And was terrified to find his hands around her throat as she slept.

# CHAPTER TWENTY-EIGHT

"Making a few home improvements?" Landry said.

For some stupid reason, Alan had answered the front door without checking to see who it was on the other side.

Now, Sheriff Landry stood with his hands wedged into his too-tight khaki pants, looking twice his normal girth within his parka. Behind the sheriff on the porch steps stood Hank, looking uncomfortable and out of place. Despite the gray afternoon, he had on reflective sunglasses and was sporting a fresh haircut.

Alan blinked and momentarily forgot he was standing in the doorway covered in drywall dust and holding a hammer. "Oh, sure," he said after a moment. He shot his gaze past Landry to Hank, but he couldn't tell where Hank was looking behind those sunglasses.

Landry took a step toward the door. "Mind if we come in, have us a little chat?"

"This about Bart's paper on *War and Peace*?" It was

meant to be humorous, but the words fell from his mouth and shattered like pottery on the ground.

Landry's and Hank's expressionless faces in the wake of his attempt at humor quickly conveyed to him the gravity of the situation.

"Actually," he quickly amended as Landry took another shuffling step toward the open door, "I'm in the middle of something. What is it you guys want?"

Landry chewed on the inside of his cheek. Then he said, "Okay. Maybe you can come out, then?"

"Like I said . . ."

"Yeah. In the middle of something." The sheriff's gaze shot past Alan's shoulder and into the house. The action made Alan uncomfortable. "Wife at home?"

"She is, yeah."

"That baby coming along okay?" The tone of Landry's voice suggested he could have been talking about a loaf of bread baking in the oven.

"Sure enough." Subconsciously, he tightened his grip on the hammer.

"See," Landry said, and Hank shifted disconcertingly behind him, "I thought we had an understanding, Hammer-stun. About the lake? You get me?"

"I'm not letting you in my house," he told them, though he was still looking past Landry and at Hank. "I'm not coming out, either. I don't have to talk to either one of you."

"Alan," Hank said. There was a tremor in his voice that made him sound almost childlike.

"You can't bully me."

"No one's trying to bully nobody," Landry said, his

voice taking on a surprisingly placating tone. "Way I see it, this whole thing's my fault. I should have been more direct when talking with you about all this. You see what I'm saying?"

"No."

"Okay." Landry smiled his shark's grin—the same one he had used that day in the community college faculty parking lot. "Then maybe you can come out here and I'll explain it to you."

For the first time, Alan noticed a second police car in the street in front of his house, parked beside the sheriff's cruiser. He could make out the silhouettes of two men sitting in the front seat.

"I want you off my property now," Alan told them. "The both of you."

"Jesus, Alan," Hank pleaded, his voice rising an octave. He sounded even more childlike than he had just a moment ago. "Can't you see we're trying to help you, man?"

"No. You're trying to bully me and keep me away from something you have no right to. This is harassment. I want you all to leave me and my family alone."

"There are other ways we can go about this," Landry suggested, and there was little room for misunderstanding his intentions.

Infuriated, it was all Alan could do not to grind his teeth into powder. "So you go from harassing me to threatening me?" He jerked his chin toward the street. "Get the hell out of here."

Again, Landry chewed at the inside of his cheek. He seemed to be assessing his options as he shifted his considerable weight from one foot to the other. Beneath him, the porch creaked and groaned. Then he smiled. "All right, son. Suit yourself." He nodded and, looking past Alan, tipped his wide-brimmed hat. "Ma'am."

Alan whirled around to find Heather standing behind him.

Sheriff Landry and Hank walked away almost in slow motion, like two men being led to their executions.

Alan stood in the doorway and watched them until Landry and his two deputies drove off and Hank had entered his own house. He expected to see the curtains whoosh aside in one of the front windows, but that didn't happen. Finally, he closed the door, aware that he was squeezing the hammer hard enough to leave an impression on the palm of his hand.

"What was that all about?"

He moved past Heather without saying a word, heading back into the living room where he had knocked out a section of drywall. Within, vines had collected around the two-by-fours like spools of wire. It had taken the better part of the morning to cut them all away. They sat in a trash bag beneath the jagged gaping wound in the wall.

"Alan," Heather said, coming up behind him. "I asked you a question."

He summoned his best lie. "They heard I was doing some work in the house. Sheriff just wanted to make sure it wasn't anything I'd need a permit for."

His wife barked laughter but didn't ask any further questions. When Alan finally looked over his shoulder, she was gone.

He thought then of Owen Moreland . . . and the sheer fact that he thought of him caused him to panic. There were no parallels between Owen Moreland and himself. Were there? So what had caused him to think of him at that particular moment?

*It's the town*, he convinced himself. *They've got me paranoid. They've got me thinking of every disgusting nightmare my mind is capable of summoning.* Shuddering, he recalled the night he'd awoken to find his hands around his wife's neck. *And not all of them are nightmares. They're driving me insane, goddamn it.*

*Gotta protect your family, boyo*, said Jimmy Carmichael. *Gotta keep on marching down them happy trails.*

Trails.

Indeed.

Outside, Alan emptied the bag of vines into the ceramic flowerpot, squirted some lighter fluid on them, and set them ablaze with the drop of a single match. The smell was caustic, the smoke as black as the ace of spades. He pulled his sweatshirt up over his nose so he didn't have to breathe the fumes.

Behind him, something released a bloodcurdling wail.

He spun around to find one of the buzzards perched on a low tree branch in the yard. It was so heavy it was causing the bough to bend, the top of it nearly brushing the ground.

"Filthy fucker," he muttered.

When the fire had died out, leaving nothing but powdered ash at the bottom of the flowerpot, he returned to the house—

And froze in the middle of the living room.

A single, threadlike vine had grown straight out of the floor in the center of the room.

How had he missed this one? How long had it been here growing without either him or Heather noticing?

*She's noticed the others but hasn't said anything before*, he told himself. *She sees them but doesn't say anything, doesn't care. Almost as if she wants them here.*

He went to the vine and knelt before it. This close, he could see the spacing between the floorboards where the vine had managed to work its way up. It was too young to have sprouted thorns; Alan wrapped it around one finger and tugged it free.

He burned that one in the yard, too.

*A house with blood on its walls—names and symbols painted with blood. Carvings etched on stone.*

*The shuddering, feathery gasp of giant wings . . .*

*"I dreamt of your arrival for six moons without break,"* says the old Indian beside the smoldering fire pit. *"Since then, I have been coming out here to the valley and the Devil's Stone, guided under the protection of the warrior* Tsul Kalu, *waiting for the day of your arrival. I'm glad it is today." Grimaces. "I'm tired and the summer days are long."*

And his eyes flipped open, a scream caught in his throat.

Literally *caught*.

Alan couldn't breathe. Air could just barely whistle through his restricted esophagus. And when he tried to sit up, he felt something tighten about his neck, digging into the flesh and squeezing his windpipe.

He gripped his neck. He felt the indentation where

something sliced into him, choking him, cutting off his air. It was pulled taut and he could not get his fingers underneath it to pry it off.

Tried to gasp for air.

Couldn't.

His legs pinwheeling in the air, he kicked the blankets off him, the bed jouncing and groaning beneath him. He twisted from side to side, then thrashed, even though the strength of such movement caused the garrote to cut farther into his flesh. His fingers, still trying to grab a hold of the thing around his neck, became slick with his own blood.

Bright spangles of light exploded before his eyes. He knew without a doubt that his vision was fading.

Somehow he calmed himself for a moment. He managed to think. And in doing so, he sucked in his throat and slipped two fingers underneath the item that was strangling him. It was as strong as piano wire. He tugged at it, and it bit into the soft pads of his fingertips like barbed wire.

*God—*

Then he slid a second set of fingers underneath—*and he pulled.*

It snapped apart like a length of elastic, and he felt wetness spatter on his neck, chest, and the left side of his face. His first thought was *Blood, my blood*, and he sat up quickly, panting and gasping and wheezing and rubbing the tender strip of flesh at his neck with both hands. His fingers were sticky, tacky, but it didn't necessarily feel like blood.

He clicked on the lamp beside the bed.

A coiled vine lay in his lap, bleeding its syrupy fluid onto the mattress.

Repulsed, he brushed it off the mattress and onto the floor. Then he looked at his hands. There was some blood, but it was mostly the juice that bled from the vine. He rolled over and looked behind the headboard. There were no visible traces of the vine. Though upon closer inspection, he could see a sliver of space between the molding and the wall behind his side of the bed.

*That didn't just happen. No way that just happened.*

With all his thrashing about, he was shocked to find that Heather was sleeping soundly. If it wasn't for the unlabored sounds of her respiration, he might have thought—

*(she died)*

—the worst. She was on her side, her back toward him, the cool *M* of her form just barely hinted at beneath the heavy cotton nightgown.

Out in the hallway, the floorboards creaked.

Alan froze.

A second creaking floorboard . . . and then he was up, snatching the baseball bat from beneath the bed and storming into the hallway.

He stood there in the semidarkness, his breath still wheezing out of him, making him sound like an accordion, the bat poised over one shoulder. Naked, he felt both foolish and vulnerable.

From what he could see, the hallway was empty.

Then something moved at the end of the hallway—a shifting of shadows low to the floor, perceptible only in the puddle of moonlight that spilled in from the foyer windows.

Alan's heart stopped in his chest.

Slowly, he moved down the hall, unable to get a firm grip on the bat due to the blood and the fluid from the vine on his hands. When he reached the end of the hallway, he flipped on the lights and winced. He was alone; the hallway and foyer were empty. Opposite the foyer, the entrance to the kitchen was a dark rectangular maw. Anything, Alan knew, could be hiding in that inky darkness . . .

"Someone in here?" But there was hardly any strength to his voice.

Again, his mind returned to Owen Moreland.

*No. Stop it.*

His face blown apart from a self-inflicted shotgun blast, the nearly headless corpse of his wife propped beside him on a mattress sodden with blood—

*Stop it!*

Alan turned on the kitchen lights and stood trembling in the doorway, not moving. It took several seconds for his eyes to adjust to the light. When they did, he found nothing out of the ordinary—no cupboards disturbed, no drawers opened, no evidence of any late night visitors whatsoever.

He felt instantly foolish, standing there in the nude with a baseball bat propped against one shoulder, his genitals dangling like a pendulum. It was an old house. Old houses settled. Old houses made *noise* when they settled. Was he really racing around in the middle of the night with a baseball bat because he heard some goddamn creaking—?

From the bedroom, Heather moaned.

Alan raced down the hall, images of that sliver of vine having somehow made its way onto the bed and around

Heather's neck—

But when he got there, he could clearly see the vine on the floor where he'd flung it.

On the bed, Heather rolled onto her back fitfully but still asleep.

He watched her, listening to the low rumble at the back of her throat.

Something beneath her nightgown moved.

Something *inside* her.

Heather's own voice rushed at him from a week or so ago: *Alan, honey, there* is *someone else in the house with us.*

He remained in the doorway and watched the soft rise of his wife's stomach, anticipating further movement. He waited for several minutes. Then, when he was satisfied it wasn't going to happen again—or perhaps that it had all been in his head to begin with—he gathered up the length of vine off the floor, carried it to the bathroom, and flushed it down the toilet. (Yet the moment he did so, he questioned his method, able to visualize all too clearly the vine snaking up through the pipes and wrapping it around him one day as he sat there unawares.)

He went over to the bathroom mirror and examined his neck. There was a red ring of flesh just below the Adam's apple and a few places where the skin had broken open. His fingertips, too, had been serrated. He washed his hands beneath the faucet, scrubbing furiously. He wondered if the vines themselves carried infection.

*Fuck it*, he thought. *Doesn't matter.*

Back in the kitchen, he poured himself a glass of Heather's water from the jug in the refrigerator. He drank some, which immediately soothed his abraded throat, then he dipped two fingers into the glass. The cuts on his fingers stopped throbbing. With those same fingers, he massaged the wound at his neck. It was like applying aloe on a burn.

Alan stayed awake all night, too fearful to go back to sleep. And when he did find sleep, the sun was already coming in through the windows. He called the college and had his classes cancelled for the day, then slept on the living room couch until dinnertime. Exhausted, he dreamt of many things in all those hours, though he remembered very little once he later awoke.

# CHAPTER TWENTY-NINE

The day before Christmas Eve, Heather refused to go to her scheduled appointment with Dr. Crawford.

"I've been doing a lot of reading," she explained to Alan, "and some doctors actually say that it's *unhealthy* to bring your unborn child into places like that. All that electrical equipment and radiation in the X-rays."

"Nobody's getting X-rays," he told her.

"But it's all there. In the building." She was sitting cross-legged on the couch, a ball of pale green yarn in her lap. The past few days she had actually taken up knitting—something Alan would have never pictured her doing in a million years—and she had made decent headway with a tiny blanket, which was splayed out over one thigh.

"I thought Dr. Crawford said not to read all those books? That she would give you reading material if you wanted to keep up on things."

"This is *from* her reading material."

"Hon, you can't skip your appointments. We're not, like, Amish."

"Don't be a fool." She would not look up from her knitting. Across the room the TV was on, some banal sitcom looping through reruns. Their artificial Christmas tree was propped up in one corner, meticulously decorated with colored lights, tinsel, glass balls. Heather had done it herself, struck this year by the Christmas spirit. She had even purchased a tiny stocking for their unborn child, which now hung from the stone hearth. "I'm not skipping *every* appointment. But these random checkups aren't necessary. Even Dr. Crawford said we could move them around."

"Yes. We can move them around, not cancel them altogether."

She paused in her knitting and looked up at him with big brown doe eyes. "I feel fine. I feel *fantastic*. And I know what's best." She reached out and touched his arm. Her hands were horribly cold. "I don't want to argue with you, baby, but I'm not going to the appointment. In fact, I've already cancelled it."

Alan didn't hound her about it further. Truth was, he had been uncomfortable about going back to Dr. Crawford's office since their last visit when he thought he'd glimpsed the profile of a monster in his wife's womb. If Heather didn't want to go and it wasn't necessary, he certainly wasn't going to force the issue.

She went back to her knitting, and he retreated to the master bedroom, where he'd pried away the molding that ran the length of the walls and sealed up all the cracks in the wood and drywall. He resisted the urge to tear down the walls and search for more vines since the weather had grown considerably colder over the past couple of days and the plants in the yard had already started to die, the trees now completely barren of leaves. He couldn't imagine the vines beneath the house, beneath the ground, still going strong in such unreasonable weather.

He finished spackling the cracks in the wood and drywall, then hammered the pieces of molding back into place. He'd worked up a nice sweat but felt invigorated by the effort. He stood, swiping a forearm across his sweat-peppered brow and, glancing out one of the windows, happened to catch sight of a police car across the street.

It wasn't directly across the street but down the block a bit, partially obscured by a stand of evergreens on the opposite curb. It wasn't Landry—the cruiser didn't possess the sheriff's emblem on the door—but one of his deputies. Even at this distance and despite the impeding pines, he thought he could make out the shape of a head and a pair of shoulders slumped behind the wheel.

They were watching him.

Keeping tabs.

He thought about Landry's last visit to the house and his not-so-veiled threat that there were other ways to take care of their little problem. Was spying on him around the clock part of that solution? Did the local sheriff's department seriously have nothing better to do than stake out his house?

Not for the first time, Alan wondered just how far Landry would go to protect his town's precious secret. Images of masked vigilantes climbing in his windows, strapping him and Heather down while Landry made off with their infant child like a wolf in the night, ran on a continuous loop in Alan's mind. Would the sheriff go that far to teach him a lesson? Would Hank Gerski and Don Probst and Gary Jones and the rest of his prying neighbors conspire against him and take his child?

They had no right. He'd already lost a mermaid and a sailor. They had no right to take this one from him.

"Nobody's taking nothing," he muttered at the window-pane, fogging up the glass with his breath.

"Alan!" Heather shouted from the living room. "Come quick!"

He took off in a sprint, expecting the worst. When he arrived to find Heather still seated calmly on the couch, he was holding his crowbar as if ready to bludgeon some-one. "What is it?"

She had both hands pressed to her belly. "I felt it move!"

He just stood there, stared at her.

"Come, come, come!" She waved him over. "It was a definite movement. And not just on the inside, but I could feel it pushing against my stomach. Here—give me your hand."

He knelt down before her and extended his free hand. She placed it against the swollen left side of her abdomen. Her fingers on top of his, she moved his hand around as if to locate the appropriate spot.

"Isn't it a bit early to feel it kicking?"

"Shhhh," she responded, as if the sound of his voice might scare the little thing inside her into motionlessness. She was smiling widely, her eyes distant and unfocused, perhaps trained on some motherly subuniverse Alan him-self could not see.

"Heather, honey, I don't think—"

He felt it.

An echoing thump on the other side of Heather's stomach. Inside her body. The sensation reverberated against Alan's palm.

Had her hand not been pressed against his, he would have recoiled.

*Something's wrong.* It was the first thought that came to him. *Something is not right in there.*

"Ha-ha!" Heather crooned. "Did you feel that? Isn't that something? Isn't that *amazing*?"

He nodded.

"Oh, wow. That's *in* me."

"Yes," he repeated . . . and managed to slide his hand out from under hers.

That night, lying in bed together, Alan was afraid to fall asleep. His dreams had become more and more erratic; upon waking in the middle of the night, he would wonder if they were really so abstract and piecemeal, or if he was just remembering pieces of a larger whole. Either way, he didn't like what he remembered.

Beside him, Heather said, "Lydia invited us over for Christmas dinner. She said she knew you and Hank had some sort of falling-out, but she wanted to help mend things. I told her we wouldn't go."

"Are you okay with that?"

"Yes. I don't want to go. The weather's getting colder and it's flu season. I don't feel comfortable taking the baby out of the house, bringing him around other people."

"Him?"

"Oh. Or her."

"Mother's intuition? Is there something I should know?"

"No. Freudian slip, I guess."

He hadn't realized Heather was aware of the "falling-out" between him and Hank and was a bit surprised that she didn't ask about it. He waited for her to bring it up, but after a few minutes of silence between them, her respiration grew deeper and she was quickly asleep.

Eventually, sleep found Alan, too, and he was racing up a midnight hillside toward the foothills of the Great Smoky Mountains, his feet on fire as he cruised at breakneck speed. When a deep gorge threatened to suck him down into the earth, he leapt and cleared it as confidently as a bird. In the gorge below, large animals moved about in tempered lethargy, some of them the size of tractor trailers.

There came a point where he was aware of both his dream state and the real world, that indistinct plateau that overlooks both worlds, and he began talking to someone from one realm or the other. He responded in hushed dream tones, but the other person shouted shrill, birdlike cries into the ether. The sound of the person's shrieks hurt his ears.

Something burned the side of his face.

He opened his eyes. Heather's fingernails were clawing at his right cheek, strong enough to draw blood. Her other arm flailed, and her hips bucked against the mattress.

Alan sat up—and found he had one hand pressed over her nose and mouth.

He pulled his arm away, and Heather immediately gasped for air. He went to her, attempting to comfort and cradle, but she instinctively shoved him away. He backed off, too afraid to approach her again and upset her further, too afraid and distrustful of himself at that moment. "Baby . . ."

"I'm okay," she wheezed. "Just . . . give me a minute."

"Fuck, hon, I'm sorry."

"It's all right." She sat up against the headboard and allowed her breathing to regain its normal, regulated pattern. "You must have been having one fucked-up dream, brother."

"I . . . I don't remember . . ."

Heather tittered like a schoolgirl. Pulling her knees up to her belly, she cradled herself and rocked slightly against the headboard.

"Honey, I'm so sorry. I don't know what the hell happened. Are you okay?"

She swung her legs off the bed. "I have to pee."

While she was in the bathroom, Alan got up and inspected the house. The tingling sensation of the intruder still lingered in that ancient, reptilian part of his brain. But as usual, the house was empty.

When he returned to the bedroom, Heather was already asleep, the blankets tucked underneath her. As he watched, he initially thought the movement beneath the blankets was her leg . . . but then he realized it was occurring at the center of her body. Something was moving on her stomach beneath the blankets.

Or *inside* her . . .

He flipped the blankets off her without waking her. She was wearing her cotton nightgown, but it had grown tight as her pregnancy progressed, and he could clearly make out the smoothness of her belly beneath the fabric. As he stood over her, he saw something *move* beneath the fabric, as if someone were slowly running a finger across the other side of her nightgown. He watched the bump circumvent the swell of his wife's belly until it vanished completely down the opposite side.

For the first time since his initial conversation with Hank about the lake, all those many months ago, he remembered something Hank had said about some woman who had backed over her Doberman with her car, breaking its hip: *She carried it to the lake and the hip was healed. But later that winter, the dog gave birth to a litter of puppies that all came out . . . well, they came out wrong.*

His heart was beating too fast in his chest.

*(they came out wrong)*

He spent the rest of the night sitting up in bed, not sleeping.

# CHAPTER THIRTY

Christmas morning, they exchanged gifts while Christmas music lilted out of the stereo. Afterwards, Heather retreated to the kitchen to prepare a large breakfast—scrambled eggs, sausage patties and bacon, sliced fruit, heavily buttered toast.

While she cooked, the smells of the food wafting throughout the house, Alan went out onto the porch. He smoked a cigarette, chilly in his sweatpants and hooded sweatshirt, and saw Landry's cruiser parked down the block. Was the son of a bitch actually keeping tabs on the house on Christmas fucking morning?

Just seeing the sheriff's car made him angry. His ulcer began to flare up. It had been several days since he'd been to the lake, and he knew he wouldn't be able to hold out much longer. Also, Heather's water jug was getting low. It was nearly time for a refill.

By the time he finished his cigarette and went back inside, Heather had laid out breakfast on the kitchen table.

They ate together, Alan in predominant silence, Heather humming along with the Christmas tunes coming in from the living room.

When she got up to refill Alan's coffee, she stood beside him, her protruding belly at his eye level. "Do you want to sing to your kid?"

He cupped his hands around his mouth and placed them against the front of Heather's stomach. "Hello-ello-ello . . ."

Heather laughed.

He took the coffee, then told her to go soak in the tub and that he would take care of the dishes.

"Can't argue with that," she said, already heading down the hallway. "Merry Christmas to me."

He cleared the table, dumping the leftover food in the trash and stacking the dirty dishes in the dishwasher, all the while keeping one eye on the windows that faced the street. Landry's car hadn't moved.

"Cocksucker," Alan growled.

He returned to the living room and lowered the volume on the stereo—weeks of Christmas music was beginning to grate on him—and proceeded to gather up the torn and crumpled balls of wrapping paper he and Heather had left strewn about the floor. He was halfway done cleaning the mess when he picked up a ball of red and green paper to find a single tiny vine beneath it, growing straight up out of the floor.

It was as if he'd been stung by an electric cattle prod.

*Son of a bitch . . .*

It was late December, and though the weather wasn't as cold as the winters up north in the city, it was surely too cold for goddamn *vines* to grow, wasn't it?

It was sprouting from the same place he'd seen it last time: right up through the narrow slit between two floorboards. But this time something new occurred to him, and it was because he also noticed (for the first time) the faint blond grooves in the floorboards that had been made months ago by Jerry Lee. It had been this exact spot that had so agitated the old golden retriever. Even now, Alan could recall the dog's steadfast determination in digging up . . . well, *something* . . . from that particular spot on the floor. At the time, both he and Heather had found it somewhat peculiar, even somewhat amusing, but had never truly given it much thought. Now, however, the memory caused a nonspecific unease to course through Alan's body, chilling his blood to ice.

As he'd done before, he wrapped his finger around it and gave it a sturdy tug. The sound of it breaking free was akin to plucking a taut rubber band. He went out back with his cigarette lighter and lit the end of the vine like the fuse on a stick of dynamite. The vine was dry enough to burn freely, and Alan held it by one end until he couldn't hold it any longer without getting burned. He dropped the charred bit into the grass where it hissed as it hit the frost.

Again, he looked out across the street at Landry's police car. *There are other ways we can go about this*, Landry had said.

"We'll see," Alan muttered into the atmosphere.

He hurried across the street toward Landry's police car, half-expecting the sheriff to step out of the car before he ever reached it. But there was no movement from within, and as Alan approached, he began to doubt if the car was even occupied.

It wasn't.

He stood there peering in through the windshield at

the vacant police cruiser and suddenly felt like a goddamn imbecile.

They were playing with him.

They were making him out to be a fool.

Of course the son of a bitch wasn't sitting out here on some ridiculous stakeout on Christmas morning. No. Hearn Landry, county sheriff, was at home celebrating Christmas morning with his wife and boneheaded kid. The bastard had just parked his car here to make Alan *think* he was being watched. Oh, that clever motherfucker . . .

Alan couldn't help it. He laughed in spite of himself.

Then he kicked a dent in the driver's side door before heading back inside.


That night Alan dreamt—or thought he dreamt—that tiny wet hands were on him. They poked and pinched and snatched up fistfuls of his pubic hair. At one point, he imagined he could feel the little creature on his stomach, wet and warm and sticky with odorless fluid. It slid down between his legs and snaked beneath the bulb of his testicles. More tiny, clawlike fingers—poking, prodding, pinching.

Seeking entry.

He awoke as always, terrified and disoriented, and spent much of the night searching the house for invisible monsters.

# CHAPTER THIRTY-ONE

Heather found Alan early the next morning, naked and asleep on the floor in the living room beside the sliding glass patio doors. She prodded him with her toes, and he snapped awake so quickly, it caused a kink in his neck.

"Sleepyhead," she intoned, standing over him. "What are you doing on the floor?"

He looked around but had no answer for her. The last thing he could remember about last night was checking under the couch for more vines. The fucking vines, it seemed, were driving him crazy.

He stood up just as it occurred to him that he had been lying in the exact same spot where he had found Jerry Lee's corpse all those months ago. He recalled without difficulty the details of that morning . . . and how one of those horrible birds had been pecking at the glass door, a blazing hunger in its soulless black eyes.

Alan showered, still thinking of Jerry Lee and that

spot on the floor where the dog had dragged its claws and how that one single vine kept reappearing. Cold weather be damned, those goddamn vines were determined. By the time he dressed—black dungarees, long-sleeved T-shirt, pullover—and had a cigarette on the front porch, he was already contemplating tearing up the living room floor.

*No need for that.* Alan remembered something he'd seen when he'd first moved into the house and began cutting the vines away from the siding. He hopped off the porch and went around to the side of the house that faced the woods, crouching until he could see the semicircle divot in the earth and the tiny wooden door against the house's foundation.

The crawl space.

Dropping to his knees, he leaned forward and brushed dead twigs and leaves aside, scooping more dead leaves and brambles out of the divot. It dropped down about two feet. The door looked much too small to accommodate an adult male, but when he got up close to it he figured it would indeed be possible for him to wiggle through it and gain access to the underside of the house.

But did he want to?

He shivered, and it was only partially due to the cold.

There was a latch on the little wooden door, a hooked handle threaded through a rusty eyelet. Alan undid the latch and pried the door open. It squealed on rusted hinges. A smell like rotting vegetation rushed up and accosted his nose, strong enough to make his eyes water. There was a deeper smell from within, too—the danker, headier scent of rotting meat.

Realizing he would need a flashlight, he hurried into the house and got one out of the pantry, then hustled outside before he lost his courage.

Bending down before the opening beneath the house, Alan clicked on the flashlight and shined the light into the square doorway.

Dust clouded the beam of light, falling like confetti in a snow globe.

*Either I'm doing this or I'm not.*

He counted to ten in his head, then swung his legs down into the hole and pushed his feet through the opening.

Indeed, it was a tight squeeze. His shoulders barely cleared the doorway, and for one horrifying moment, he feared he might get stuck. But he managed to climb all the way through and soon found himself crouching beneath the house in a space that was maybe three feet high.

He turned the flashlight toward the center of the crawl space, and his breath caught instantly in his throat.

His first thought was, *It's alive.*

His second thought was, *That's the goddamn heart.*

In fact, the entire assemblage was suggestive of the inner workings of a living creature—all the organs and veins and arteries and bands of musculature accounted for. The heart was at the center, a pulsating, gel-coated muscle approximately the size of a grown man's head, dangling like an immense hornet's nest from the beams at the center of the crawl space. As he watched, the thing actually appeared to respire like a single lung taking in and releasing air. Branching off from the heart was a network of intertwined veins, crisscrossing the beams in the ceiling of the crawl space and burying themselves into the soft soil. The veins themselves were as thick as power lines, layered with rows of thorns that looked more like the teeth of a deep-sea behemoth.

The veins were vines, hundreds of them, and they weren't diving *into* the ground but sprouting *out* of it. The heart at the epicenter was not actually a heart—not in the traditional sense, anyway—but some strange purplish plant. What Alan had at first mistaken for respiration was in fact the curled fingers of tricornered leaves rustling in the breeze coming in through the open crawl space door.

Nonetheless, the sight was horrifying.

*We can't live here. This house is poisoned by those things.*

Like the voice of a ghost, George YoungCalfRibs spoke up in the center of Alan's head: *The lake is like a magnet. Your house is the closest thing to it. It's too close to the forest and sits on the soured land. Your house rots with you and your wife in it. Rots like carrion. Vines keep it tethered to the soil like a balloon. They are channels, conduits, for the transfer of power. You can cut them away but they grow back. They come up through the earth. They are the lifeblood, the beating veins, of that house now.*

Twenty minutes later, armed with an electric saw and an entire box of Glad trash bags, Alan went back beneath the house and began cutting. The vines were thick and stubborn, and they bled their juices on him. He tried to uproot them from the soil, but many of them seemed to pull farther down into the earth before he could grab them. When he took the electric saw to the dangling mass of tissue-like fruit that looked so much like a heart, it cracked down the center like an overripe watermelon smashed against a rock.

It vomited greenish gunk onto the ground and spattered Alan's clothes with it. Its insides reeked like fecal matter, and twice Alan had to climb out of the crawl space for fresh air.

It took him much of the afternoon to cut the vines down. When he was finished, he had filled five extra-large trash bags with the foliage. He was exhausted, his muscles strained and weakened, and his mind was already returning to a quick dip in the lake as he dragged the trash bags out to the curb.

This time, Hearn Landry was across the street, leaning against his parked cruiser and smoking a cigarillo.

Alan froze, glaring at the man, his hands balled into fists around the plastic pull straps of the trash bags.

Casual as could be, Landry raised a hand in Alan's direction. He looked like a lazy sheriff in an old western.

*Fucking cliché*, Alan thought, practically snarling.

He continued carrying the bags to the curb, ignoring the sheriff as best he could. A number of buzzards had alighted on the trees at the opposite end of the property toward the street. They weren't as big as the ones Alan had been seeing lately, but their presence was no less daunting. This was the closest he'd seen them to the road since he'd moved into the house; something about their nearness to civilization—to the other houses on the street—carried with it the sensation of impending doom.

He wiped his hands on his pants, surveying the crowded trees. He counted five birds weighing down the boughs.

Hearn Landry glanced up at the buzzards. Then he tipped his hand down over his eyes and zipped up his parka.

After he'd finished with the trash bags, he went back

inside and tugged off his smelly pullover and dungarees while still standing in the foyer. The muck from the podlike plant had dried to a vomit-brown crust on the front of his pants and pullover.

Heather was asleep on the couch. She had a book opened on her chest, *Everything a Mommy Needs to Know (and a Few Things More)*, and she looked almost childlike in her stretchy maternity pants that were still too big for her. A band of white belly flesh protruded between her pants and loose-fitting blouse. At that moment, Alan was overcome by the sheer love he had for this woman and temporarily forgot about Hearn Landry, Hank Gerski, and even the lake at the end of the wooded path through the woods. It was just the two of them again, young and in love, having each other's backs, and they couldn't be touched by the world. Couldn't.

The band of exposed flesh rippled. Something was moving beneath the skin.

The baby.

A bitter taste flooded his mouth. As he watched, a distinct handprint stretched the skin of his wife's stomach, tiny yet perfectly and hideously detailed, all five fingers—

*(biohazard bag)*

—accounted for.

A second hand, its little fingers splayed, pressed against the inside of Heather's womb. The skin stretched like putty. Both tiny hands pushing out. Alan imagined a seam appearing at the center of his wife's stomach, a vertical mouth that gushed blood and amniotic fluid onto the couch cushions, and it widened as those two hands conspired to tear out of Heather's womb.

*Heather was right but she didn't know it*, he thought, too

terrified to move. *You are the intruder. You are the violator. You are the thing I sense moving about the house at night. We are not alone because you are here with us. I just didn't know it at the time. But I do now. I do now.*

The litter of Doberman pups. What had Hank Gerski said? *They came out wrong.*

*They came out wrong.*

Between the two handprints, a face appeared. He could make out no other details other than the convex shape of a smallish skull identifiable by the nub of a nose at its center.

In her sleep, Heather moaned.

"Leave her alone." It was his voice, but he did not think he'd spoken.

The face moved from side to side, as if shaking its head in slow motion. Each time it turned to afford him its profile pressed up against his wife's flesh, he could see the suggestion of a sharp little cheekbone.

". . . me . . ." Heather groaned from the couch.

He wanted to rush to her but didn't want to *touch* her.

The face retreated. One of the hands pulled away, too. The first hand lingered a bit longer, its fingers working individually against the tautness of Heather's flesh.

Alan recalled a memory from his early childhood when he'd been at a birthday party and he and some of the other boys had gone around stomping all the balloons. They'd picked up the broken flaps of rubber and, pulling them taut across their faces, made funny noises into the rubber and stuck their tongues out and pressed down their noses . . .

The hand retreated, leaving the band of navel flesh undisturbed.

On the couch, Heather rolled onto her side. The book

fell on the floor, but she didn't wake up.

Alan stood above her for a very long time, waiting to see what would happen—waiting to see if she would come suddenly awake, screaming in pain. But nothing happened.

He threw up in the toilet, then showered.

# CHAPTER THIRTY-TWO

Alan did not fall asleep that night. Nor the following night. He found time during the day to catch quick naps on the couch, but his lack of sleep was making him lethargic and was evident in his face and around his eyes. Soon he prayed for winter break to be over so he could get back to school and give himself some time to settle, to rest, and to be away from the house. *And Heather.* He quickly chased the thought away. That wasn't what he wanted. They were finally a family again. Finally. What was he thinking?

Heather quit her job at the art gallery. Alan wasn't sure when it had happened, exactly. She hadn't told him when she'd done it, and he only found out about it when he asked her why she hadn't been going to work.

"It's over," she said simply. "It's done."

"Heather, you love that job. Why would you quit?"

"Germs," she told him. She was doing some pregnant woman style of yoga on the living room floor, glancing occasionally at an open textbook with diagrams beside her. She had one of the classical music CDs playing low on the stereo, convinced that it was turning their baby into a genius with each passing minute. "There are germs everywhere. Also, have you seen all the cats in the neighborhood?"

"Cats?" He thought of Patsy the Cat for the first time in a long while. How it had hissed when Cory Morris had picked it up and how Alan had found it sometime later out in his yard, torn apart. He'd dumped it in the woods that afternoon. "What do you mean?"

"Cat feces can cause toxoplasmosis. It can make him retarded. Do you want your kid to be retarded?"

"No, of course not. And you're still calling it 'him.' Did you open the envelope Dr. Crawford gave us?"

"It's just what I call him. I don't like saying 'it.' You shouldn't, either."

He shook his head. "What's wrong with you?"

Heather laughed sharply. The sound resonated in his marrow. "*Me*? What's wrong with *you*? You've been acting like a fucking head case lately."

He frowned. "Real nice. You play all that classical music hoping to make this kid into the next Albert Einstein, yet you'll toss around the F-bomb like a baseball. Real classy."

"Leave me alone. Don't make me upset. It's not good for the baby to get my heart rate up. You'd know that if you read any of the books."

He turned to leave the room.

"And get some sleep, will you?" she called after him. "You look like hell."

• • •

In the kitchen, Alan went to the fridge and took out the plastic jug of lake water. There was very little left in it, but it was enough. He popped the cap and drank it all. Almost instantly he felt his throat open up, his capillaries breathe, his body lighten. He hadn't realized his ulcer had been acting up until the pain in his stomach quelled. Then he threw the jug into the recycling pail.

He didn't like what that water was doing to Heather now, anyway.

That night, he tried to stay awake by sitting up in bed with headphones on while reading a Jack Ketchum book beneath the light of the bedside lamp. But he was working on days of sleeplessness now and, even having finished the water in the jug, his body needed rest. Soon his eyelids grew heavy. He got up at one point and walked through the house, already confident that he would not find an intruder, because he knew where the sensation was coming from. The wellspring was in his wife's womb. The baby. The baby was the intruder. It was the baby he'd been sensing all along.

Standing in his pajama bottoms and a sleeveless T-shirt, he stood wavering at the end of the hallway, breathing deeply, listening to the sounds the house made all around him.

He was on edge. Maybe he would never sleep again.

But he did as soon as he climbed back into bed beside his wife. His exhaustion carried him down like a weight, sinking to the ocean floor of his dreams. Massive shapes moved through his subconscious. He found himself blinking, freezing, and standing out beside the road that ran in front of his house. Cory Morris was across the street, dressed all in black and wearing white greasepaint, cradling something in his arms.

—*Mistakes have been made*, the boy said, though Alan could not see his mouth moving. *Mistakes have been made and they need to be rectified.*

The thing in the boy's arms was Patsy, his dead cat. The lifeless creature was draped over one of Cory's arms. It bled black blood down the front of the boy's hooded sweatshirt.

When Alan opened his eyes, he was temporarily disoriented. It took him several moments to realize he was in bed beside his wife and in his new house and that he had fallen asleep. He sat up and listened in the darkness. Only Heather's breathing returned to him; the house was otherwise silent.

But still . . . the creeping sensation that—

Something moved down the hallway. He heard it. The sound was like someone dragging a chair across the hard-wood floor.

He sprung out of bed and rushed into the hallway, moving so quickly and reactionary this time that he forgot his baseball bat. The hallway seemed to cant to one side. He fumbled along the wall for the light switch and flipped it on, bathing the tilting hallway in yellowish light.

At the end of the hallway, something was banging around in the kitchen. Someone—or something—was going through the cupboards, moving things around, making a racket.

Sprinting down the hall, he skidded into the kitchen while simultaneously turning on the light. Harsh fluorescents burned his retinas.

The kitchen cabinets were open, the lower cupboard doors ajar. There were pots and pans strewn about the floor.

Something shattered behind him.

Alan jumped and spun around, his heart like a locomotive in his chest. The foyer behind was pitch-black, though he thought he spied the silhouette of something moving across one of the windows. He couldn't tell if it was outside the window or in the house. He couldn't tell what it was.

Steeling himself, he went into the living room and turned on the lamp. A glass vase lay shattered at his feet. He was sweating profusely now. It felt like his ears had been stuffed with wads of cotton.

At the opposite end of the house, he heard Heather cry out in her sleep. He turned and ran out of the room, sprinted down the hallway, and switched on the bedroom light upon entering the room.

She was still asleep, lying on her back, all the blankets kicked onto his side of the bed. Her cotton nightgown was hiked up past her hips, leaving her upper thighs and the vague cleft of her genitalia exposed to him.

There was something coming out of her.

He tried to speak her name, but it came out a petrified gasp, more breathy and indistinct than any actual utterance.

There was a little bit of blood on the mattress and a smear on one of her inner thighs. The thing coming out of her—elongated and flesh colored, horrifically wormlike in its appearance, maybe six inches in length—bent at an angle that suggested a knee or an elbow. It made a sound like a cicada. The appendage was grotesquely *footlike* . . . and then it retreated inside his wife. In disbelief, Alan watched

Heather's labia close upon it like stage curtains after an encore performance.

The mound of Heather's belly rose. It was obvious something was moving around in there.

*What have I been chasing around this house for the past month?* he wondered . . . but could not bear to consider the notion for longer than a second.

Heather broke out in laughter.

He went to her side and spoke her name several times, but she would not stop laughing. Disturbingly, she still appeared to be asleep.

*(they came out wrong)*

*(came out)*

The sounds of cicadas echoed in the center of his brain.

# CHAPTER THIRTY-THREE

When Heather awoke, it was still night. She startled him from his own slumber, where he slumped on the floor against her side of the bed, by standing above him, legs spread, hair tousled into a mop.

Groaning, still half-asleep, he blinked and scooted against the wall. "Heather, honey . . ."

She did not move. In the dark, he could not make out the details of her face, could not see if her eyes were open and she was awake or if she had gotten up in her sleep, a somnambulist.

"Hon . . . ?"

She said nothing. The silence was like the aftershock of a tremendous explosion. Then he heard the sounds of what he at first mistook for the crackle of a distant burning fire until he felt the wetness spray onto his bare feet, and he realized his wife was standing before him, urinating on the bedroom floor. Alan groaned and hugged his legs to his chest.

Once she had finished, she climbed back into bed and pulled the covers up to her chin. Two seconds later she was snoring.

# CHAPTER THIRTY-FOUR

And when Alan awoke, it was to the sound of running water in the bathroom down the hall. He sat up, his neck stiff, having fallen asleep on the floor with his back against the wall. Heather was no longer in bed. The room reeked of ammonia; the puddle of urine was a clearly visible pool on the hardwood floor between his feet.

She was soaking in the tub, a washcloth on the dome of her belly.

"We need to make another ultrasound appointment," he said, standing in the doorway.

Heather wrung out the washcloth, then draped it over her eyes as she rested her head against the tiled wall.

"Are you listening to me?"

She made a *hmmm* sound but didn't remove the washcloth from her face.

"I'm calling Dr. Crawford's office and scheduling another ultrasound. Something isn't right."

She threw a fist down into the water, splashing. With her other hand, she swiped the washcloth from her face. The expression there chilled him to the core.

"What's the matter with you?" She was practically seething. "Why are you doing this to me?"

"I'm not doing anything. I want to have the baby checked. Something's not right with the baby."

"You leave us both alone."

"Something isn't right. We need to see Dr. Crawford."

"Lesbian cunt," Heather growled.

"Something isn't right with you, either." His mouth was dry and tasted like old tube socks.

She sat up in the tub, sloshing water onto the floor. Her hair was stringy and wet about her face, her eyes larger than he had ever seen them. "I know what you're trying to do."

He shook his head. "I'm not trying to do anything."

"You are. You're weak. You never wanted children. You were happy the other two died."

Her words stung him worse than anything she had ever said to him. "That isn't true."

"Isn't it? Your father was a criminal and a lousy dad, and your mother split before you were even old enough to stop shitting in your pants. You're weak and you think you'll be just like them. You never wanted children, and you were happy when the other two died. You were *happy*."

"Heather, baby, no . . ."

The mound of her belly glistened in the water. She caressed it. "Take your weakness someplace else. You are not taking this baby from me. Do you understand? I won't let you."

"None of that is true. I've been heartbroken over all of this, just like you have."

"You've been afraid I'd do something to myself, and you feel bad about what happened to me, but you never wanted to be a father. You never cared about our two dead babies. Where are they now? Ashes in a trash heap? The city fucking sewer? They were *babies*. You never fucking *buried* them."

He took a step backward. Her eyes never left him. He could feel them piercing straight through to the core fibers of his being.

And just like that, her face went slack, expressionless. She dipped the washcloth into the tub water, wrung it out again. As she eased back down, resting her head against the wall, she draped the wet cloth over her eyes.

The glistening mound of her belly rose like a leviathan out of the water.

# CHAPTER THIRTY-FIVE

Alan spent the remainder of that day falling apart.

After her bath, Heather had returned to the bedroom wrapped in a terry-cloth robe and a towel turbaned around her head, humming softly and pleasantly as if nothing had ever transpired between the two.

Alan had cleaned up the urine from the bedroom floor with a wad of paper towels, then retreated to the backyard where, in the cold midafternoon air, he smoked an entire pack of menthols. Beyond the hedgerow that ran along the curb, he saw Landry's cruiser parked down the street. From this distance he couldn't tell if the sheriff was in the car or not. Then he lifted his gaze to the line of pines along the street's edge. He could make out the weighty black shapes weighing down the boughs, the hooked beaks and fire-flecked eyes of the great birds. There were more of them now. Many more. They had come out of the woods and were now nested in the trees lined up and down the street.

One of them was even perched atop a nearby telephone pole, surveying the neighborhood.

—*You fucked up good, old sport*, Owen Moreland spoke up beside him. The man's words were garbled, and Alan knew it was because his face had been torn apart from the shotgun blast. *What now?*

Alan shook his head. "I don't know."

—*I'm not part of it*, Owen said. *You may think I am but I'm not. I'm a casualty, just like you.*

"I'm not a casualty."

—*Maybe not yet. Maybe you can still fix things.*

"What do you mean you're not part of it? Part of what?"

—*Doesn't matter. Only thing that matters now is that you fix your mistake.*

"How do I do that?"

—*I can't tell you what to do. You just have to think about it and do it.*

He looked down. His hands were quaking.

—*You're a good kid, Alan.*

And it was then that he realized he'd been talking to his father all along.

Alan stood out there in the yard by himself—or seemingly so—for the next three hours. He hardly moved. He was watching the birds.

Only once did Heather poke her head out, and her disposition was one completely different from that morning in the bathroom. "My water jug isn't in the fridge."

"I'll get you more water," he told her, and she let him be

for the remainder of the afternoon.

Alan Hammerstun gave thought to a lot of things. By the time he went back inside, more birds had come out of the woods and gathered on the branches of the evergreens that ran up and down the street.

After Heather had fallen asleep, Alan got out of bed and padded to the bathroom. Opening the medicine cabinet, he rifled through bottles of aspirin, a tub of TUMS, ointments and skin cream, hair products, and various other hygiene products. When he found the bottle he was searching for, he didn't reach for it immediately. He just stared at it, listening to the whoosh of his heartbeat amplified in his ears. It sounded like the heartbeat on an ultrasound.

On the bottle's label in all capital letters: PREGNANT WOMEN SHOULD NOT INGEST.

He recalled the day he'd picked up his first prescription from the pharmacy and how, after reading the label, he'd let out a pained and ironic laugh all the way to his car. The pharmacist's eyes had gone as large as lightbulbs. Now Alan just began to tremble.

Misoprostol. Little white octagonal tablets that helped reduce the agony of his stomach ulcer.

He was thinking of Heather's words to him from earlier that morning. He was thinking about the mermaid and the sailor. He found he couldn't consider her accusation for longer than a few seconds. To do so meant to convince himself of its authenticity.

*None of that is true,* he thought now. *I want to be a*

*father. I can be a good father.*

Then what was he thinking? What was he about to do?

He thought, *Pregnant women should not ingest.*

After his father's death, he spent the remainder of his life being self-sufficient. There hadn't been a family there to support or advise him. He had been utterly and completely alone.

Until Heather . . .

*You never cared about our two dead babies. Where are they now? Ashes in a trash heap? The city fucking sewer?*

He took the bottle of ulcer medication from the medicine cabinet and carried it to the kitchen. With the wall clock ticking overhead, he dug the empty water jug from the recycling bin and filled it with tap water. He listened as the house's old pipes rattled and chugged through the walls. After the jug was filled, he set it on the counter, then opened the bottle of misoprostol. He shook several tablets out into his hands and put them on a paper towel on the counter. From one of the kitchen drawers he withdrew a table spoon which he used to crush the tablets into powder. Then he poured the powder into the jug of water, screwed the jug's cap back on, and replaced it in the refrigerator.

Around three in the morning he awoke screaming, certain that something had been squeezing his genitals. Despite the scream, Heather never stirred beside him.

In the morning, Alan prepared his wife a large breakfast and pretended that everything was fine. He smiled a lot, and each time he walked by Heather he made sure to rub her head and pat her stomach. She ate all her breakfast and never once remarked about the taste. She did the same with the lunch he prepared for her, which was tuna salad, and he knew she could not taste the things he had put in there. (He'd cut his hand opening the tuna can and it bled freely. He rinsed it under a stream of water at the sink. The cut did not heal.)

New Year's Eve, and there were fireworks in the distance over the trees. Alan and Heather went out on the front porch and watched the dazzling display.

Across the street, some neighborhood kids cheered, carving swaths of light through the darkness with twirling sparklers. Hank, Lydia, and Catherine were on their front porch watching the fireworks, too. Hank waved to him. Alan did not wave back. When he saw Hank rise from his seat, he rubbed Heather's shoulder and told her it was getting cold and they should get inside.

"It's probably not very good for the baby," Heather agreed, hustling through the front door.

Alan had expected Hank to knock on the door moments later, but the knock never came.

Alan told the college to find a substitute once winter break was over—that there were issues at home he had to attend to, complications with his family. He hung up before anyone could ask any questions. When the phone continued to ring, he unplugged it.

Dinner that night, he lit candles on the kitchen table

and dimmed the lights. Outside, the wind was blustery; the nearest tree branches scraped against the windows and the roof. He cooked and placed the food on the table in large ceramic bowls. Yet he hardly ate.

Heather ate much of it, saying it was all very delicious. "What did you put in it?" she asked.

Something tickled the inside of his throat. He affected no expression and simply said, "I made it with love."

Heather smiled and cleaned her plate. Then she retired to the bedroom, complaining of gas pains.

Alone, Alan cleared the table, then sat before the fireplace, a small fire cooking in the hearth, while he knocked off a bottle of red wine. Sleeping in the same room with his wife had become an exercise in mental torture; the thing inside her womb had found a way to work the tendrils of invisible fingers into his brain. It knew what Alan was doing. It tried desperately to stop him.

Twice that evening, he heard Heather rise from the bedroom and scamper down the hall to the bathroom. The second time, he closed his eyes and leaned his head back against the couch cushions and tried not to think of much in particular.

He listened to the scrabbling of buzzard claws on the roof instead.

Two days later, Alan drove into town and refilled his misoprostol prescription at the pharmacy. A young woman attended to him at the counter, but he did not forget that the pharmacy had once belonged to Owen Moreland.

No, he did not forget.

He drove home in the rain, singing along with a Bruce Springsteen song on the radio.

When he arrived home, Hank was standing at the end of his driveway in a puffy red ski jacket and a baseball cap. Alan swerved around him and pulled up the driveway toward the house. In the rearview mirror he watched Hank move up the drive. When he got out, Hank took his hands out of his pockets in a symbol of surrender. Of peace.

"I'm sorry," Hank called to him. "I want to be friends again."

"Please go home." His voice sounded cold, even to his own ears. "I've got things to attend to here at home. I don't have time to talk to you."

"Alan, please—"

"I don't have time to talk to you." He went inside and, without turning on any lights, peeked through a part in the curtain over the foyer window.

Hank stood there for several moments, looking lost and hurt and afraid, before stuffing his hands into his ski jacket and turning tail back across the street.

In the morning, Heather complained of cramps. "I feel dizzy a lot, too," she said after refusing to eat the breakfast he'd made.

"Should I call Dr. Crawford's office?" It came out sounding like an empty threat.

"I think I'm going to be sick."

She spent the next several minutes vomiting in the bathroom.

Hank was knocking on the front door. Heather, ill in bed, never commented on the noise, if in fact she even heard it. Alan sat on the living room couch, his wife's purse in his lap, and looked at Hank through the foyer window. Eventually, Hank gave up and sauntered dejectedly across the lawn toward his house. The black humps of buzzards moved behind the hedgerows near the edge of his property. One of them squawked at Hank, and the man put his head down and hurried home.

In Heather's purse, Alan found the envelope Crawford had given to them. But it had been torn open. When he looked inside, he found it was empty.

*Him*, he thought. *He.*

Behind him, the living room wall cracked as something pushed up through it.

# CHAPTER THIRTY-SIX

The baby came on the evening of January 15, five months premature.

It was after two in the morning and Alan was sitting on the couch, watching an old Humphrey Bogart movie with the volume turned all the way down. A bottle of Jameson was tucked in his lap and he was feeling pretty good, despite the burning ember in his gut. Having used all the misoprostol in Heather's food and water, it had left none for him. He would have to go to the pharmacy for another refill eventually. In his head, he cursed Hearn Landry and his deputies who rotated surveillance outside his house.

At the end of the hall, Heather cried out. It wasn't a sleep moan; there was real strength, real agony behind it, causing Alan to spring up from the couch and knock the bottle of Jameson to the floor.

His heart hammered.

*"Alan! Alan!"*

His mind whirling, he gathered his legs up under him and commanded them to move. When he hit the hallway, he could see his wife had turned on the bedroom light: a crooked rectangle of yellowy light spilled out of the bedroom doorway and fell against the opposite wall.

*"Alan, come!"*

It was time.

It had come.

When he arrived in the bedroom doorway, he saw his wife buckled over in a fetal position on the mattress. Her face was a mask of pure agony and fear, her long hair plastered to the side of her face with sweat. She clutched the bulb of her stomach with both hands, the loose cotton fabric of her nightgown riding up one pale thigh.

"Oh, God," she moaned.

"I'm here," he said, moving to the side of the bed. But he didn't touch her, not right away. He stood there looking down at her.

"Something's *wrong*!" There was a rattle in her throat.

"Shhhhh."

*". . . hurts . . ."*

"Shhhhh, baby." He brushed some of her sweaty hair from her face.

She glared at him. Her eyes were wide and fearful. Distrustful.

"Something's . . . something's happening . . ."

He sat down beside her on the bed, rubbing the side of her face. She was burning up. He sang, "Mama's gonna buy you a big black bird . . ."

*"Alan!"*

Her back arched. Her legs straightened. The cotton nightgown rose up to her hips. Alan could see the darkened *V* of her pubis between her legs. The lower portion of her swollen belly looked as taut and sturdy as the flesh on a piece of overripe fruit.

Heather cried out. She tossed her head back, wiping his arm with her damp hair. "Oh my God," she panted. "Oh my God, oh my God, oh my God . . ."

"Lie back." He pushed gently on one shoulder.

Like a turtle, she wheeled backward onto her back and repositioned herself.

"It's okay, hon. It's fine."

"No!" she barked. That rattling—

*(death rattle)*

—was still prominent in her throat, her voice. Tremolo. Vibrato.

"Alan, *please*!"

Leaning forward, he helped reposition her legs, bring her knees up and her thighs apart. The hem of the nightgown was over her hips now, and he could see the swollenness—the redness—of her down there.

"It will be okay," he promised her. He surprised himself with the steadiness of his own voice. "Everything will be okay, honey."

*"Hurts! Alan! Alan!"*

Much of the rest occurred with her screaming and with his eyes shut. Snapshot images were all he retained, but they were enough to piece it all together and formulate a single, cohesive picture.

There was blood. It was black as squid ink and soaked

the mattress and the sheets. It came out in sudden squirts, arcing like a fountain. Heather shrieked and grabbed fistfuls of the sheets, slamming her head back against the headboard while gritting her teeth.

There was a smell, too—of feces and blood and the vague artichoke smell of semen.

Heather's hips bucked. The flesh of her stomach rippled, the stomach itself changing shape. There was a sound like brittle fabric being torn in half. Alan felt something warm and wet splattered against his left hand.

It was less *born* than it was *rejected*—coming out as if through a wet and bloody flume, coated in lumpy, reeking gelatin on a wave of amniotic juices that nearly burned his flesh as they sprayed him. The thing itself—the *him*, the *he*—wriggled wetly, brokenly, rubbery . . . though Alan couldn't tell if it was because the thing was alive or because its frail and unformed body was easily jostled into lifelike movements in the course of its expulsion from its mother's womb.

It spilled out and rolled across the mattress, landing almost soundlessly against Alan's right knee.

He wanted to scream.

Didn't.

Held his breath.

On the bed, Heather's cries gradually lost their potency. Exhausted, her entire body seemed to cave in on itself. Her head hung forward, wet hair draped over her face like a veil, and she released the grips she'd had on the sheets. Her blood-slicked thighs quivered. She moaned, then sighed, her sour breath momentarily all Alan could smell.

"Shhhhh," Alan whispered. He was looking at her, not

at the thing that was slumped against his knee. He could feel its wetness bleeding through the fabric of his sweat-pants. "It's over, honey. It's okay."

Heather just sobbed behind that curtain of wet hair. Her entire body hitched.

Alan climbed off the bed, aware of all the wet places on his clothes and body, as well as the tenseness of his muscles. How long had the whole thing lasted? Ten minutes? An hour? He had no idea.

He leaned over his wife, kissed the top of her head. Heat radiated off her in waves like desert blacktop.

"Is . . . is it . . . ?" She couldn't finish the sentence.

"Just relax," he whispered in her ear. "I'm going to get some towels. I'm going to clean this up."

She sobbed almost painfully. "Alan, no . . . please . . ."

"It's over," he told her. "It's okay now. We're done."

In the bathroom, he gathered bath towels from the linen closet. Then in the kitchen he retrieved the box of Glad trash bags from beneath the sink. When he returned to the bedroom, Heather's sobs had tapered off in her exhaustion. She lay slumped nearly on her side, her head craned at an awkward angle, her respiration labored.

He happened to glance at it as he gathered it up and dumped it in the trash bag: pale, fishlike, appendages like twists of intestines. The face was only a face in the most generous of terms, unfinished and malformed, one eye cut to a slit, the other a horrific, staring emerald with a vertical pupil, its mouth a ragged, lipless slash, its ears mere canals drilled into the sides of its narrow, oblong head.

It had something that looked like a segmented tail . . .

*Fuck . . .*

He dumped its lifeless husk into the trash bag, then mopped up the afterbirth and what blood he could with the towels before throwing them, too, into the trash bag. By the time he had finished, Heather was asleep, though she cried out periodically, a sound like a distant summer loon.

He set the loaded trash bag in the tub, then went back into the bedroom and fell asleep on the bed, spooning his wife.

Moments before sunrise, Alan arose and dressed quickly and quietly in a pair of old dungarees, an NYU sweatshirt, and a ratty old Miller Lite ball cap. Heather was still sound asleep in bed, and he walked through the house without turning on any lights. He collected the trash bag from the bathroom tub and carried it out the back patio doors.

The wind was bitterly cold, the sky a mottled undulation of stars. There were things all around him, movement all around him, and he paused just outside the doors and held his breath.

Buzzards. They were in all the trees surrounding the house, even the ones down by the street. They had gathered on the roof and chimney, too, the sounds of their clicking talons like typewriter keys.

He waited for them to shriek but they remained silent.

"Okay." His voice was tremulous, shaky. "Okay, then. Good."

He kept a trowel and a shovel leaning against the back of the house beside the large ceramic flowerpot he'd used to burn the strands of cut vines. He took the shovel now and, carrying the trash bag over one shoulder, tromped into the field to the edge of his property, where the yard abutted the line of trees, now mostly bare for the season. He dropped the bag at his feet, then thrust the head of the shovel into the earth. The soil was cold and hard. He kept digging.

Once the hole was large enough, he kicked the trash bag into it and shoveled the dirt back on top, covering it up.

He didn't know how long it took, but by the time he returned to the bedroom, he was breathing heavily and his arms were sore from digging. That fecal stench hung stiflingly in the stale air of the bedroom. Soundlessly, he stripped out of his filthy clothes, then crawled into bed behind Heather. She stirred just the slightest bit. Beneath them, the mattress was sodden with blood.

It coated their legs.

# CHAPTER THIRTY-SEVEN

A part of Alan Hammerstun never got up from that bed. Or so he wished. But the truth was, his actions of the following morning were actions taken by a man who was not completely *there*, not fully aware of what he was doing, what he was thinking, what he was being. It seemed his movements occurred before he actually thought about doing them, as if he were controlled by someone or something else. So, in truth, perhaps a man named Alan Hammerstun never *did* get up from that bed. Or even more likely is the possibility that he had disappeared even long before that . . .

Either way, when he awoke, it was daylight. There was a horrid, metallic taste in his mouth, and when he rolled over, all his bones and muscles ached. It unleashed a pathetic cry, one hand sliding across the crusted bedsheets.

He sat up, blinking stupidly. The mattress was black with blood, and the room stank of death.

Heather's side of the bed was empty.

Rolling quickly out of bed, he stomped into the hallway but froze when he saw the bathroom door halfway open, light spilling out into the otherwise darkened hallway in a vertical sliver.

*Jesus, no . . .*

He went to the door, shoved it open.

Haggard, vacant, lost, she looked up at him from where she sat on the edge of the tub. Her nightgown was covered in dried blood as were her legs—dark runnels of it straight down to her ankles—and her hair was a rat's nest of twisted wires.

There was no life left in her eyes.

He went to her, hugged her clumsily. Pressing her head against his chest, he could feel her heartbeat reverberate through his body. He imagined he could feel the thoughts clanging around in her skull like shrapnel in a tornado. When he eventually pulled her away from him, she stared at him with those vacant, haunted eyes.

"We're broken," she told him flatly, soullessly. Then she stood and walked to the bedroom.

It took Alan another thirty seconds to get his wits about him and follow her. He seemed to be leaving contrails of Alan-shaped electrons behind in his wake. When he stopped in the bedroom doorway, he saw her climbing onto the bloodied mattress and scooting backward until she struck the headboard. It was as if she didn't see the blood anymore.

"I love you," he told her.

"We're ruined now."

He shook his head. "We went too far. But I can fix things. Do you trust me, Heather? Do you trust me to fix things?"

She looked away from him and stared out the window

into the yard. It was an overcast morning.

"You're weak and you're hurt," he said, moving around to her side of the bed. She continued to look past him. "But if you come with me, I can make you feel better."

"The baby—"

"Is dead. It isn't meant to be. Some people get sick and some people die. But I can fix *us.* I know how to do it. You've just gotta trust me and come with me." He extended a hand to her. "Will you come with me?"

She looked at him, and there were tears in her eyes. "No. It ends here. No more."

Anger welled up inside him, fueling his determination. The ulcer had returned in full force now, too. "No. God-damn it, I'm not going to let it end this way. I can *fix* us."

She folded her arms and refused to take his hand. Tears spilled down her face.

Outside, there was a dull crash. Alan felt it in his bones. He went quickly to the window and scanned the yard, the trees, the street. Across the street, he saw Hearn Landry's cruiser still parked down the block. The sheriff walked around the car, pulling his hat off, one arm pinwheeling in the air as if swatting away swarms of gnats. He stared per-plexedly at his own vehicle, and for a second Alan had no idea why. But then he saw the windshield and the webbing of cracks that spread out along the glass. At the center was something large and black and . . . *feathery* . . .

"One of the birds," he muttered. "Goddamn it. That was one of the birds."

Indeed, they had overpopulated his yard. And as he watched, they flocked closer to the street. There were some perched on the cement curb and others roosting on the tops of nearby cars. Some had migrated across the street and sat like gargoyles on the peaks of neighboring houses. While he looked on, the birds all opened their wings in a gesture of intimidation. That was what it looked like to him at first, anyway. But then he realized what they were doing when their heavy network of wings blotted Sheriff Landry out of his line of sight . . .

They were providing concealment.

Alan turned around and snatched one of Heather's arms. "We need to go now!"

"Alan!" She tried to pull herself free, but his grip was too strong. "Let me go!"

"Come on! You've got to trust me."

He dragged her from the bed and onto the floor. Her legs gave out from beneath her, and she collapsed in a heap. Bending down, he scooped her up, suddenly all too aware of his aching muscles. Nonetheless, he carried her down through the hallway as she began sobbing against his bare chest. He carried her through the living room and to the sliding patio doors.

*"Alan . . ."*

Despite Heather's cumbersomeness, he managed to slide open the door. He stepped into the yard and into the cold morning, his naked body suddenly accosted by the frigid air. It hadn't even registered with him that he wasn't wearing any clothes. In the crook of his neck, his wife cried, her entire body hitching. He walked quickly with her through the wet grass toward the path, aware of the tornado sound of wings at his back shielding him from the street and Sheriff Hearn Landry.

The path materialized before him. He wasted no time, moving swiftly beneath the clawlike branches of overhanging trees and taking each curve of the path like a stock car driver. In his arms, Heather grew heavier and heavier with each passing second. By the time he reached the clearing and the lake, his arms were burning and he'd nearly ground his teeth into powder.

Alan went to the cusp of the lake and set Heather down on the grass. She collapsed in a ball, shielding her face with her hands. His shadow loomed above her, and he caught his breath while the cold morning air bit into his naked, sweating flesh.

"You need to get into the water," he told her.

She continued to sob, paying him no attention.

After a few more moments, he repeated the command. "Honey, you need to get into the water. Do you understand me?"

"I understand you're an *animal*," she screamed, whirling around, her eyes on fire. There was genuine hatred behind them. *"What did you do to us?"*

"No, no, I'm going to *fix* us. This time it'll work. This time we'll be careful. We'll take better care of each other and not lose our way."

*"Fuck you!"* Heather struggled to her feet, the hem of her bloodied nightgown coming up over her hips. Shoving past him, she turned to run, but Alan was quicker and had anticipated this mutiny, so he grabbed a fistful of her hair and yanked her backward.

She jerked to a stop and fell against him, the back of her head cracking his jaw. Vinegar spirals capered briefly before his eyes.

*"Let me go, goddamn you!"*

Still clutching her hair, he dragged her around until she faced the lake. She was flailing, struggling, but she was much weaker than him. He managed to get his free arm around her, bracing both her arms to her body. She sobbed weakly next to his ear.

"I'm going to fix us," he whispered. "I promise you."

Then, without even taking a breath, he launched forward and carried them both down into the lake.

# CHAPTER THIRTY-EIGHT

The freezing water struck him like a punch. The wind was knocked from him. Momentarily, Alan lost all sense of place and time, and he became nothing more than a pinprick of light floating in the seminal fluid of some giant, nonexistent creature of myth.

A high-pitched keening sucked him back to reality: it was Heather, crying out before him, scrambling through the water toward land. Her hair was a dark fan down her back. He grabbed her, pulled her backward. She didn't understand. Screaming, she went under and swallowed mouthfuls of water, breaking up through the surface choking and sputtering. Her wet hair looked like seal fur.

"Stop it," he told her, his voice eerily calm. A flag of vapor billowed out of his mouth. He grabbed her with a second hand and attempted to steady her in the water. "Heather, stop it."

*"Let me go!"* she shrieked, and he could hear her teeth rattling—

*(maracas)*

—in her skull from the cold. He spun her around so that she faced him. Her skin was already turning blue, her lips quivering, her wide, colorless eyes sunken into dark, fleshy caverns. A banner of hair was plastered down the center of her forehead, bisecting her face, and Alan thought of dramatic masks symbolizing good and evil, happy and sad.

"You have to—"

*"No!"*

"You have to—"

*"Get . . . off . . ."* Heather pulled one arm free of his grasp. She swung and belted him on the side of his head.

Something exploded in twisting red flashes of light before his eyes, and he both felt and heard the sound whoosh out of his left ear.

She was wading toward the edge of the lake, carving a *V* through the surface of the water in her wake.

*(It's deepest at the center. I've never touched the bottom. Don't know if anyone ever has.)*

Alan lunged for her, gripping a fistful of her nightgown. He felt the fabric tear and come apart, unfurl like a roll of paper towels.

*She doesn't understand . . .*

Just as she was about to climb out, he yanked her toward the center of the lake. He had been the one who swam here, and swimming was how it helped heal him. It stood to reason then—

"Drink it," he said, pushing her head down.

Splashing. Struggling.

"Mermaid, *drink.* Mermaid, I *love* you."

One hand, hooked into a claw, raked the flesh of his left

arm. The bloody tracks healed almost instantly.

Bubbles ruptured the surface of the water. Her hair was tangled about his wrists like an undersea plant. The water too deep here; her feet could not find purchase on the bottom to hoist herself up.

*Drink*, he thought. Willed it.

Holding her.

Underneath.

Momentarily, he was a teenager again, standing in the morgue with Jimmy Carmichael at his back, gazing at the pale lump of flesh that had been his father splayed out on a stainless steel table. A crisp white sheet was draped over his father's waist. There was a dime-sized hole ringed with dried blood at one side of the man's head.

—What am I supposed to do now? he asked Jimmy.

*Guess you can do whatever you want.*

*Happy trails.*

Once Heather stopped moving, Alan felt a sharp tremor quake from the base of his skull to the tip of his spine. He wasn't sure how long he stood there, the lake water up to his chest and freezing his skin, his hands submerged beneath the surface and buried in the strange undersea plant that was Heather's hair, but the dark and brooding clouds overhead had changed position by the time he blinked and looked down.

Nothing. And nothing. And nothing.

Then: the billowy white fabric of her nightgown floating like seaweed to the surface. The pale white of her body came next. Her hair fanned against his chest. A bare buttock rose through the surface, a pale and glistening orb. His heart was racing like a locomotive, yet he felt strangely calm.

"Heather? Baby?"

She didn't move. Facedown, her hair continued to spread out across the surface of the water.

"Honey . . . ?" And his voice cracked. "H-H-Heath—"

Trembling. Rising mercury. Something hot rushing through the very epicenter of his soul.

Fists clenched, he threw his head back and screamed into the air.

Gathering his wife's body in his arms, Alan waded through the water and climbed out onto the grass. His muscles, which had been sore and weak just moments ago, now felt rejuvenated and strong. Powerful. In his arms, Heather's body was practically weightless.

At the line of trees, the opening to the path seemed much larger. Absently, Alan wondered if it was just a trick of perspective since the trees had shed their leaves for winter. But he didn't think so.

He stepped onto the path and crossed through the woods. At one point, an enormous lumbering beast walked alongside him, shrouded mostly by the trees. Alan could smell its fetid stench and hear its tremendous footfalls punching craters in the earth. Many times he was tempted to look at it, but each time he refused to give into the temptation.

The walk seemed to take forever, but he eventually found his way back to the house.

# CHAPTER THIRTY-NINE

Inside, Alan shut and bolted all the doors, made sure the windows were locked. He had laid Heather's body in their bed on bloodied sheets. Then he went to the kitchen and peered out the windows at the street. The birds had retreated to the trees, and Sheriff Landry, along with two other men from the block, had scraped the dead buzzard off the cruiser's windshield. The sheriff was now in the process of dumping the twisted carcass into a trash pail. Hank joined the sheriff and the other two men.

Alan let the curtain whisper back into place.

Behind him, the walls crackled. It was a sound like breaking bones. He turned and, for seemingly the first time in days, actually *saw* the house: the gouges he'd knocked in the walls; the trails of vines and ivy sprouting from jagged fissures in the drywall; snakelike chutes jutting up from the separations in the floorboards; tendrils curling down from the light fixtures in the ceiling, stinking of rot and dripping a pinkish ooze onto the floor, couch, tables, and chairs.

*It has become a bad place.* It was George YoungCalfRibs speaking in his head. *It no longer hides and offers rejuvenation to those worthy enough to find it. Now it calls to whoever is careless enough to seek it out. That is its revenge on the ones who have soured its waters and poisoned its land.*

His left eyelid twitched.

*The lake is like a magnet. Your house is the closest thing to it. It's too close to the forest and sits on the soured land. Your house rots with you and your wife in it. Rots like carrion.*

He went to the kitchen sink and bent down, opening the cabinet. He found what he was looking for.

*Leave that house immediately. Burn it to the ground so no one else can live there after you. Do it before it's too late.*

Laughter bubbled up inside him. Alan couldn't help himself. He stepped into the foyer and uncapped the bottle of lighter fluid he'd retrieved from beneath the sink and began spraying down the walls, soaking the stalks and vines. Some of the leaves seemed to curl up and turn brown upon contact.

From the foyer windows, he saw Hank moving up his driveway toward the porch. Alan ignored him, spraying the remaining lighter fluid onto the spots in the floor where the vines were corkscrewing out of bored holes. When Hank knocked on his front door, Alan did not acknowledge it. Once he emptied the bottle, he returned to the kitchen and got two more. The second bottle he used to spray down the hallway. Vines were everywhere, and great handfuls of them were spooling out of the holes he'd smashed in the walls. The floor itself was tacky with their purplish blood.

From the front porch: "Alan! I know you're home! Open the door! Please!"

Finally, in the bedroom, Alan emptied the final bottle of lighter fluid. He soaked the walls, the floor, the heap of dirty clothes atop the hamper. He sprayed the bedsheets and the comforter. The lampshade. A stack of paperback novels on his nightstand.

"Alan! Please, Alan! Open the door!"

But that sound could have been coming from a dream or shouted by someone submerged underwater.

Still naked, he climbed onto the mattress. The bed squeaked, and he could smell the mix of blood and lighter fluid in the sheets. He propped himself up against the headboard, then rolled Heather onto his chest. She weighed next to nothing. Her body was cold, her skin malleable.

"Shhhhh," he whispered as he stroked her head. "Shhhh, mermaid. Shhhhh."

"Alan!" A louder voice on the porch. A different voice. "This is Landry! Open the goddamn door, will you?"

Alan laughed and tasted the salt from his tears as they ran into his mouth. He grabbed his pack of Marlboros and a lighter off the nightstand. He lit the cigarette and inhaled deeply. It tasted of lighter fluid but he didn't mind.

"Shhhh, my baby, my mermaid."

He smoked it down to the filter. Flicked it onto the mattress.

Then laughed once, sharply, as the sheets burst into flames.

# DECEMBER PARK

## RONALD MALFI

In the quiet suburb of Harting Farms, the weekly crime blotter usually consists of graffiti or the occasional bout of mailbox baseball. But in the fall of 1993, children begin vanishing and one is found dead. Newspapers call him the Piper because he has come to take the children away. But there are darker names for him, too . . .

Vowing to stop the Piper's reign of terror, five boys take up the search. Their teenage pledge turns into a journey of self-discovery . . . and a journey into the darkness of their own hometown. On the twilit streets of Harting Farms, everyone is a suspect. And any of the boys might be the Piper's next victim.

Horror
Trade Paperback
US $14.95/$14.95 CDN
ISBN# 9781605425887
MARCH 2014

# FLOATING STAIRCASE

## RONALD MALFI

To Travis and Jodie Glasgow, the house in the idyllic small town seems perfect, the surrounding woods and lake like a postcard. But soon after they move in, things begin to . . . change. Strange noises wake Travis at night. His dreams are plagued by ghosts. Barely glimpsed shapes flit through the darkened hallways—shapes bearing a frightening resemblance to a little boy. Footprints appear. Strangest of all are the wooden stairs rising cryptically from the lake.

The more Travis investigates, the more he uncovers the house's violent and tragic past . . . and the more he learns that some secrets can't be buried forever.

Horror
Trade Paperback
US $14.95 / CDN $16.95
ISBN# 9781605424361

# MEDALLION
## P R E S S

Be in the know on the latest Medallion Press news by becoming a Medallion Press Insider!

<u>As an Insider you'll receive:</u>
· Our FREE expanded monthly newsletter, giving you more insight into Medallion Press
· Advanced press releases and breaking news
· Greater access to all your favorite Medallion authors

Joining is easy.  Just visit our website at
<u>www.medallionmediagroup.com</u> and click on
*Super Cool E-blast* next to the social media buttons.

---

medallionmediagroup.com

# MEDALLION
P R E S S

Want to know what's going on with your favorite author or
what new releases are coming from Medallion Press?

Now you can receive breaking news, updates, and more from
Medallion Press straight to your cell phone, e-mail, instant
messenger, or Facebook!

Sign up now at www.twitter.com/MedallionPress to stay on top of all
the happenings in and around Medallion Press.

For more information
about other great titles from
Medallion Press, visit